Sparrow in the Keep

Jean Ann Hudson

Jean Ann Hudson

Copyright © 2014 Jean Ann Hudson
All rights reserved. Without limiting the rights under the copyright requested above, no part of this publication may be reproduced, stored in or introduced into a retrieval system or transmitted in any form or by any means (electric, mechanical, photocopying, recording, or otherwise) without prior written permission of both the copyright owner and the above publisher of this book. The characters and events portrayed in this book are fictitious. Any similarities to real persons, living or dead, is coincidental and not intended by the author.
ISBN:1494716410
ISBN-13:978-1494716417

Dedication

To all those who love and care for animals.

1
An Enchanting Forest

Seventy feet above the forest floor the crowning leaves of the sweet gum tree flutter in golden flashes and tinkle like tiny bells. Huddled in the tree top is a nest with two eaglets who tremble along with the branches as a muttering, cursing voice disturbs the peace below them. The baby birds' big black eyes look out with alarm and dismay. It is a human there below, and humans are strange. The eaglets, bald except for a few spiky white tufts of hair, bob and blink, peering across the rim of the nest, but there is only a sea of treetops all around them. The shaking gets stronger, the cursing gets louder and then there is silence. The eaglets can only await the return of their mother. They cannot fly, their beaks and talons are too small to do much harm and they can easily be squeezed into a human hand. After a minute the shaking subsides and they hear a thud as a human hits the ground and runs off. Then they hear their mother's piercing scream:

"I see you two men; get away from my babies before I rip your eyes out. Yes, run; go deeper into the forest and let a wolf find a meal in you." I'll circle overhead to check for other dangers before I land and tend my babies. The woods are full of humans today; there at the edge of the forest are more; six with horses and two in a wagon and some dogs alongside. I scream again; "More humans close to my babies; I warn you, stay away." Circling around I also see the girl named Sparrow, sitting high up in a tree, the only human I have ever understood. She raises out her arms to me in greeting. I tip this wing, then that one, I greet her back. Drifting down and towards the nest, my eaglets are there, safe. But when did a snake climb this tree? It must be a snake, with a long brown body and dangerously close to my babies; but I can easily kill a snake. I land right on it, grasp it in my talons; it doesn't even try to strike. It will be dead soon and I will chew on it and feed it to my babies. But this one grabs me back; it won't let go of the tree, or me. I am caught.

Trevka heard the eagle overhead and saw it fly into the treetops, then heard it scream again and saw a great flapping of wings and fluttering of leaves and twigs and knew that it was caught somehow high up in the branches of the tree, right under its nest. He leaped off his horse and ran towards it, shouting and pointing with his usual exuberance. Trevka was a page to the recently crowned Count Gustav of Wilker, whose entourage was making the annual trip to the hunting lodge in the forest, high in the mountains of his realm. Three more men on horseback, all officers of the Count's, and another page driving the wagon, had by now caught up to Trevka standing at the base of the sweet gum tree. The two girls in the wagon bed shaded their eyes and craned their necks trying to see, nervous but silent. The men milled around the base of the tree, also trying to determine what was going on, while the Count listened to the eagle screaming and pondered whether the malevolent forces that had set such a trap were human or otherwise. The Imperial Eagle was revered by royal decree and to hunt or eat one was to toss up sovereignty and call forth chaos. Another scream rained down upon them. Trevka looked anxiously from one silent face to another. Were they just waiting to see if the eagle freed itself without help? Or were they going to stand by and watch as it struggled so fiercely it broke its leg and bled to death or slowly starved? A wing feather drifted down as the eagle flapped strenuously. Gustav did *not* want to witness the unnatural death of an Imperial Eagle. It was a baleful omen, especially for the very beginning of his reign, but trying to save it meant risking someone's life.

If you leave, the curse will follow with you! Gustav heard those words in his head and wondered why, if they were his words, it sounded as if a girl had spoken them. Trevka was trying to say something and perhaps in his distress about the bird, he was sounding more high pitched than his seventeen-year-old voice. *You cannot leave!* Well if Trevka was that concerned, perhaps he would prove brave enough to help the bird. He hadn't proven to be very much as yet. Even so, was it worth risking Trevka's life? If he fell out of the tree trying to climb it, was perhaps harmed by the eagle or merely inept, he would either be dead or wishing it by the time he hit the ground. Then Gustav could contemplate the deaths of both man and beast upon his conscience. Gustav decided with a heavy sigh which he did not let the others hear and commanded, "Trevka, get back on your horse." Trevka hesitated; didn't anyone else think they should help the bird? But instantly the officer nearby kicked him with a booted foot and ordered Trevka to get on his horse and be quick about it. No one pauses when the Count commands. Gustav gave more commands; one officer tucked a knife into Trevka's jacket with a grunted warning not to drop it on their heads, then another pushed Trevka's mount into the tree trunk to keep either from moving off. There was silence while the Count paused, willing Trevka to be up to this expectation of his. He didn't think he'd have to make such a request so soon into his reign. He said,

"Trevka, climb the tree and free the bird." Trevka was frozen in place but his eyes were moving up the tree. He had imagined that somehow they would all take part in helping the eagle, and yet how could they? He alone was being asked to do it; he knew all faces were upon him, expecting him to balk. He had never been entrusted with such a responsibility. The girls in the wagon were watching, eyes wide and worried; the other men in the party took sidelong glances at each other. There was silence and no one prodded him this time. Before another silence could pass, Trevka launched himself into the branches.

Gustav watched him climb, fighting the urge to order him back down, for the tree was tall and this risk was perhaps too great to help a bird, even an Imperial Eagle. If he fell, it would be more than an unfortunate accident; it would be a third death. For his mother had died in June and his father, the late Count, in July. There was a month of mourning and then an August coronation ceremony. The annual hunting trip was almost canceled, but in the end, just shortened. Gustav had decided that going was a way of showing his subjects that all was well. He wanted them to know he gave no weight or reverence to the adage on everyone's lips:

If two deaths close to a sovereign lie, expect misfortune by and by. If a third one happens then again, expect the sovereign's line to end.

Trevka was climbing the tree with steady determination and strangely the bird, instead of becoming more frantic, seemed to give up and sit calmly without concern for the advancing human. Trevka refrained from looking down, not wanting anyone to see his face damp with sweat trickling over a nervous visage. He was approaching the top of the tree and paused to consider. Five feet away, the eagle waited, magnificent and staring. Talons like blacksmith tongs gripped the thin branch on which it sat, eagle and branch bobbing pendulously as a breeze swept through. Trevka studied the leather noose, wondering how to cut it without yanking the eagle off its perch and into his face. If he could pin the leather against a limb, he might be able to slice through it, but the bird might also reach down with its hooked beak and rip the blue vein out of his hand like a worm. He closed his eyes and swallowed. He climbed three more feet, wiped his palm on his jacket and took the knife out.

Everyone below was transfixed heavenward, horses shifting beneath them as they tried to see through all the lower branches. Trevka sprung forward, planted the knife blade and sawed with fury. Suddenly the eagle was flapping its wings madly, spindly branches snapped and splintered and there was a loud shriek amidst frantic thrashing. The branch under Trevka's armpit broke, his feet slipped off their perch and he was falling through the air when his elbow plunked with a thud onto another branch and he swayed limply. The bird swooped into the air, leather strap and talons hissing past scalp flesh and a flutter of leaves and feathers sprayed Trevka's body with a hail of confetti to the chorus of cheering and clapping from the girls below.

The eagle flew off in an arc around the treetop, then landed in the nest and tapped each eaglet's head with its beak several times. Trevka was gasping and pedaling for new footholds; he finally found them and steadied himself enough to look up and see the nest jiggle with activity. Thinking he should get away from the mother eagle before she changed her mind about him, Trevka began climbing down, going as fast as he could with his shaking hands and feet. He dropped gratefully the last eight feet onto the ground, stood up and brushed himself off with nonchalance while hoping for an end to the zinging pain in his heels. He looked up to see everyone taking a rather surprised notice of him, which he would have begun to loudly protest, but he didn't trust his quavering voice so instead he merely remounted his horse in silence.

"Very good, Trevka," Gustav finally said, leaving out any note of surprise. "Recognition will surely come to one who frees an Imperial Eagle." Still too unsteady to speak out loud, Trevka merely bowed slightly and touched his forehead. Thus he displayed humility for perhaps the first time in his life, but merely because he had been too unnerved to speak. Sparrow, witnessing the whole scene from her tree perch nearby, was overwhelmed with surprise and gratitude: *He heard my call for help and answered.*

'How great is a man who helps one so small!' Sparrow thought towards the tall man in charge as she breathed relief for the mother eagle and her babies. The young man who had climbed the tree would never have done so without the prodding of the taller one. The man in charge made the decision and caused the rescue to happen. She had done what she could, sending encouraging thoughts to the climber, thinking softly to him, *you can do this- look up and have courage.* She reassured the eagle to keep it quiet and stop its struggling and fortunately it listened to her. She had been watching the nest for many weeks now, and the eaglets were growing fast, but they would not survive without their mother. And although Sparrow could have climbed the tree herself, she was probably too far away to get there in time, and she didn't have a knife in any case.

On this morning she had been following and watching the two men she had come to call the Rogues, saw one of them climb the tree toward the eagle's nest, then jump down and hide when the royals approached. But she had not understood what they were about until the eagle started screaming. *Rogues* was the word her father used when describing an animal that left their herd and acted aberrant and vicious (usually because of a sick head). The Rogues hunted for food and furs, but were not like usual hunters; these two killed more than they needed and killed just for the fun of it. They were strange and dangerous, and she kept expecting them to die of disease or be killed by their own or even each other. She had been told by her parents that poaching in the royal forest was a crime punishable by death. Did they not know this law? Why did they so flagrantly disregard it? Now unseen by her or the royal party, the two rogues had also witnessed the saving of the eagle, and with disgust and fear they slunk away unnoticed.

She watched the party with the wagon mill around. They were stopping for lunch, not chasing the Rogues who had moved off but probably lingered nearby, lurking behind a ridge. The rescue party seemed ignorant of how close they were to these criminals, how easily they might catch them. How unwise they seem and yet, she mused, *they are different from all the others I've seen come and go. And without mother and father alive any more, I can watch them all I want.* So she studied the tall one; she soon understood he was the ruler, even though he wore nothing on his head or around his neck denoting his rank - ah yes, because it would be foolish to draw attention to his true identity where he has only five men to protect him. His clothes too were simple for this reason, although his jacket was unusual. Just then the "snake" that had confounded the eagle was ripped off its leg by its sharp beak and the slice of leather it truly was came down from the sky and landed right at Gustav's feet, surprising him and causing his horse to shy away. He picked it up and tossed it to Trevka, saying, "Here; if you ever have children, you'll have this to show them when you tell the tale, as no doubt you will many times." The officer nearby laughed, then added,

"And find out who it belonged to. It will make a good ending to your story." Trevka studied the leather strap in his hands; how would he ever find out who had owned it? An unremarkable strap! But oh, if he could, yes, that would bedazzle people.

Sparrow was amazed, dismayed and impressed all together. She was firstly amazed that such a portend from Heaven had fallen at the very feet of a Count; dismayed that he had so casually tossed his good fortune to a page, and impressed that these people not only stopped to save an eagle, but were planning to capture and perhaps punish the criminals responsible, and they apparently had all the time in the world to do so. Gustav's largesse towards his inferior page was certainly unselfish, imprudent though it might be. She would send another good luck charm his way and hoped he would hold onto it, as her favor was for him.

Trevka was carefully examining the leather strap that had so recently been in the tree, tied around an eagle's leg. Someone had made a noose out of it; the harder the eagle had pulled away from it, the more it had tightened. Sparrow could sense the malice of the

Rogues through Trevka's fingers as he examined their object of entrapment. All she had to do was to look at it and sense the miasma emanating from the leather; she wondered how he could continue to hold it in his hands, then suddenly he dropped it onto the edge of the wagon and Sparrow saw why. Food had been uncovered from the canvas bags by the two girls and he was quickly reaching for it.

Sparrow thought about all the times the royal hunting party had come into the forest in the past. As soon as they drew near, her parents would make important business out of going far away from them, even though Sparrow always wanted to stay and watch. It was because her parents themselves had come up to the mountains to escape their own people that they were never sure if whomever ventured into the forest might be looking for them. Leaving their families had been an unruly and wicked thing to do. Sparrow had been reminded time and again that people were not to be trusted; they overwhelmed your childhood with chores, decided which work you would do your whole life, even arranged your marriage without a thought to your heart's desire or suitability. Her father had told her the tale often:

"Your mother and I fell in love over the stream that ran between our lands. She was washing one day, very early because she wanted to get out of the house, away from her mother. She looked up at me and our eyes met. I shouldn't have been there, I was there late because my father made me re-shoe each hoof when he found one horseshoe worn down. As she washed the family laundry she slipped on a rock and got all wet; I went over to help her and we talked to each other, even though we weren't supposed to. We met then as often as we could, but it was difficult, they were keeping an eye on each of us because they had already chosen our spouses and looked forward to matches that would elevate them by some slight measure. We both disliked the mates they had chosen. So I convinced her to come away with me to the forest. I told her we could hide there until our intendeds gave up and married other people, then we could return, proving that we would not be forced into anything any more." Sparrow had heard the story many times. Her father was always trying to prove to her that people were manipulative and scheming, and one had to out-smart them. And if it were true of ordinary people, then it was especially true of royal people. She had never been permitted near them, royal or ordinary. There was more to the story:

"After our first winter here, we found our resourcefulness served us well. I was good at trapping animals for dinner and mother was good at gathering food and making our home comfortable. She knew how to make useful items from things she found. And you were on the way..." Here he often trailed off in his telling. They were never legally married and now they had a child together; this would mean people would treat them as outcasts or at least be uneasy talking to them. Their parents would cast them out, mostly because they would be unmarriageable to the people they had chosen. Returning became less and less of a possibility. "After a while, our families gave up searching for us or perhaps had never even tried. We did fine without them, so why go back? Your mother especially was afraid of her intended fiancee; he was supposedly rich, high class and heartless, and her mother always had airs and dreams of being higher born than she ever was. She was a bitter woman. Then you came along, our dear little Sparrow, and we simply never thought any more about going back. You have been raised like no other person; you know the animals and nature spirits without inhibition, you understand them as we never could. Never go back to that life we left, you don't know how wicked it is, there's no telling how they would treat you." And thus all her life Sparrow had been taught that people should be disliked, feared and avoided. But she had always wondered, was that true of everyone?

Sparrow watched as the hunting party reassembled their sacks and boxes, rearranged the cages holding the oddly fat and strangely clucking birds. Gustav rode next to a black-haired man but they did not lead the party. Anyone leaping from behind trees would have to contend with the larger man in front. The wagon with the girls came after Gustav and his companion, then Trevka, still examining the leather strap. Around them as they traveled, four very tall, wiry-haired dogs trotted alongside. Finally at the end was a slightly older man with red hair, green eyes and his thoughts in the clouds; he wasn't one of them, she realized, but he was accepted by them. By watching them Sparrow would be able to discern their names and personalities, between what was said out loud and how they interacted and of course, what she heard in their thoughts. If she became very curious and nosy, she could dig more deeply and probably sense their feelings, if their feelings were close to the surface, which they usually were.

Sparrow waited until they were far up the trail, with the redhead glancing back and assuring himself, although not convinced, that they were not being followed. She climbed down from her perch and loped through the forest ahead of them. The trail was winding and gentle for the horses and wagons, but Sparrow knew how to reach the path ahead of them much faster. And of course she knew they were headed to the hunting lodge, and she was curious to get closer to it, which had never been allowed by her parents when they were alive. But then they had only just died.

They had both fallen ill at about the same time. Illness almost never visited them. Once, Sparrow had had a fever after a cut on her leg, but her mother knew which herb to put on it and it was better after that. But when both her parents fell ill at the same time, neither one was able to tell Sparrow what to do. She made them teas out of all the herbs she knew to be good for fevers, good for ill stomachs, good for bad innards. Nothing helped, even though it should have. They died after only two days and she had to drag them a ways off. Now she was without human companions for the first time in her life. But she had spent most of her days in solitude even before her parents died, and knew everything died eventually. She was well able to take care of herself. Her days were filled with ambling through the forest, gathering food to eat along the way, mingling with the animals and conversing with the vibrations and emanations of anything in the forest that was interesting. Perhaps people only lived to her parents' age anyway, whatever that age was. Now she felt it was time for her to have a baby of her own, just like the mother eagle. And here was a good man who cared to see that eagles were saved. She knew nature would somehow provide her with what she needed.

She had climbed into a tree above the hunting lodge. This was a well-chosen area for a lodge, easy to defend, although it hadn't needed defending for many decades. She settled in and waited for them to catch up with her. Until then, she closed her eyes and focused her mind down the pathway they were traveling up. It wasn't long until she met them on their way. They were amusing, their little worries and thoughts, so unrelated to what was really going on around them. Her parents weren't correct in thinking all people were so wicked, but perhaps they were correct in how unwise they could be.

The procession was now wordlessly making its way through a maze of lodge pole pines, having grown tired of talking and having to keep a keener eye on the path underfoot. Through the canopy of leaves overhead, only spangles of sunlight glittered intermittently onto the riders. The trees were gathering around them in increasing numbers, making it harder to advance up the road, across rocky streams and further into the forest. The sounds of twigs snapping and wagon wheels groaning disturbed the peace of the place. The girls hushed themselves, knowing that as they entered this very darkest part of the forest they must be careful not to frighten the elfin spirits surely hiding under poisonous toadstools, and even more careful not to offend any evil trolls blinking out from the shadows under the log bridges. The girls' eyes grew wide as they imagined what creatures were lurking behind the trees, silently observing a heavily-laden wagon carrying two attractive females.

Sparrow easily caught their thoughts and giggled, but eight people all together was confusing. Even though none of them spoke, still their minds chattered on and on. She could separate out the lustful thoughts; these were not Gustav's. She sensed from several of the men an alertness about the road around them. There was always risk when traveling. But this was not Gustav's job, and she pushed these vibrations aside as well. One of them was contemplating concepts and ideas so intricate and foreign to Sparrow that – ah yes, the red haired one with his head in the clouds. That was easy to ignore; those thoughts made little sense to her. Finally, she was able to isolate Gustav, knew it was him because he carried heavily the burden of being the Count. But he wasn't congratulating himself on saving an eagle; his mind was on his responsibilities.

She had been taught that powerful leaders were always scheming ambitiously for the future, never tortured by memories of the past, never bothered by those in discomfort. Gustav had power and influence, yet he did not plot about how to exploit it. He had possessions uncountable, but did not dream of them or of new ones he wished to acquire. He had responsibilities enumerable, and yet had managed to delegate them successfully. One matter did nag at him deeply, and it accounted for the stony expression he was usually wearing. He was a handsome man until he began contemplating his marriage. And what was privacy to Sparrow? Unchecked in her curiosity, infatuated with his rescue of a mother and her babies, she followed his thoughts down their long, lonely path.

A long, lonely path. That is what stretched before Gustav as he remembered Gertrudis, his bride-to-be, walking down the aisle of the church on their wedding day barely a year ago. How she had flounced with a pompous, affected air as if she were marrying the crown prince, heir to the throne of the whole kingdom. *I'm just a Viscount, you'll just be a Viscountess.* And she could take but little credit for becoming the wife of the future Count of Wilker. She had done nothing to charm Gustav, who saw her as silly and feckless. It was their fathers who had arranged it. Gertrudis was from Uluvost, a backward province Gustav thought he might elevate by association with Wilker. To his father, the ruling Count, it was a naive and easily swayed county, and advantageous alliances would fall into their laps. It had become unavoidable. As Gustav neared the age of 35, he was practically required to marry and have children. He would have preferred some simple woman, there were many to choose from, but this was not allowed.

Sparrow was surprised to realize that rulers could be trapped. This was sadder than when her parents had died, for with them she would always have good memories to look back on. Sparrow also had a whole family of companions in the forest, always keeping her company. Gustav's situation yawned into his future, an annoyance threatening to turn from mild discomfort into aggressive bitterness. She shrank into the arms of the tree, recoiling from the feeling of entrapment. But her plans would change that; the plans she had been concocting for a while now and into which her noble Gustav would fall into perfectly. She leaned forward to finish watching the scenes in his head, not wanting to be ignorant of anything important.

Gertrudis became pregnant just when Gustav began to understand that his wife was utterly self-absorbed and that few distractions gave her any pleasure. She was greedy for attention and poked at life like a squeamish child with a caterpillar, afraid to embrace it, unable to put it down and simply admire it, too impatient and ignorant to wait for its beauty to unfold, and threatening with her carelessness to destroy it. She was completely unsuited to royal life; how this had been omitted from her upbringing in the Uluvost court baffled him. She barked at servants like dogs and was dismayed when they didn't bother to pretend liking her. Her baby had been born late last spring, and to everyone's relief it had lived, despite the mother's complete disdain for pregnancy and torment when confronted with the trial of childbirth.

Sparrow again shrank back. The trial of childbirth, which she had witnessed many times in the forest but never experienced. Animals just laid down, some even stood, and let it slowly take place. There was no fighting against it, although she knew it was a trial for them. Sparrow compared herself to Gertrudis and wondered, then dismissed her fears. *I will know how to give birth and not be afraid.* She was almost finished with this private intrusion that she had had no idea would be so complex.

The royal child was thankfully a boy. He lived and was cared for by nannies. Neither mother nor father saw him much, and neither felt much attachment to him. No thought was given to providing siblings. Sparrow sensed its lonesome heartbeat. The wee baby's grandfather, the elder Count of Wilker, had lived only a few months to see his plans bear fruit, this grandson and heir to the throne born well and healthy.

The party was now making itself heard on the path. Sparrow held herself entirely still in the tree. As the humans approached, the animals nearby moved off temporarily and a hush fell over the lodge. The sun was behind the trees on the mountain top and dusk was falling.

2

A Hunting Lodge in the Woods

The heavy timbers have stood for a hundred years, carved from the trees that once lived there, and shaped into this form that now stands as a home. The people have returned most every summer to open the windows and doors, walk the halls, rustle the curtains as they pass and wear ever smoother the wooden floor. There are stuffed animal heads adorning the walls; an elk with a huge rack, many deer, a bobcat and a snowy owl perched on a tree limb gaze down, ever at the same spot, but now there will be movement below them to watch. The walls around the bedrooms will hear laughter, sighs, sounds. From the kitchen will waft aromas of meat and bread cooking, strawberries hulled and apples baking. In they come, so lively and glad to be here at last. They light fires where it has been empty and cold, they pile food on the tables, they plop down their bodies on the sofas and furs and once again the hides have life in them. The dogs trot around and sniff every corner, waking all the slumbering spirits.

As each one in the hunting party made their way into the lodge, Sparrow was now able to put faces and bodies to the thoughts she had been picking up and trying to keep separate. Suddenly she realized she had only accounted for five men, and there were six. Gustav was inside with the foreign redhead and the hefty leader. The young one who had climbed the tree lingered with the horses, while another young one identical to him was headed inside with the two girls. That left the man who had ridden next to Gustav and who bore a vague resemblance to him. He was so careful with his thoughts that Sparrow had not picked up on them at all. When the twin helping the girls glanced over his shoulder to his brother and said, "Better stay out here with Harz," Sparrow knew his name.

Harz was Gustav's cousin. Sparrow watched him leading his and Gustav's horses into the corral adjacent to the lodge while Trevka brought in the rest of the team. When all the horses were inside the corral, Trevka put some oats into the mangers and checked the cistern for water. Luckily, due to the good rains this summer, the level was high and did not require retrieving by the bucket-full for emptying into the trough. But Harz did not dismiss him, so Trevka took up a brush and began smoothing down the horses' flanks. Trevka's eyes were on the girls as they walked to and from the kitchen. His twin brother, having driven the wagon of supplies, was now enjoying the task of unloading it under the girls' supervision. Trevka brushed the horses absently while Harz assessed the horse shed. It was still standing solid, roof intact, walls upright. He noticed that he couldn't say the same for a falling-down smoke shed nearby. Harz came back around and watched Trevka brushing, all his attention on the girls' parade and none of it on the horses. "Trevka," Harz said. Trevka turned around and saw that he had been brushing a saddle blanket and not a horse's hide.

"Oh," Trevka muttered. He yanked the blanket off and folded it hastily, pitching it with the others in a heap. Harz meanwhile picked up the brush and was smoothing the horse's coat. Without turning or saying anything, he tossed his head to indicate Trevka could go into the lodge at last. As Trevka sped off toward the kitchen, Harz admonished him to be sure to ask first before helping the ladies. Harz knew Trevka would forget to ask. He also knew that Trevka was uneasy around him; knew he was overly self-conscious about Harz's ability to know when someone was lying. With black hair, fair skin and just as tall as his cousin, Harz seemed unremarkable. He often remained in the background, but he could tell when someone was making a great story or evading the truth with silence, especially if he looked steadily with his blackish brown eyes at them. He was glad to have the ability because it meant he could be singularly helpful to his cousin. Most people were only telling little white lies anyway. Women, mostly. Yes women always seemed to have something to hide, if he was concerned enough to wonder. He had tried to warn his cousin not to marry Gertrudis, but to no avail. It wasn't much consolation that now he was proved right.

Ruling would be a wily business and Gustav had just begun his reign. But Gustav didn't just have his cousin to help him but also his uncle Ambrose, Harz's father, to rely on for advice. Ambrose understood court life better than any of them, knew everyone, and remembered farther back than any of them. He was not along on this trip, which had been a matter of some discussion. He was always on the summer hunting trip; he was a great hunter and knew the countryside and the mountains well. But that would have left practically no one of authority in the castle, and so he stayed behind to be the royal presence of the ruling family that had so recently been decreased. When they had departed on their journey this morning, Harz had gazed back at his father waving slowly good-bye from the castle gate, smiling with reassurance, and then turned to amble along the path without him.

Harz was disrupted from his reverie and stopped brushing a moment. He turned his head and listened. He was still mindful that there were brazen, eagle-snatching criminals in the forest who might have been following. Harz put down the brush and walked to the stable door. The horses munched their oats and grass, one raising its head with Harz's curiosity. Standing in the darkening doorway, Harz scanned the edge of the forest in the last remnants of daylight.

In her treetop perch Sparrow froze, still and silent as Harz gazed in her direction. Were there any animals nearby to help her? Harz took one step out of the stable, certain there was someone hiding nearby, but then a Great Horned Owl flew right in front of him, taking off for the night's hunt and startling him. Since when did owls dive at people? He watched it go and then retreated into the lodge, forgetting the idea of anyone hiding nearby.

Trevka had stepped into the kitchen asking, "Where's Vatra?" The older girl, Genivee, replied,

"Your identical twin is lighting the fires. Why don't you be just helpful and pluck this chicken," and she tossed the bird with the broken neck across the table to him. Genivee sat down and proceeded to pluck her own chicken while Trevka reluctantly sat down as well, but his attention was on the other girl, Liesse. She was a beauty.

Young and curvy, Liesse had the biggest brown eyes Trevka had ever seen. They were like an innocent doe's eyes, sweet and inquisitive. She had thick brown hair that was always framing her rosy cheeks in a halo. And her lips, Trevka mused, her lips were full and red and so often parted in a laugh.

"Pluck!" Genivee barked. Harz appeared in the doorway and asked if Trevka was making himself useful. Trevka indignantly thrust out a fist full of feathers as evidence. Harz glanced at Genivee to see if she rolled her eyes. He would throw Trevka out if he was being annoying. She smiled up at Harz and went back to her work. Trevka would do for now.

Genivee was unlike Liesse in several ways. She was older by five years, but Genivee had lost a lot of silliness on the way to 26. Her fine blonde hair was not loose and seductive but braided around her head. Her hazel eyes were not huge but they were bright. Vatra returned and the twins exchanged glances. To everyone's great relief, Trevka and Vatra had, since the age of 12, kept themselves completely discernible via their clothes and demeanor. They would be impossible to tell apart otherwise. Trevka was loud, flamboyant and so often protesting, making his opinions known on all topics of interest to him. His shifty eyes darted about and often squinted with suspicion. He was always well adorned with special cuffs, boot buckles or a feather in his hat (now an eagle feather). Vatra was quiet and hardworking. His eyes were placid, thoughtful and perceptive. He usually knew what to do before being told and was halfway through doing it while his brother was still arguing, or wondering.

As Harz headed for the door to the lodge's main gathering room, he took a swipe at Trevka's unkempt mop of hair and admonished him quietly to *pluck faster, page*. When he had gone, Trevka muttered about the iniquity of having saved an eagle only to now be plucking a chicken. "And with a broken arm, too!" He winced and rubbed his elbow but when Genivee showed no sympathy and Liesse just smiled at him, he went back to plucking.

In the great room of the lodge, everyone was relaxing. One wolfhound lay at the Count's feet and the three others were in an overlapping pile near the fireplace. The large man who had led the party up the mountain trail was tsk-tsking at how narrowly Trevka had escaped death earlier and was recounting a tale about once saving the life of another page who had been so inadvertent as to catch an arrow in his ear. "Just the outer ear, mind you. Three inches to the left and he'd have been dead before he hit the ground with the shaft of an arrow through his eye socket and an eyeball skewered at the tip." All eyes were on Boris as he told the tale with one foot propped against a low table in the center of the circle of loungers and sofas. Gustav was resting in a bearskin-covered chair, drinking from a tankard of sack. As he sat listening to Boris, he lifted each foot in turn for Vatra to remove his boots. Boris planted his forearms on his bent knee and continued. "The boy's ear wasn't even bleeding at that point, but the impact of being impaled had caused him to spin around twice and he hit the ground with a thud like thunder and a snap like lightening. The arrow had broken in half, you see, but a bit of the shaft with the point was still lodged in his flesh." Boris took a long sip from his mug while the others waited patiently to hear the outcome. "Girls nearby fainted at the sight of him sitting up and turning his head around in confusion with an arrow stuck in his noggin." Vatra took the Count's boots over to the fireplace and added some more logs to the fire, then sat down on a footstool to brush and polish each boot. "Well, they ran and found me, I was just a barber back then, known for pulling teeth and such. But I was all they had, so they brought me and I carefully examined the young man and told him he'd just have to live with that arrow in his ear." The listeners scanned their memories for a page of that description, and could think of none. "Well he raised such a racket about it that I pushed the arrow through and pulled it out while he was busy complaining." Gustav reclined back and closed his eyes. Boris concluded, "The wound didn't even bleed due to my skillful technique." He took a long gulp of sack. "And that is when I became known as the best surgeon in the realm."

Vatra continued brushing boots while Gustav raised his tankard in salute to his surgeon and body guard. Harz entered the room, scanned it and sat down in a corner chair near the fire. In a few minutes and what seemed like too short a time for an entire rooster to have been plucked properly, Trevka came in and joined the group. Boris dropped onto the sofa behind him and loudly plonked each of his heels onto the central table. Trevka went over to him and proceeded to pull each of Boris's boots off in turn, but it required several tugs and Boris helped out by planting the sole of his other foot against Trevka's backside. They were quiet until the Count spoke, indicating he wasn't yet too weary and they could converse for a while. He said, "Tomorrow we'll go falconing if the weather is good." Boris then asked Trevka,

"Have you got those birds safely put away for the night?" Trevka nodded vigorously, still tugging on the last boot in his hands. Suddenly he lurched forward with it, regained his balance, then went to sit next to Vatra to polish and scrub.

Gustav only half listened to the mild conversation. His mind was on the last leg of the trip up to the lodge. He had been thinking he heard birdsong in the forest. He even imagined he had seen a bird flying past him and brushing his cheeks with its wings. He reached his hand into his jacket and found his fingers touching on something light and wispy. He pulled the item out from his jacket and gazed at it; a short, brown feather. He wondered why and when he had put it there. Slowly contemplating, he smoothed the barbs down his cheek and across his lips. It had the aroma of spruce and he seemed to forget everything else.

The room began to fill with the smells of chicken frying in a skillet of fat and there were more sounds coming from the kitchen. The wolfhounds lifted their heads but kept to their places. The men became quiet. The great room was like a village at dusk, with a glow from the fireplace resembling the setting sun and glimmers of light from the sconces on the walls twinkling like stars rising in the night sky. The candles on the various tables were like little lamps shining from cottages. The animal heads hanging on the walls were lit from below and loomed over them like gods plotting their fate. The numerous tapestries softened the stone walls and helped hold in the warmth. The wool curtains over the few windows faintly rustled from time to time as the usually-cold room now warmed with shifting currents. The gentle plunk of tankards set onto solid wooden tables and armrests were the only sounds for a time, as well as the creak of leather jackets and the planting of tired feet, followed by long exhalations from the tired travelers.

Just as Gustav was almost nodding off, the women came through the doors of the kitchen with chattering talk, platters of food and the aromas of supper invading the great room. The girls' lively voices stirred the men and they all rose to take seats at the table. The last one to arrive was the red-headed man who had trailed the party as it progressed up the mountain, making sure they were never being followed. He had been reading by the strongest light in the room, a place where the glow from the fireplace and an overhead sconce intersected. He closed his book but his mind was still in it as he took his place at the table. Only then was Magnus's attention turned to food.

Magnus was the only one at the table who was not a Wilker native. He had come from up north, across the bay, which was well known for being a developed and advanced realm. It had the advantage of being on an isolated peninsula. While other realms spent the centuries fighting each other over prized ground and borders, Brylle had built cathedrals and a great city with a busy trade port. They were fabled for their university and its huge library, but many of the peasants in Wilker simply didn't believe it existed. Five years ago when Magnus's wife had died suddenly, a friend urged him to travel as a way to keep the sad memories from lodging in his mind. Such tragic events had a way of doing that, and the mind should be given better things to contemplate. When Magnus arrived in Wilker, he was awarded an introduction to the Viscount of Wilker, the same Gustav who now sat across the table from him. Travelers from so far away were rare and Gustav was curious when he heard about him. At their first meeting, Magnus entered the royal hall and the introduction was belted out by the Speaker of the Chamber:

"The right honorable Sir Christian Magnus presents his salutations to the Viscount of Wilker, his father the Count, and all the people of Wilker in friendship and good will." And after that all formality vanished. Gustav was very curious to speak with a traveler far from home. Traveling for pleasure was rare enough, and a trip as far as this was very unusual. After a bit of conversation, Gustav began to sense that here was someone who did not dress up or disguise his opinions merely because he was in the presence of the Count. He also began to detect a superiority that he was eager to test or disprove. So he asked Magnus at length,

"If it were possible to improve Wilker, how would you go about it?" Being its future ruler, Gustav was keen to believe his realm was the best, even when humbly compared to Brylle, a land far away and thought of as legendary, but in truth unknown to most. But instead of grasping for some vague suggestion, Magnus was quick with an answer.

"A bridge across the river Wilker far upstream would be most beneficial. I crossed into Wilker on its northern boundary, and could almost view the bluffs upon which your castle stands, yet was compelled to travel many leagues south in order to cross the river where it is wide and flat and can be forded on foot. Thence I had to return north along the eastern side of the river until finally arriving at your kingdom nearly a fortnight after having first glimpsed it from afar." Magnus ended there, as if this alone was a remarkable revelation. Gustav well knew the route and could find nothing exceptionally smart in the idea of reducing the length of the trip. Indeed, such isolation meant that the threat of invasion was nearly non-existent from that side. He noted to Magnus,

"We have enjoyed decades of peace thanks to our rocky river banks. What advantage do you see in bridging that?"

"I see the advantage of easy trade with lands that have much to offer you. While your realm is filled with craftsmen and merchants, most are still in only plain circumstances due to the lack of greater volume of trade. If they had an easy route to buyers eager for their unique goods, the trade in coins and intellectual commodities in the other direction could only be of value to your realm. Your craftsmen are a great asset to Wilker; make it easy for them to prosper through the advantage of efficient trade and travel and all Wilker will prosper." Gustav paused there to consider the idea, then casually checked with his scribe to see that the information of their exchange had been duly recorded. He then turned back to his guest and invited him to stay for a month of food and hospitality, in recompense for how long it had taken him to arrive.

A month went by but Magnus never left. After a while, the books he had brought with him had become great objects of interest among the court people and were talked about in the village. Even among those who could not read, they were held in high regard. He lent them out and did not want to leave before getting them back. Magnus found it novel to be so singularly regarded. In his own land, he was one of many with education and thoughtful intelligence. Here he was revered and held in a certain amount of awe. The accent in his speech and even the color of his hair was unusual. So Gustav made him an honorary member of his court and he was often consulted on matters of nature and foreign affairs, having traveled widely. Otherwise he was left to study what volumes of science and literature he could obtain. For it was not that Wilker was without books or learned men, only that they were fewer and somewhat far between.

3

Dreams and Totems

The meal was ended and the women were taking the empty platters back to the kitchen. Vatra took a scrap of chicken skin and held it up to the vigilant wolfhounds; all of them were on the floor lying on their bellies, heads obediently resting on paws, eyes shifting, mouths drooling. He gestured to one of the dogs and it promptly stood while the others watched. The chosen dog held his paw up and Vatra tossed the scrap of food in the air; the dog caught it in his mouth and sat back down to eat. Vatra had carefully divided the left over food into four equal parts and proceeded to single out each dog in turns for its share. Next to him, Trevka had his own chin propped on his stacked fists on the table, his eyes shifting from table to kitchen to table as the ladies carried away the plates, goblets and silverware. Boris continued with another tale from his past.

"That maiden used to follow me when I went into the marketplace.

Her mother had to lock her up finally on Saturdays just to keep her from wandering off and getting lost in the woods while trying to follow after me." Liesse took the empty plate in front of Trevka and he smiled up from his fists at her. She winked at him and went back to the kitchen. "They say she became a nun when she couldn't follow me any more. A shame really, for she was a comely lass, with breasts that swayed like goat udders in the morning." Boris sighed into his tankard of sack. "Pity, flesh like that buried under a frock of black wool for all eternity and me the cause of it." Harz had his arms crossed and was leaning back in his chair, watching the twins and regarding Boris only occasionally. Magnus had left the table and resumed his reading. Gustav appeared to be listening but in fact was rather lost in his own thoughts. He kept imagining that a girl was giggling, flirting, tickling his ear. He glanced at Genivee and Liesse as they retrieved more empty plates but dismissed his imaginings. He looked up at the stuffed Snowy Owl perched above the fireplace. It stared back down at him.

Outside, Sparrow was reclined in a crook of tree limbs; she could sit for hours like that silently watching and listening. It was something she did when she didn't feel like hiking all day. She had been trying to get Gustav's attention, to see if he responded with delight or indifference. He would be curious, which she smiled at, but then he'd shake his head and dismiss his imaginings. His thoughts were often pulled back into the castle from which he had only just retreated. He wasn't yet completely away from it.

Gustav had reminded her of a time when she had come upon a rabbit caught in a leg trap. The rabbit would have become somebody's meal soon except that she spotted it first. It was wide-eyed and panting. The injury was something she could splint and wrap and the rabbit would likely be fine but the animal was so afraid that she feared it would kill itself struggling to get away. She backed away from it and laid down on her back, making herself as flat as possible so the rabbit would be less intimidated and could get used to her presence. She lay there imagining herself freeing the leg trap; she knew how they worked for many poachers used them, and many had been left in the forest, forgotten or abandoned. She imagined wrapping the leg with a twig for a splint and a lock of hair from her own head. She saw herself caressing the rabbit's frightened body and protecting it gently in her arms. She repeated the image of removing the leg trap and the rabbit became quiet. She was then able to remove the trap and wrap up the little leg. She took the rabbit back to her abode and fed it and cared for it, until one morning it hopped off on its own. Now she wanted to take Gustav back to her abode and bind up his sadness.

When she thought of Gustav saving an eagle, she wished her father had been present to see it so that she could say to him, 'You see, here is a good man. They are not all bad as you say.' Memories of his wife Gertrudis held him down, however. Sparrow didn't like seeing him this way; she wanted to see him again as she had when he journeyed up the path toward the lodge, chatting with his cousin and casually plucking a feather from some tree bark and tucking it into his jacket. It was difficult to keep his mind listening to hers. It kept wandering off again, like a curious young mouse following its nose.

"The feather," Sparrow whispered to him again. "See me in your mind; I am the one who has worn this feather before I gave it to you. It connects us now." But she could only distract him for a few moments at a time. He would look around as if trying to remember something, his attention off the feather again. Fortunately, he tucked the feather back inside his jacket and she spent the rest of the evening imagining herself tucked inside his jacket, softly sighing and breathing in the scent of him. The women had already gone off to bed in their room over the kitchen, most of the men fell asleep in the great room near the fire and the Count went up to his own room on the second floor.

Just before dawn, a band of light appeared on the horizon and the wolfhounds' ears perked up, because to them the light had made a sound like chimes in a breeze. Inside, Gustav was asleep and dreaming. He was back at the edge of the forest under the sweet gum tree with the nest. He was looking up into the tree, trying to see if the eagle and her eaglets were there, to see that they were all right now. He heard a noise from the forest and turned to look for it. It sounded like a whisper or a sigh. Then there was a slight rustling, a flutter of leaves and she seemed to float down from a tree and land in front of him: A girl with long brown hair dressed in only vines of flowers and feathers, standing barefoot and gazing at him, looking both curious and knowing at the same time. She turned suddenly and pranced off, glancing over her shoulder, making sure he knew to follow. She was staying just one step ahead of him, but he might catch her if he was lucky. A flower petal came off her dress and fluttered back to him and touched his face, soft and fragrant. It slowed him down and now he had to run faster to catch up again. Then a downy feather was carried back to him in the wake of her path. She giggled and twirled in her running and more petals and feathers drifted back at him, and more of her skin became visible between the vines and leaves of her dress. He watched her body take shape and willed more of the scanty dress to fall away, and it did but still he couldn't catch her. He made one great effort to run forward and reach out and grab her arm, but just when he would have caught her she turned into a bird and flew away, swooping above the trees and out over the meadow. He watched her from the ground as she flew farther away, getting smaller and smaller. Dogs were howling for her not to go. Then there was the very real howling and barking of the dogs as they bounced and scattered like moths at a candle and waking him up when he should have been allowed to sleep as late as he pleased.

Trevka should have been keeping the dogs quiet or trying to find out why they were making such confusion in the first place. Gustav rolled over and buried his head in his eiderdown pillow, wishing the dream back, trying to capture the image of her face. Now he remembered it; hadn't he been thinking of her last night? It must be a woman he'd met before. No, that's not right. He had never met her before, no one in his realm wore clothes like that. When he had dressed and gone downstairs, his eyes still sleepy and dark, he asked Trevka why they had all been awoken so early. Trevka answered,

"The dogs were all running around in circles; I thought they must have caught the scent of someone about the place, but when I went out and commanded them, they could give no direction to the scent, so there was nothing for me to follow." Trevka paused, then added in a whisper, "They say ghosts carry a scent to awaken the living to their presence." Trevka rocked back on his heels and rolled his eyes slowly overhead, because a ghost with a scent could certainly listen as well. Gustav ended further conversation by sitting down to wait for the food to arrive. Trevka sat and waited too, not mentioning the thought that nagged at his mind: Whomever had tried to trap an Imperial Eagle might have followed them up the mountain despite their watchfulness. He didn't know which was worse, ghosts or poaching thieves, and certainly had no desire to be ordered to chase criminals through a haunted woods.

The rest of the men came to the table and the women brought bread and ale and dried meat and they all ate quietly at first, then with more conversation about where they would go and what they would do. Gustav listened as Harz and Boris considered the various options. It might be better to head for the meadow now, before any more rain made it too boggy. If the ground were dry enough, they might be able to go as far as the pond on the far side. Harz told Trevka to weigh the falcons and get the lightest one ready for a trip.

When the horses had been assembled and a dinner was packed, they set off with their falcon and two dogs, venturing higher up into the woods until at midday they crested a small ridge and were on the rim of a mountain meadow. In the meadow was a small lake as big as the entire village of Wilker. They ambled toward it, but not too closely because they didn't want to scare off all the game to be had. They dismounted and allowed the horses to graze and their echos to fade, and waited for the wild animals to come back out of hiding. Trevka carefully moved the box with the falcon onto the ground and peeked inside, then quickly re-shut the cage and went to find his gloves. Everyone watched him as, now gloved, he balanced the bird on his hand and set it on top of the box, allowing it to get its bearings while he backed away from it. It could sit there tied to its perch with its hood on for hours as far as he was concerned. They all rested for a while, eating their packed provisions, twisting grass around their fingers and dozing off. They had been anxious to arrive in plenty of time to hunt, and now were overtaken by the warm sun and an overwhelming desire to be lazy.

Trevka stuffed the last two bites of food into his mouth, flicked his fingers, and still chewing, pulled a pack of cards from his jacket pocket and began turning them over, trying to invent a game of solitaire. They were not suit cards but pictorial cards. He had just acquired the deck at the market. An old woman purportedly painted the cards, with drawings of animals and scenes from nature. They were supposed to teach people the wisdom she felt was disappearing from common knowledge. However, she herself had not sold him the deck, there were no instructions and he didn't know how to use them. Boris noticed Trevka's cards, then reached over and grabbed one, and with a dismissive squint snorted, "A squirrel?" Cards without kings were clearly worthless. Trevka snatched the card back and said in a low voice,

"It means something." Unfortunately he wasn't sure what. Boris answered instead:

"It means your nuts are in short supply and hard to find." Trevka frowned. He wished the cards came with some explanation. Boris relaxed back onto the grass exhaling a sputtering dismissal. Harz was on the other side of Trevka and extended his arm; Trevka put the card reluctantly into the outstretched hand. It was actually a good little drawing of a squirrel with its cheeks full of nuts and one big acorn in its paws, ready for winter. Its big bushy tail seemed to protect it from behind and Harz thought Trevka could do with as much industry and foresight. He handed the card back to Trevka and said,

"You might learn something from these." Then he too closed his eyes and allowed his sleepiness to overtake him. The sun was directly overhead and the men all sank into a torpor. Some of Trevka's cards flipped over in the wind as he dozed off. The breeze sighed through the grass and the horses munched and chewed while the two dogs slept soundly. The hawk bells on the falcon's legs jingled now and then as it adjusted its stance, unconcerned with the passing of time. Gustav was lying back on a tree stump with his hands laced behind his head. The others were scattered along the trunk of the long-ago fallen tree. His eyes had started to close when the wind carried one of Trevka's cards towards him. He picked it up and viewed a drawing of an owl. Three words were written along the edge of the card: *wisdom, magic, fertility*. The card fell out of his hand as he dozed off. A gust of wind rushed through the meadow as if an enormous door had opened, heralding the entrance of something important. The breeze settled again but there was something different now in the meadow.

A rustling was heard. The men opened their eyes but were careful not to make any noise. At first all they could see was the chest-high grass moving independently of the wind direction. Then there appeared a fluffy brown body which rumbled and grunted. The grass moved again, or rather parted for the passing of an immense, stocky animal. All they could see was the spine of it; a large curve of backbone covered with fur, it seemed to be like a boat keel parting the waves of grass as it passed, but this one was sailing upside down. It heard something or smelled something and looked up. Two spikes resembling drinking horns popped up, attached to a solid brown head with large brown eyes that seemed to regard them for a moment. Then it disappeared again into the tall grass.

Trevka jumped up and pointed, exclaiming with a whisper, "A wisent!"

The wisent was the central character on the Count's coat of arms.

Gustav had never seen one alive, and was quite surprised to see one now. An animal native but rare to this country, the wisent was a symbol of wealth and power. With rounded shoulders taller than its head and spanning half the length of its body, its backbone was sometimes all anyone saw of it. Its large head was close to flat on each side, giving it a huge profile with a forward-pointing skull and a long, shaggy beard that hung nearly to the ground. Its hindquarters were streamlined and trim. It was as heavy as 15 men. It was so rare and unusual for people to see one that it was often thought of as mythical.

The men watched it lumber through the meadow, then emerge clear of the grass to stand at the water's edge. Its stout and formidable body made it apparent why it had been chosen for the Wilker coat of arms, but the tiny shadow of a symbol drawn on shields and doors and tunics conveyed so little of the massive, strong body now regarding them across the meadow.

*There they are, just as Sparrow said they would be. Yes, I am impressive. I am abundance. See my great horns? They point to the heavens; you should be so attentive. You have drawn me on your Flag. I am honored. But do not let that small image rob you of my wonder; see what I really am and carry **that** in your hearts.*

The wisent drank quietly, then raised its head and ran full charge along the edge of the pond and then away, giving them a display of its graceful speed, so surprising given its bulky body and short-looking legs. It was the long, knotty fur that gave the impression of it being a lumbering beast, but in fact it was swift and clever, and the running display entertained them, and they watched in silence as it cleared a distant ridge line with a lilting gallop, leaping for fun. Gustav pondered the lack in his education that had failed to ever convey to him the full import of the totem on the Wilker flag. He wondered if there were a sculptor in the realm who could do justice to the animal and create something to display in a prominent location.

On a rim of the meadow opposite the one the wisent sailed over, Sparrow watched the animal go and thanked it silently for coming. She had had to call it over from quite a distance away with the lure of the lake as incentive; it was necessary to suggest some sleepiness to the group of men to make them delay their falconry and wait for it. A wisent seemed to have significance for Gustav, and she was pleased she had been able to tickle some joy out of Gustav's serious demeanor. "My dear, solemn man," she sighed to herself, wondering what exactly a sculptor did.

Once the wisent had cleared the ridge and was out of view, Trevka leaped from his spot of flattened grass and quickly retrieved his wandering cards. He began shuffling through them, looking for the depiction of a wisent. Surely there was one in the deck. Harz told him to put them aside and bring the falcon, which he jumped to do, then remembered his gloves, bent to get them, then slowed as he approached the bird and carefully coaxed it onto his hand. He walked over to Gustav and gladly handed the bird over to him.

Gustav took the hood off the falcon and allowed it to gaze around at its surroundings. Boris said, "Let's give those lasses who cook for us something better to roast than old hens," which gave the signal to the pages to bring the dogs and begin walking through the meadow with sticks, beating at the grass to flush out a rabbit for dinner. Suddenly the falcon took off flying and circled high over the lake, startling a flock of geese resting on the far side. The geese took to the air and the falcon singled one out and dove down to it. It knocked the goose on the head and the goose fell to the ground stunned while the dogs bounded around the water's edge toward it with the pages running off after them.

By the time they returned, both dogs and pages were panting from the exertion of running and of carrying a twenty pound goose. It would be more than enough for tonight's meal. Gustav held up his hand as the falcon landed and gripped tight with a jingling of its bells. It was rewarded with some jerky and then returned to its box. Trevka proudly hung the goose on his saddle and they set off on their horses back to the lodge. As Sparrow watched them go from her vantage in the distance, she wished she could make the other men in the party return to the lodge by themselves and leave her and her Count alone in the meadow. She put this idea into their heads, trying to shoo each one away, and although they made a rather mixed-up departure from the meadow, they all left together. After a time she followed them at a distance.

Returning to the lodge late in the afternoon, Trevka jumped off his horse and carried the goose into the kitchen. He swung it around in an arc before depositing it onto the central table, but it intercepted a copper pan hanging on a hook. Genivee ducked from the flying pan and said, "Nice goose," Trevka chased after the errant pan and placed it on the table next to the bird. He figured they could cook the goose in the pan. He looked up at Genivee and asked,

"Anything else I can help you with?" Genivee shook her head and pointed him out the door saying,

"You rest your broken arm."

There was a rule in Wilker that men were not permitted to touch a woman in any other than a helpful way, so men were often asking women if they could help. It was a way of starting a conversation with them and also because to fail doing so could mean that a woman might accuse a man of wrong-doing simply by saying she had never asked for his help. Even men who knew nothing of cooking or housekeeping might offer help, but wise women didn't accept such offers, as men often proved to be both really poor at housework and really offering something else.

Vatra had finished taking care of the horses after their day's journey and stood in the doorway of the kitchen until Genivee looked over to him. He asked her, "Would you like me to dress that goose for you?" Genivee nodded and set several knives on the table for him.

She could do the job herself, but it would take her quite a while and she was busy with other things. Vatra was experienced and would finish the job quickly. Liesse was busy making bread and stoking the fires in the ovens. Although the two girls had had the whole day to themselves with only two wolfhounds for company, they had not accomplished very much. They had spent most of the day exploring the lodge, looking into every room and taking an especially long time to examine the closets and wardrobes. It was part superstition and part curiosity. In a royal hunting lodge such as this, there must surely be secret passageways, hidden compartments, mislaid treasure, possibly even the skeleton of a long-dead kitchen maid hanging behind a false wall. Perhaps beside the bones would be a note scribbled by her as she slowly suffocated, confessing to all her grisly sins and explaining her reasons for turning so evil and poisoning everyone excepting her final prosecutor, the only knowing one among them. But there was nothing like that, only a forgotten but telling undergarment gathering dust under a feather bed.

They were young women hoping to corner an advantageous marriage one day. Not that they had designs on any of these men, who were all too far above them in station, except perhaps the pages. But to be thought well of by them, to be able to do one of them a small favor that would be remembered, that in itself would be a very useful recommendation. It was their first trip away from the castle, a privilege only a few were ever granted. They intended to make the most of it and be able to tell tales about it for the rest of their lives. For all they knew they would never again have such an adventure.

It would be hours before the meal was ready and in the meantime there was bread and cheese on the dining table. Magnus was setting up a game of backgammon and Boris was talking by the fireplace with Trevka who was arranging the kindling for the evening fire in a very precise way. Boris said sagely, "A wisent, my boy, is like a woman. They may look harmless and scamper off when they think you've noticed them. But don't believe those coy maneuvers. They can come back to plague you." Trevka continued to arrange the wood, saying under his breath,

"That wisent didn't look harmless to me; he looked like he could swallow me up without even belching."

"*She*, my boy, *she* looked harmless," Boris corrected Trevka.

"That was a female?" *Heaven help the males*, Trevka thought to himself. Then it occurred to him, "How do you know?"

"My page, a wisent is a creature that can change form; look smaller if it needs to, look bigger when it wants to. Just like a woman. They're never quite what they seem." Trevka pondered this. He had studied women quite a lot. They always seemed to be what they looked like. Now he grew suspicious and glanced in the direction of the kitchen. Harz came in from outside and noticed no warmth or crackling from the fireplace. He went over to Trevka and, rubbing his hands together, asked him if that great pile of logs would ever ignite or if they were doomed to pass the night in cold and darkness.

Trevka warned him: "Prepare to stand back – you may get scorched." He picked up his flint and steel and examined them carefully. Boris and Harz looked down at him, then at each other. Harz leaned over and whispered to him,

"Liesse has the fire going in the oven; I'm sure she'd let you light some fatwood." Trevka extracted a stick from his careful arrangement and headed to the kitchen to borrow some fire.

After an evening of backgammon, a huge meal and at length a blazing fire, Gustav climbed the stairs to the lord's bedroom. It was near one end of the long building. The lodge was constructed in the shape of a broad semi-circle such that looking out any window on the front side, a person could see whomever might be approaching from the road below, and looking out any window along the back, could see a panorama of the mountainside and whomever might be sneaking in from above. Being so long also meant it would be more difficult to quickly surround the lodge. The builders had been thoughtful enough to leave many trees still standing at the ends of the lodge, which meant protection extended even beyond its ends. But such tactics were hardly exploited any more. It was mostly poachers and squatters who were the problem now.

Once in his room, Gustav went to the window and looked out. The moon was a narrow crescent just setting and by chance visible between a few trees, looking as if it were caught on a limb. He thought back to the eagle they had saved only yesterday, relieved the rescue had turned out well. Wasn't it a good portend for the beginning of his reign as Count? Then he did hear a bird, an owl softly cooing into the night. He listened but there was no responding call from another owl. Perhaps it wasn't looking for a mate. The words on Trevka's owl card came back to him: *wisdom, magic, fertility.* He wouldn't have minded a little of all three. He took off his jacket and fell onto the bed.

Dreaming he was back at the edge of the forest, Gustav gazed up into the sweet gum tree and knew something was perched on a high branch. He couldn't see, but it sounded like a girl sighing softly. 'My babies,' she said, 'They are here in this nest, but will not survive without your help. There is one more bird for you to engage with. Do not leave the task to another.' Gustav tried to see through all the branches of the tree. He hadn't known there had been eaglets in the nest; it came as a surprise. He had a sudden feeling of great importance about the rescue, of fatherly protectiveness. But something had been left undone; something started now needed finishing. The eaglets in the nest still teetered on the brink of existence. He tried to question the voice in the tree, but it only returned soft humming like a lullaby, for him or the eaglets he wasn't sure. The dream faded and a pink sunrise filled the room but still he heard the humming of a melody, soothing and sweet. She must be just outside his window. He listened to her soft tune for a minute but it stopped when suddenly Genivee chirped to Liesse, "Eight this morning!" and realized she had been the one humming a tune while gathering eggs laid in odd places by the chickens.

4
Investigating a Rogue River

After breakfast, Boris and the pages were outside gathered around the smoke shed that had been damaged, probably in a winter storm. Boris proclaimed, "Take it all down, there's no saving it." But Trevka countered with,

"All we need to do is rebuild this one wall." Vatra had yet another opinion:

"There aren't enough good boards; we'll have to make a smaller shed."

Magnus was sitting on a bench outside the kitchen. It seemed obvious to him what design flaw had led to the structure's failure. None of them seemed concerned with that, though. He could draw them a sketch how to rebuild it, but had no desire to be in the midst of such activity, and besides that, the only paper he had was bound into the book in his hands. He regarded the three discussing repairs, then looked back down at the pages of his book and continued reading. The men continued pointing and arguing, but no one lifted a hammer.

Harz also turned away from watching the smoke shed discussion and sat back down at the dining table across from Gustav. He waited for him to speak first. Finally Gustav said casually, "Well, what shall we occupy ourselves with today," ignoring the possibility of taking any interest in the smoke shed. Harz leaned back in his chair and gazed at the ceiling for a moment, then proposed,

"We could take a trip. Word is there was a flood last spring in the Marianna Valley and that the river shifted. Now there is more farmland on the Wilker side." Gustav raised his eyebrows. After a silence during which Gustav didn't disapprove the idea, Harz continued. "Some Elster farmers are saying they've been robbed of their former farmlands and they intend to take their case to the Elster Ministers. As long as we are halfway there, we could go ourselves to see how much truth there is to this." Gustav thought about it and said wryly,

"You mean their story might have changed by the time it got to the castle?"

"Yes," Harz answered, "assuming their stories even came out of the valley with truth in them." Gustav glanced outside at the smoke shed; one board had been removed and was being discussed and examined. Yes, he'd rather take a trip far away. He nodded to Harz, who concluded,

"It should take about three days, all together." Gustav nodded again. Harz stood up and glanced out the window; all the men would want to go along, but one of them would have to stay behind with the women. They couldn't leave them alone for three days and nights with only a few dogs. Harz considered Trevka, now trying to grab the board from Boris who seemed to be threatening them with it. But Trevka would only pester and annoy the girls worse than a bed bug, and he could not be entirely trusted alone with them; for that matter neither could the girls. Vatra, moving away from the waving board, was not a good choice either because Trevka would be so jealous he would make life miserable for everyone and complaining endlessly to cover his envy. Boris was the Count's physician and bodyguard. Harz had heard the complaints. Magnus would certainly know the territory and any foreign languages they encountered. But by the same token, he was also a good choice to leave behind, in case any visitors, friendly or otherwise, showed up at the lodge. He would know how to deal with them, as well as a forest fire or other odd happenstance. These were all rare and unlikely, but Magnus was ever calm and intelligent, even in dire circumstances.

Harz went into the kitchen to explain to Liesse that they would be taking a trip of a few days, and to pack provisions into saddlebags for five men for three days. She and Genivee would remain behind with Magnus, and this seemed to disappoint Liesse a little, but she turned to her tasks in the kitchen. Cooking all day and then doing less work for three days seemed a fair trade.

Harz then went to the doorway and looked out on the yard where the smoke shed still half-stood, half-drooped, as the three men around it argued like schoolmasters over a delinquent child. He glanced down at Magnus and told him he'd have the lodge to himself for three days while the rest of them took a surveying trip. Except the women, of course. Magnus nodded, glanced as Trevka swung a hammer and nearly missed hitting Boris, then went back to his reading. Harz shouted at the three that they had only the rest of the day to finish, and they glanced over their shoulders at him. Boris grabbed the hammer out of Trevka's hands and started swinging while both twins ducked.

The following morning, Gustav, Harz, Boris and the pages set off on a path heading east from the lodge. Two of the dogs went with them while two stayed behind. Magnus watched them go, then took the dogs with him on a circuit of the lodge; he wanted no surprises now that it was all under his protection. By the time he returned to the kitchen side of the building, the girls had disappeared somewhere back into the lodge or wherever girls went all day long. They seemed forever busy but there wasn't always much to show for it.

He remembered his wife, now dead these five years. She had been fathomable; was it just because she was from Brylle also? Was it just his imagination or true that stunning beauties were more prone to be either silly or mean? To him integrity was beauty, which was much harder to recognize at first glance. Familiarity with these conundrums made it easier for him to shun the obsessions that so possessed the younger pages. Would the pages settle into more decorum if they married? It was an idea worth contemplating, and Magnus looked forward to three quiet days in which to ponder these and many other ideas.

After dinner Magnus settled himself next to the fire in the great hall with several books around him, and the women knew they would get no more than one-word replies and nods from him. They went off somewhere and Magnus enjoyed the unusual solitude. Having the lodge and his books to himself was quite pleasant, only a backgammon competitor would be nice. Although he liked riding and exploring well enough, having a roof over one's head was preferable to being rained or snowed on. He had noticed some very high altitude clouds drifting above that morning, but it might all come to nothing.

Along the mountain trail to the Marianna valley, the party of five moved along making good progress in spite of Boris' greater attention on recounting a tale than keeping his eyes on the rock-strewn path that wound around the northern tail end of the mountain ridge separating them and the Marianna Valley. Fortunately, the pass did not have snow or deep mud over it. That was always possible, even in late August. Boris declared, "I once rode for three days over a pass like this to a lass that had sworn her allegiance to another man. But I knew that was a made-up tale to confuse her mother, who didn't like me." Trevka considered this, then asked,

"Then her mother had had the opportunity to get to know you?" Boris narrowed his eyes and said,

"My lad, no mother ever thinks her daughter can choose the right man for herself. It is always the duty of a mother to choose for her daughter a man like the one she herself let get away twenty years before."

"So you *did* know her mother. Were they *both* running away from you?" Trevka appeared to be the only one listening.

"Young man, they were not running away from me. I gave the mother the slip and was intending to catch up to the daughter, who had pretended to run away with the fiancee arranged for her. It was the only way the girl knew to get away from her scheming mother." They all walked along in silence for a while. It seemed like a desperate plan for star-crossed lovers, but no one wondered about the outcome; Boris was still a bachelor. Finally Trevka asked him,

"But she disappeared into the night and you never saw each other again?" Boris coughed deeply, then replied,

"Well, after a manner. Somehow the fiancee got wise to us and intercepted my lass." Boris' voice rose loudly and bravely. "They were married," he declared in the same flat tone one might use to say, *they found her dead body.* "And after that, it pained my heart to look at another girl who possessed the same magical glint in her eyes." Boris' solemn tale came to an end just as they reached the edge of the pass. The horses ambled around a rocky outcrop and instead of facing another rocky outcrop, before them was suddenly a vista so broad and vast that Trevka pulled up on his reins, thinking his horse was going to walk right over the edge of the earth.

"I had no idea the valley was this big!" Trevka said in surprise. His horse was turning in circles as he held the reins tightly against his chest. Behind him Vatra came upon the view and paused beside his brother, making the rotating horse stop its whirling. He whistled long and slow as he tried to see where the river came into view and where it left, but both places were too far away. The valley was checker-boarded with square fields of green, gold and brown, except where the silver ribbon of the Marianna River meandered through. Where the river bordered the fields, there were sinuous boundaries, some of them nearly an entire circle around. Boris remarked to the pages,

"Where did you lads think all the food to feed the kingdom came from? The grain to make the bread, and all the grass and hay to feed the cows and horses over the winter comes mostly from here. Not to mention your occasional beet, your parsnip and even your poor pathetic turnips." There were miles upon miles of farmland, far more than they could cover in a day. Even locating the flooded land would be a feat of exploration.

It was going to be dark well before they could reach the river, so they turned their attention to finding a place to spend the night. They found an outcrop of rocks that formed a shelter of sorts and made camp. The pages built a fire in the center of the enclosure and rolled out rugs for everyone to sleep on. The horses were tied together at the place where the rocks were farthest apart. It offered a fair amount of protection, in fact, which made Harz relax a little.

They ate jerky and bread and cheese and were sitting around the fire, glad to be resting. Boris played his rackett, a small instrument that fit in his hands and made soft little twangs while Vatra worked on braiding some leather for the horse's tack. Trevka was examining the leather strap that an eagle had been trapped by and was now his. It had shaded stripes across its length, and one deep scratch that he was sure had been made by an eagle talon. It was some kind of sign, he felt sure, like his cards.

There was a chill settling over them and Harz dug his hands into his jacket pockets for warmth and found something wrapped in a cloth. He hadn't expected to find a surprise and it made him suddenly nervous. He had been imagining all day that they were being followed, but could never spot anyone. He pulled out the cloth and unwrapped it; it was a small apple turnover. This didn't make sense as all the food was carried together in saddle bags. He was about to suggest to Trevka that a gift meant for him had found its way into the wrong pocket, but instead he ate the treat, tucking it back in his pocket after each bite.

Before the last of the sunlight faded from the sky, Harz got up to look around. Standing outside the ring of boulders, he spotted a campfire in the distance somewhere along the same broad slope they were on. It was too far away to investigate with what little light was left. Were they poachers on royal land? Or were they mere Elster hunters camping a little too far to the west? Harz studied the boulder enclosure. He hoped their own campfire did not send out a beacon to these distant persons unknown. He estimated the line of sight from their bright fire back to the campfire in the distance. But when he looked back in that direction, he couldn't find the fire again. The pediment before him was completely dark. It was getting cold and he yanked his jacket around him tightly, grateful for the strand of fur around the collar. He walked back into the ring of boulders and took his place by the fire. He gripped the empty cloth around the crumbs in his pocket. The wolfhounds were fast asleep by the fire; they would wake up if there were something to hear or smell. He could put his trust in them. He laid down and wrapped the rug around him.

From outside the boulder enclosure, Sparrow too saw the campfire far away. She noticed it being extinguished and knew that people who intend to stay put and sleep well do not extinguish a fire at sunset when the chill is settling in. Those people were headed towards the royal survey party, and at night under a moonless sky. Sparrow sensed who they were, and had thought for a little while that Gustav was hunting down these two poachers, but she knew now this was not true. It was just coincidence that the two parties had been converging. The royal party had settled down for the night and were ignorant of the fact that headed for them, with bad intentions in total darkness, were the Rogues.

Sparrow felt the Rogue's thoughts coming towards all of them, even though they were still very far away. Their thoughts didn't make sense to her, but they were violent and driven. She had always been able to scare these two away, and perhaps she could still do so tonight. But with the five other men involved, a confrontation could erupt, during which she would be nearly powerless. Without enough confidence in her ability to sway the royals (it hadn't worked trying to make them leave Gustav alone at the meadow), she conjured up a rhyme, because animals of all kinds understood and liked better lines that rhymed:

Great Horned Owl, use your expertise-
Frighten two rats who carry disease
They think of evil and plan great harm
Dissuade them with your shrill alarm

She called out in her mind and turned around in a circle to watch for its approach. When she had completely turned around and again faced the direction of the advancing Rogues, she at last sensed a large female owl flying from beyond the Rogues' direction and straight towards all of them. They would never hear it approaching, making its screams even more terrifying. Sparrow relaxed and sat down to watch the event.

The Rogues, escaped convicts from the south, had no idea they were bearing down on a royal party. They only knew someone was alone on the mountainside and likely had things of value; stores of food, heavy clothes, weapons, and of course horses. They had no intention of starting a melee in which they might not be victorious. They had perfected a trick in which they imitated forest noises and then waited for men to investigate one by one, silently picking them off. Men didn't wake up other men to say they had heard a noise and what could it be? Women did that, and women rarely camped out, but if they did, so much the better.

The Great Horned Owl heard the "Rogues", the rats Sparrow spoke of and saw them, even in the pitch blackness. She beat her wings and flew her fastest, gliding silently towards their heads. Their wild hair made them look like especially tall and deranged rats, and she flew at them while letting out a shriek so strident one of them fell flat to the ground. The other one ducked but the owl had her sights on his matted hair and grabbed at it with her talons, piercing his scalp with a gash that immediately bled. He flailed his arms above him and shouted,

"A witch! A black moon witch has my blood!" He fell to his knees and clutched his scalp, feeling warm blood ooze out. But as instantly as the owl appeared, it was gone. They both caught their breath and waited; nothing could be heard in the night air. There was still a great prize ahead of them, and they were nearly halfway to it. The uninjured one began to think it had just been a trick to frighten them and he stood up and barked, "Curse your hurting - get up!" The injured one moaned and stood up. They began to move forward again. Again the owl came out of nowhere and swooped over their heads. This time it took a chunk of flesh off the other man's scalp and he screamed like a rabbit. The first man turned and headed away from the camping party and the owl, which seemed determined not to let them go on. The other man followed, slouching like a werewolf in the hopes of staying below the flying witch that plagued them. She wasn't getting any more of his skin with which to cast a spell.

Gustav woke up in pitch darkness because of a noise and because something heavy was on top of him. Something that breathed and was warm and had both his legs pinned down. He pulled his arm out from under the rug and felt the long wiry fur of a dog sleeping soundly on top of him. The fire was nearly out and the last of the light it cast reflected off the gray boulders. Whatever had awoken him was now silent and instead he heard the distant cooing of an owl as he drifted back to sleep.

The next day they were all anxious to speak to some people who lived along the Marianna River. Trevka was looking forward to posing stern question to wily farmers. They made their way down the pediment to a bluff overlooking the river valley. From there they spotted a small hamlet and headed towards it. Behind them, Sparrow watched them head into civilization and trusted them to take care of themselves. The chance of finding Gustav alone were now nearly none and she wasn't dressed or ready or meet people. Was she even ready to meet Gustav? She had been following him in his thoughts and felt comfortable around him – in her thoughts. How she would ever meet him face to face she still didn't know. But his trip to this place showed even more his interest in his people and she was even more enamored with him and the idea of his being the father of her child. But for that she would need him to *herself*.

By midday they had reached the knot of cottages and stalls that served as one of many hubs for the merchants and tradesmen who had commerce with the farmers along the valley. They stopped at an inn and were served a simple lunch with fresh meat and some vegetables that were so sweet and crisp that Trevka felt sure they were bewitched vegetables, and they would all soon fall into a sleep from which they would be robbed of their few supplies. But then remembering that their supplies consisted of dried meat and old mushy vegetables, he stopped worrying and had a second helping. After finishing only one course, Harz got up from the table and went to speak with the man who appeared to be in charge of the inn. He said to him in a low voice,

"Might you have some rooms for the night; we are far off from our Count's estate." The innkeeper stared back at Harz in amazement. He too spoke in a low tone,

"You men are from the Count's castle? Be ye merchants for him?" Harz replied,

"We are the Count's Sheriff and deputies, here to investigate the reports of a recent flood changing the fields belonging to the Count." The innkeeper turned and grabbed a jug of sack and thrust it into his daughter's arms and poked his finger towards the lunching party. Turning back to Harz he said,

"Sir, your indulgence please, I did not realize. My wife will have two rooms for you all ready very soon. Until then, be comfortable, please." Harz nodded his thanks, then asked,

"Do you know to whom we could speak who has first knowledge of the flood or of whose fields were changed?" The innkeeper searched his memory, then as the daughter returned from filling mugs, told her to go and fetch a certain crofter. He turned back to Harz and said,

"In a moment, Sir, such a man will be here in a moment of hearing your request." Harz nodded and went back to the table where the rest were still eating, reassured they would be given the best while avoiding tiresome ceremony.

In half an hour, the crofter they had sent for came in and nervously stood by their table telling what he knew of the flood and the farms affected. He refused to sit in the presence of the Count's men even though they invited him to and promised never to tell the Count. He said,

"That Elster field were all surrounded by Wilker land before the flood. It was a circle o' land sticking out into Wilker with the river winding all around it; good land, too. Then this spring the river jumped o'er the small bridge o' land what connected Elster to this patch and now flows straight on where once it flowed clear 'round. That Elster farmer can't cross that river, not wi' plow horses and them big hay carts. He do glare down on our Wilker farmer now, but naught he can do 'bout it. He be right red, he is, but naught he can do." Gustav asked him if the river jumped like that often. The crofter said,

"Naught in my lifetime had I ever seen it so; my grandfather do talk of it happenin' way back, and how thems that lose just has to face it and wait for the river to make fair again one day. But it don't happen much in a lifetime, and sometimes it do take generations to right the land again. Always seems someone thinks they be owed some land." Boris thanked the man, who bowed his head and then left. The "deputies and sheriff" got up to leave and the innkeeper assured them their rooms would be ready when they returned. As they left, the innkeeper and crofter leaned together and watched them go.

The Count and his men spent the afternoon walking through the hamlet and speaking to other people who had their own stories to tell. There was nothing much different in their tales, just that the amount of land gained for Wilker varied from person to person. The exact amount could only be estimated, but most agreed it was a large gain, with some complaining it was still not large enough to right all past wrongs.

They returned to the inn and found their rooms ready. Harz suspected they were actually being put up in the innkeepers' own rooms, but he was not going to complain. It was only one night and the innkeeper already seemed to be enjoying a brisk business at his bar. It seemed no one believed the story that deputies of the Count's had actually come this far. As the party was shown to a private dining room, whispers about which one was the actual sheriff were made. "The big one, he's the sheriff." "No, the tall one, of course he is the sheriff; he asks the questions." The five men sauntered past with Trevka, last in line, especially keen to be a part of their imaginings. He was also keen to catch the eye of the innkeeper's daughter. When she came into the private dining room with several jugs of sack to be left for their convenience, he winked at her and watched her exit, hoping he had at least made her nervous to be noticed by a deputy of the Count. Adding to her consternation was Vatra, standing by the door, not winking.

Long after dinner was over, only the two pages and Boris were left in the dining room. They sat listening to another tale. They were actually there to make sure interest in the Count's men had sufficiently faded away, and to make sure no one tried to follow them to their rooms. While Boris spoke with his forearms resting on his propped knee, the pages watched the daughter come and go. She was being very conscientious about not leaving them unattended for more than fifteen minutes at a time. On her third visit to see the three of them, Trevka asked her if there was any more figgy pie and cider. But Boris cut off his own story to say that she needn't check; they were retiring for the night. He headed towards the stables where the three men, plus one dog, would all be sleeping to ensure that the horses were not switched or stolen, or even their horseshoes traded during the night. Trevka, stomach growling, frowned and followed. Vatra let the chair he'd been leaning back in fall to all fours with resignation and walked out following last. The serving girl watched them go and hoped one of the twins would turn and wink at her again, and just before they were out of the room, one of them did.

Back at the lodge, Magnus was spending the second night of the party's trip away the same way he had spent the first. The day had passed quietly, with the women doing things like mending and giggling and finding reasons to go from one room to another with amazing redundancy. After a quiet dinner, Genivee and Liesse retired to the bedroom they shared over the kitchen and Magnus continued reading by the firelight in the main room with the dogs asleep by the fireplace.

After a time Magnus glanced over the top of his book to see that one of the dogs was sitting up in front of him, either reading the title of his book or else wanting his attention. There was a faint thump somewhere in the house, and the dog turned its head to the noise but did not move from its spot. Man and dog then gazed at each other. Another noise, Magnus supposed, for he didn't hear it, and the dog moved its head again. The second dog lifted its head from its nap and regarded them both. Were they going to investigate or watch each other? Magnus decided a walk would not be unwelcome and closed his book. He was conscious of the fact that he would have to be careful not to startle the ladies; they would assume he had no intention of leaving the great room and he had no way of knowing if they were related to the noises or not. He went into the kitchen, softly whistling, dogs following. Magnus studied the tools and utensils hanging all about; it appeared that cooking would require a certain amount of intelligence and application of skill. Then both man and dogs regarded the remnants of dinner on a platter. There were no more thumps or fading glances from the dog and Magnus considered going back to his book and warm fire when a door squeaked on its hinge and the dog woofed softly in recognition. Magnus knew the dog knew more than he did so said, "Fetch," and the dog trotted happily off towards the women's room. Magnus wouldn't have considered going first, unannounced. They arrived at the room, its door open, and still Magnus was reluctant to glance inside. But the girls greeted the dog happily and cheerfully assured them both that everything was fine. Magnus studied them for a moment, knew they had been moving about through the lodge, knew they were hiding something and knew he would receive no intelligence from these two silly creatures. He nodded, said good night and went back downstairs.

The following morning Magnus woke up to a very quiet lodge. It would be the last such morning. The girls were either not awake yet or taking advantage of the fact that Magnus did not require an early meal, or perhaps they were just going about things quietly. Magnus enjoyed the unusual silence.

At the same time, Gustav was waking up to the sound of softly falling rain on the roof of the inn. The mountains were shrouded in fog, and likely receiving a light snowfall, possibly even the lodge was being dusted with snow. There were voices and aromas from downstairs; bacon and eggs were frying in a pan and the innkeeper's wife was ordering her daughter about. They went down to their breakfast and were served by the wife, and discussed over the meal their arduous return via the northern pass. As they left, Harz gave the innkeeper several gold coins, amounting to three times the cost of a day's hospitality and board. He said to him, "The extra is for your daughter's dowry."

They trotted off north, but on the far side of the same bluff they had stood on just one day ago, they turned and headed south. Anyone overhearing their plans and hoping to follow them would find themselves alone on the northern road. The royal party would have to pass through some Uluvost land, but would get home much quicker and without the threat of snow, and Gustav was in a hurry.

5

A Guest at the Lodge

After breakfast, Magnus took bow and arrow and both dogs and went off to hunt for a better dinner than poorly plucked chicken. Hunting was perhaps not his finest talent, but he possessed a great patience which usually meant eventual success. He returned to the kitchen around noon with several rabbits on a string and laid them down on the kitchen table. Genivee and Liesse were beginning to cook for the return home banquet. They saw the rabbits and cooed over them and then smiled at Magnus. Maybe he had mistaken femininity for silliness, but he wasn't sure.

On the road back from the Marianna Valley, Sparrow stopped following Gustav's party when they were near to the mountain meadow they had come to the first day. She knew they would be all right from here on, she knew the Rogues had gone very far away, being superstitious and believing in flying witches. Sparrow went to the meadow and laid down in the tall grass. It was mid-afternoon and the sun was warm, the early morning storm long past. Wisps of clouds scattered across the sky and she gazed up at them, wondering how she would ever attain her heart's desire. She had sent Gustav so many messages that she wanted to be with him, but he never came out to where she was.

She had dreamed of having a baby ever since seeing a mother deer browsing grass and sniffing flowers while her speckled fawn hid under her belly looking out on the world. It seemed that being a mother was her reason for living. If she never had a chance to do that, what was her life for? She had felt important following and protecting the royal party, as if they were her children. But soon they would be gone and there would be no one to watch over, no one to share her knowledge and experiences with. *Please, Gustav, give me a child before you go. Don't leave me all alone.*

She heard something at the edge of the meadow but didn't look up. Instead, she sent a gentle hello to the noise and asked if she could look up and be seen without frightening. The message she got back was, *I am very protective of my baby and we want to drink here.* Sparrow almost sprang upright, but stopped herself for fear of alarming what was out there, some kind of deer. She whispered her thoughts to the deer, *I will look out for you both; drink here and be safe.* When she felt it was time to look up, she slowly raised herself, wondering exactly what she would see. Fifty paces away was a furry deer-like creature with antlers like tree branches. She'd never seen one, although her father had drawn one in the sand to tell her that they did exist and brought their own message, just like all the other animals. He'd explained,

"This is a reindeer, Sparrow. They used to be much more numerous here, but since there have been so many people hunting these woods in the last decades, they have all pretty much moved further on, keeping to themselves. There is a legend about deer in general; that they draw village people back into the wilderness, and lure nobles, even kings, deep into the woods for some novel quest. They are among the gentlest of creatures, yet not fearful, and have succeeded in surviving in all kinds of circumstances." Sparrow watched the reindeer. It scanned the area for possible threats, determined there was no danger and then sauntered over to the pond, her fawn close by. They touched their noses to the water and then drank, although the fawn soon went back to its preferred meal, milk straight from the teat.

Sparrow watched the little fawn nuzzling its mother and wondered to herself, *How can I find the courage to ask Gustav for a child? I've never spoken to another human being except my own parents, and my thoughts have not been strong enough to bring him to me.* The deer lifted its head and conveyed the message, *You have seen there is no danger, so go toward what you want; it may be gone soon.* If she was to have her own baby to love and raise, she'd have to be much braver than she ever had been before, and go against the very things her father had warned her about. She had thought it would be easy to lure Gustav out to her, but he was too attached to his own ideas to be easily removed from them.

The party returned to the hunting lodge late in the afternoon, feeling weary but fortunate to be back where they belonged. There was a huge meal and they all ate heartily and talked animatedly about the rigors and accomplishments of the trip. When the reporting from Trevka seemed at an end, Gustav asked formally how things had gone while they were away, and Magnus said mildly that all was fine. Harz eyed him carefully but Magnus looked down at his empty plate. Then Trevka resumed his recounting of how he had successfully interrogated hostile farmers from Elster, cowing them into admissions of ill-gotten gains.

That night the twin brothers settled into their sleeping nook in the corner of the great hall, as usual. But Trevka had forgotten something, he said, and went to retrieve it. Vatra was too weary to care what, and fell into his spot sleeping. In fact, Trevka had forgotten nothing, other than that it had been three days since the pleasure of teasing a lady had been his privilege (it was never actually his, but he tried it just the same.) He caught Liesse in the kitchen mixing bread dough for the next morning and startled her. She was quite put out and insisted he go back to his place in bed immediately, without the usual coyness. He was surprised and backed away from her, disappointed. Genivee came in as he left and snapped, "What's he doing here?"

"Looking for trouble, as usual." Liesse answered. Genivee shook her head, knowing there'd be trouble.

The next morning Gustav awoke with a sense that his little nymph had whispered in his ear, *I'm here, come be with me.* But wherever *here* was, he did not know where. That is what dreams are like, he thought: Very real at night with only the moon's reflection, but faded and impossible in the full illumination of the day. The forest was enchanted and he had enjoyed dreaming of a creature who desired him. When he returned to the castle in a few days, the dreams would not follow him, the enchantment would be gone and although there might be women who desired him, they would be within the curves of their own shadowy spider webs.

He dressed and went downstairs and sat at the dining table next to Trevka, who was there early, as usual. Trevka had brought his pictorial cards to pass the moments before breakfast and was scanning each one, determined now to find the wisent card. "It's a sign," Trevka said. "It's a sign that great fortune is at hand, somewhere close by." Gustav waited alongside him watching silently with his chin on his hand, slightly amazed at this page's simple diversions and superstitions. Suddenly Trevka barked out triumphantly, "Here it is!" But in that moment the food was carried in and he put the card aside forgotten and began to eat. Gustav picked up a piece of bread and his gaze fell onto the cast-aside card. He narrowed his eyes and looked closer. He picked up the card and stared at it. No wonder Trevka had a hard time finding it before; the wisent depicted was only a small portion of the card's picture, merely an icon on the coat of arms draped across a horse's back. Most of the card depicted a place uphill behind the lodge. It was a place Gustav knew, where the trail swung around a ridge. The horse on the card was under an ancient cedar tree with a distinctively twisted trunk, said to be the oldest tree in the forest. Gustav stood up and pushed back his chair. The table was jarred and Trevka planted his hands down to steady it, but did not pause in his chewing.

Gustav bolted outside to saddle his horse; how dearly he wanted to just ride off. But the Count who rode off on his own would soon be followed by men sworn to protect him. He waited impatiently for someone to emerge from the front door. When Harz came down the stairs for his breakfast, Liesse was looking out the window and said to him, "He's headed off somewhere, looks like." Harz looked at her dubiously, then out the window, then at the table where Trevka was eating in silence. He liked this time of day and wanted very much to sit and eat, but instead sighed, took the piece of bread Liesse offered him with a smile and walked outside. He jumped on a horse and followed Gustav, already heading uphill.

They rode in silence for a ways. Gustav wasn't forthcoming with any explanation about where they were going or why. Finally Harz asked him, "Going hunting?" Gustav looked back, no one followed; looked ahead, no one waited, and considered what to say. 'Yes,' seemed adequate. Then he added,

"I'm looking for a certain cedar tree up this hill. It's very distinct."

Sure, Harz thought, a tree. It was probably there, but not the reason for riding out before breakfast. Harz knew how to get Gustav's attention and the truth at the same time, so he declared loudly,

"Gustav, I think you should promote Trevka to Squire immediately." That made Gustav jerk a look directly at his cousin, and Harz saw right away what was actually on his mind. Unfortunately, Harz was not the man to consult on matters of how to find or captivate a woman. He had been in love only once, and that was half his lifetime ago.

They reached the ridge with the bend in the road when the sun had risen just above the treetops. They dismounted and let the horses browse. Gustav looked around, spotted the twisted cedar and sat down at the foot of it, his mission apparently accomplished. Harz surveyed the land around with a newly keen eye. He wondered what female his cousin was apparently obsessed with. He commented, "How unusual to find a girl in the forest. She must have followed you here from the village."

"Oh she's been following me, but only in my dreams. And she's not from a village." Harz scrutinized the woods, wondering why they had needed to come up here so he asked,

"You dreamed of *here*?"

"Sort of, I saw this spot in one of Trevka's cards." *Trevka's cards*,

Harz thought with wonderment. Maybe there was something to them. He looked around carefully, then as if seeing the twisted cedar for the first time declared, "Ah yes, the tree in question. And perhaps this girl will appear just as unexpectedly."

I'd like for her to find me alone; I'd like for her to appear in my bedroom, Gustav thought. He blamed Harz for following him up here and probably scaring her off. But it was his duty. And there was no one here to scare off. The two of them lingered for a while and then got back on their horses and rode away. Behind some trees nearby, Sparrow had sat listening and was now wagging her head slowly at the inscrutable rules of royal society. *So that's why he hasn't come out to me.* For one thing, his people won't leave him alone. For another, he didn't actually believe she existed. *Well all right,* she thought to herself. *I know what a bedroom is, and if that is the only place you will meet me, I'll go there.* She was only just beginning to realize how easy it was to hide from these people. What in the world had her father ever been so afraid of?

That evening, Sparrow watched and waited in a tree near the lodge. Two of the dogs roamed around, passing by, taking no notice of her. They would be no problem, in fact they would be helpful. The locked door at the front of the house would not. All the knowing and sensing in the world wouldn't get her past a bolted door. She thought about how to get around that and in the meantime she was happy to sit outside the lodge and listen to these people entertain her some more. They certainly did a lot of talking, much of it redundant or contradictory and some of it downright dishonest. She had lost interest in listening to the birds and squirrels after spending a week around people. Birds and squirrels were not nearly so cagey in their interactions with each other. Either a female bird thought a male bird would do or she rejected him. The squirrels barely had that much discernment; a female who found a male had a nice bushy tail was probably well satisfied. The males weren't picky at all.

Human males spent a lot of time *pretending* to be picky, when in fact felt most any female would likely do, and *actually* spent more time trying to calculate which ones would accept them. The women thought in rather the opposite way. They debated back and forth with themselves about the various virtues of each man they knew. They weighed qualities back and forth, thinking of reasons to justify being with them, all the while pretending they were far too busy and disinterested to even consider such a possibility. In truth, they had usually made up their minds and were trying to justify the decision.

Sparrow wondered how much time they could spend making these assessments, probably years from the sound of it. How much easier it was to simply see into someone's heart and decide if they were good or not and if they noticed you in return. She had seen into Gustav's heart and found him to be a man grand enough to command a county but humble enough to help an animal. He was a good man, an honest man. He welcomed her into his dreams. As he sat in the lodge passing the time playing backgammon with his friend, trying to focus on the numbers and discs, she giggled into his thoughts and distracted him. After losing the third game, he headed up to his room for the night wondering at his poor gaming. *Don't feel bad,* she thought, *I made you lose. But you'll cheer up soon, trust me.* Now she could finally get to work.

Sparrow got down from the tree she was in and the two dogs came over to her and sniffed affectionately. One of them stretched out with a quiet whine and sat. They had been a little confused by her a week ago, but now they understood. They all walked over to a door at the far end of the lodge, the side farthest away from the kitchen. Sparrow found a spot nearby and then gave a signal to the first dog. It began to howl and bark as if the devil himself were outside, then backed away from her growling. Sparrow stood frozen in her spot.

Soon Trevka came bursting through the door, calling to the barking dog. He needed to know what the dog was so upset about, and at the same time had no desire to confront whatever that was. The dog barked with a viciousness Trevka knew meant real trouble. In order to quiet the beast, he would have to go out to it, as it refused to come to him. Trevka stepped outside and went towards the howling animal. Behind him, Sparrow and the other dog stepped quietly around the open door and went inside, immediately climbing a flight of stairs. When they had reached the top of the stairs, the dog outside suddenly stopped barking. Sparrow looked down the long hallway and the many doors before her; she would have to trust her dog to show her the right door, but she waited a moment to take a deep breath and gather her courage.

While she hesitated, Trevka came back into the lodge with his dog trotting alongside. He scolded the animal, "What was that all about? I was winning for once." The dog whined and whimpered, and its companion next to Sparrow looked down the stairs in its direction. She knew that downstairs, Trevka's dog was looking upstairs. In the next second, Trevka would call to her dog and it would either trot downstairs obeying him, or else stand by her and Trevka would be up to investigate. Either she'd end up alone in the lodge without the dog having shown her the right door or she would be meeting Trevka very soon.

"Trevka!" Boris' voice boomed down the first floor hallway. "Get back in here fast or your winning streak is over." Trevka swore something and bolted down the hallway, his dog running along behind him and Sparrow's dog standing faithfully by her side. She looked down at it and reminded it what to do. They started down the hallway, her heart beating hard in her chest and her knees swaying like meadow grass. They came to a door. Sparrow would have to trust the dog's instincts, as her own were unreliable in her agitated condition. Maybe this was his room, maybe it wasn't; maybe he wasn't in his own room tonight, maybe someone else was. Maybe he, or they, weren't in it alone. She wasn't sure what to do; her heart was beating too fast to be sure of anything. She put her hand on the door, barely touching it. In a soft whisper, gazing down, she said, "Help me," and suddenly the door flew open.

Gustav had landed on his bed on his back and lay there with his arms stretched out wide. He heard Trevka chase after another barking dog and scold it and then all was calm again. The sudden quiet in his room was complete, so when one of the wolfhounds padded softly down the hallway, he noticed it right away. It was a very soft noise, he just barely heard the tail brush the wall, the toe nails tap the wood. Then it stopped outside his door. He knew in an instant the dog wasn't alone; dogs don't come calling, which meant this one was being led here by someone. He took two strides to a door four steps away and yanked it open. Sparrow blinked at the figure in the darkness, knew at once it was him, paused only a second and then flung her arms around his neck before she could change her mind or say anything.

She flew into him and he didn't let go. He teetered backwards with her hanging on until he felt the bed at the back of his legs and they fell backward onto it together. *I've materialized you right out of my dreams,* he thought to himself and confirmed how real she was by squeezing her tightly and pulling at her dress. She read his mind very easily in this state, it sent images clearly and quickly and while some of them seemed unlikely to contribute to the conceiving of a baby, she trusted him and enjoyed him. It was a bit different than it seemed having glimpsed animals at it. She had never known how lonely her existence was until she was held like that.

Gustav was finally too exhausted to kiss her more or run his hands through her hair and across her face, so he laid on his back and pulled her on top of him, his arms around her. She waited until she heard him fall into a deep sleep and started to move away from him. His arms tightened around her and she waited again for him to fall back asleep. But then his foot planted itself over the back of her legs. She realized he wasn't going to let her go.

In the morning when his eyes opened she smiled at him and said, "I'm Sparrow." She wondered if all the others in the house were in bed with a partner. She wondered why they wouldn't be, but then people did odd things. Or neglected to do things. But then there were sounds from downstairs, and aromas wafted up.

Eventually, there was a knock on the door and Liesse asked through it, "Some breakfast for you?" Without moving or turning, Gustav called out, 'In my room.' After Liesse came back with food and had set it on a table at the other side of the room, Gustav asked her to fetch her smallest dress, which would be replaced later with a better one. She left and came back soon after, laying the dress on a chair but unable to spy anything of his companion. Gustav got out of bed and put some clothes on, then took the dress and pulled it over Sparrow's head, tying its front laces up, reluctantly, and pulling her to him while their food got cold. They sat down at the little table beside the bedroom window and ate. She tried to ignore the tightness and itch of the fabric against her skin and glanced around the room, amazed and confused by most of what she saw. There were items she had never seen before, some of which she could figure a use for, others which were too strange for her to make sense of. Gustav wondered how to fill an entire day until they were together in bed again tonight. Finally it occurred to him to say,

"Oh, I'm Gustav." Sparrow smiled and nodded.

Downstairs, Harz asked Liesse if the Count was all right. He was usually down early for food. "I imagine he is," she answered, feeling one dress poorer. "He's not alone." This made all the men turn their heads in the upstairs direction, but in actual fact it wasn't really extraordinary news. It seemed that women had an uncanny way of finding their way to the highest ranking man.

In his room, Gustav had finished eating and now watched Sparrow slowly try the food in front of her. She was used to roots and nuts, berries and rabbits. She thought the bread was some kind of fake meat, and the cider was some kind of water gone bad. But since he had eaten it, she ate it too, hoping it didn't make her sick later on. When she had eaten a small amount of everything, Gustav took her hand and said to her, "I'm afraid we can't avoid meeting my friends downstairs. No more sneaking in and out." He smiled at her. Actually, sneaking in was fine. But he didn't intend to let her sneak out.

They went downstairs and the room turned silent. Gustav simply told everyone Sparrow's name, and he told her the names of the others. "This is Magnus, he can give you any scientific information you might want."

"Honored," he said, studying her in an analytical way. She

wondered what facts he could have that she would want; it seemed to her eventually there could be many.

"This is Boris, teller of tales and healer of ills." Boris touched his hand to his head and bowed slightly but charmingly. What healing he could know that she didn't know herself made her wonder, but there must be some.

"Genivee and Liesse can bring you any food or articles you might need." The women smiled and nodded at Sparrow. "And Harz," Sparrow turned to the black haired cousin who had hidden so well from her in the beginning, "Harz can tell you anything you might want to know about me." Harz looked her in the eye, the first person to really do so. Maybe he was a man who wouldn't be so easy to hide from, but she had managed it so far. She smiled and thought to herself, *Gustav, there are things I could tell you about him.*

Then looking around for his pages and not seeing them, Gustav said, "And somewhere are Trevka and Vatra, who look exactly alike and are probably not good for much of anything." Genivee suppressed a chortle and went back to the kitchen. Gustav and Sparrow went outside to spend the day in the forest.

Gustav suddenly believed that he understood exactly how this girl had come to be in the forest and was impatient to have only the details filled in. He asked her, "How long have you been here? In the forest, I mean?" She must have become lost; it could not have been for long. She must now feel very grateful that someone found her and would take her back to a village. How good of Gustav to be here to do this, perhaps saving females in need of help would be a legendary trait of his. "Did you become separated from your family? Did they beat you and drive you to run away?" Gustav could not stop asking questions even before getting answers. Sparrow found it hard to have so many words thrown at her at once, but she managed to answer,

"No, my parents did not beat me, they were wonderful to me, but yes I have become separated from them recently." Of course; a little family goes off on a picnic and naively gets lost. The parents disappear and the girl wanders about, despondently eating whatever she can find, praying that someone will rescue her.

"Well, how fortunate I have found you, I can take you back to your home and you will be safe there." Sparrow was very confused by his logic. She said,

"There is nowhere to go back to. I do not know the village my parents came from, I have never been there. This is my home, I have lived here all my life " Gustav stopped in his tracks.

"All your life? But what were your parents hiding from? Were they criminals?" Sparrow realized her parents were right about one thing; for people to leave their village was rare and incredible, and others could not understand it.

"No, they were not criminals, they chose to leave. If they were hiding from anyone, it was their families who had dictated a life for them they did not want to live." Gustav was surprised, not that young people didn't like the lives before them, but that they might run off and succeeded in escaping those destinies.

"But how bad could those lives have been, to run away forever from their families?" Arranged marriages were not unusual, although a bit old-fashioned. But usually they were good arrangements, made to benefit everyone involved.

"Perhaps they weren't so bad, I can't tell. I only know they were not what my parents wanted for their lives, so they left." She made it sound so easy. The way Gustav understood things, people in difficult circumstances complained and bore their lot; very few had the independence to abandon everything they had, just to avoid something they disagreed with. And nobody he knew thought living alone in the forest was possible, let alone preferable. He shook his head in disbelief, saying to himself,

"I thought you must be lost..." Sparrow marveled again at how little he seemed to know for a man in a position of so much power. Sparrow had watched these eight people, all friends, display behavior that showed they did not truly communicate with each other. They thought they knew one another, and there was caring and kindness for one another, but true understanding? They barely understood themselves. She had been sending him thoughts of herself all the time, and yet he did not understand the first thing about her.

"I am not lost," Sparrow said to him gently. "But I fear you may be." Gustav was unaccustomed to having his actions questioned. Of course she did not know he was the Count of Wilker, and he was on the verge of declaring that to her when he heard it in his mind and stopped. He had never in the past been certain that any woman had loved *him*, but instead loved his status or what he could provide. Now here was this very woman in front of him and he was about to bring it all into question just so that he could feel superior. He had never been humbled by one so humble. Why would she think he was lost? She said,

"You love this place, this huge structure in the forest, filled with the things it provides, like shelter and warmth and greenery and solitude. But here tomorrow you plan to leave it and return to something that does not feed your soul. Why would you do this if you were not lost?" Again Gustav was on the verge of saying he was the Count of Wilker with powers and responsibilities. He was not some ne'er-do-well free to ramble about. Again he stopped himself. After all, if he were so powerful, why was he not able to spend all his life at the hunting lodge if he so wanted? He couldn't solve this riddle. He pondered it while forgetting she had seemed to read his mind. Finally he said quietly,

"Perhaps instead of you coming back with me, I should stay here with you." Sparrow wondered for how long he would be happy here. If he was to give up so much power and responsibility, what would replace those, here in the forest?

"I think you would miss your life," she said. She seemed to be already resolved to his leaving. And how did she know he was leaving, anyway? If she didn't want to be taken back to civilization, then why wasn't she begging him to stay in the forest with her? Yet she was not asking him to do either. He wasn't used to people not wanting anything from him. She added, "But I have wanted something from you, and now I have it." She was not at all what he expected, an innocent, distressed, timid girl needing rescue and protection. She was keen and forthright without being treacherous. He said,

"Then I am lost no matter which place I go." He poked the stick he was carrying into the ground and flicked the pine needles up. They walked on for a ways and Sparrow wondered about it. She felt she knew where she belonged, but did Gustav know where he belonged? Did Sparrow even know? It was one thing for two peasants to run off, no one caring enough to follow, soon to be forgotten. For a Count to run off? It was either selfish or insane, and neither one was a help to his subjects. Finally after a while she stood in front of him and made him stop walking, his head down deep in thought, the joy of the night having faded. Her eyes looked into his with a gentleness and sympathy for the many burdens upon him.

"My darling Count, do not let the power at your hands overpower you. Yes, you must rule over your people and your place, but you must rule over your own life first of all, for if you neglect it thinking your duty comes first, you deprive everyone of the person they look to and depend on." Gustav didn't know whether to wonder why she had called him Count, or whether to listen to what she said. Both ideas surprised him. They continued walking and came to the top of a ridge overlooking a valley. They sat down and Sparrow sat behind him and perched her head on his neck, nuzzling his ear until he almost laughed. She picked up his hand and pointed it towards a distant tree top. As they watched in that direction, an eagle flew off the tree and sailed across their vista, turned and circled above them, then flew out of view.

"Thank-you for saving my babies, she says." Sparrow whispered into his ear. Then she wrapped her arms around his shoulders and kissed his cheek. The joy of last night came back to him. He pulled her around and laid her across his lap. She was placid and intent at the same time. She was yielding yet avid. He was more used to women who were either too submissive or too eager. If it was the former, he had to wonder if they really wanted it; if it were the latter, he had to wonder what else they wanted. He wanted to remember how she looked, this unique creature, but couldn't resist finally leaning over to kiss her lips that smiled up at him in knowing wonder.

She thought he certainly was persistent. Males did seem to repeat some behaviors compulsively. They didn't have to come together again because she was already pregnant. But perhaps there was a reason. And there was such a pleasant warmth to his hands, slowly untying the laces on the front of the dress and letting the cool air chill and tickle her skin, then warming her breasts with his hands and his mouth. Her legs were cooled as the air touched them, then warmed again as he touched them. Every pleasure was replaced by a greater one, every touch followed by a more intimate one, every warmth by fire. His body was forceful and strong while hers melted and flowed.

Hours later, after napping and waking and eating some of the lunch they had with them, Gustav asked her, "You couldn't have seen that eagle in the tree, she was too far away. How did you know it was there?" Sparrow thought about it, then said,

"One develops keen vision and eyesight living here." It wasn't the truth, but how else could she explain that she just knew? It never made sense to her parents either.

"And what else have you developed living here? Besides making do quite well finding your own food and making your own clothes and getting through the winter..." It still seemed impossible to him. Maybe she was making it up and just not telling him the truth. Maybe she had followed him here from a village, but he knew this was impossible. She answered,

"How do the animals who live here do it? Of course there is much my parents taught me and left me. There are many furs from animals my father trapped, still good, and things he made from wood, some things they brought with them that are still solid and useful."

"And you never wish to see other people, acquire new things?" Gustav had marveled at how women could spend so much time enjoying the process of acquiring things. Sparrow answered,

"I acquire many new things all the time, most of them I leave back where I found them or somewhere further on. The only thing I have wished for that I could not find here, you have given me." She smiled and hugged herself. She was obviously quite naïve and he warned her,

"Well, that pleasure does not last." She giggled and agreed, but added,

"Yes, but you *have* given me something permanent." She was young and dreamy and couldn't possibly be so sure she was pregnant already. He patted her face with polite condescension. She smiled back at him and let him believe he was wiser.

Before they left the vista from the ridge to head back to the lodge, Sparrow pointed again, holding Gustav's hand out in the right direction so he would see something very far off. He would not have seen it if it hadn't been standing on the next ridge over, silhouetted against the sky. But it was recognizable as the wisent. "There she is again; she bid you hello when you came and now says goodbye you are leaving." Gustav had never been greeted by a wisent, and could only say,

"Tell her I have enjoyed her, she is magnificent."

"Yes, she is. But she is also a symbol that there is much abundance at hand. She has huge shoulders, just as you have a huge responsibility on your shoulders. Her large head and horns are even more powerful than her mighty legs. Whatever drives her is inspired first by her divine intuition, her strong body follows after. I wanted you to meet her so that these qualities could become known to you and more used by you, if you want."

"And what animal inspires you, Sparrow? What visits you?" Sparrow thought about this; all the animals brought wisdom. She said,
"The reindeer came to me yesterday with her fawn; that's how I know the time is right." Gustav had been listening to her tales of animal lore and said,

"The reindeer that lures kings to new adventures? And village people back to the wilderness? I think that would be good for people, even a king. Perhaps we would all be better off if we spent more time in the forest and had your understanding of things; if we had you for our friend." Maybe it was just a ploy to get her to come with him willingly. But she wasn't sure of either idea.

"I don't think it would be good for the forest. People don't seem to understand things; animals, trees, nature spirits. They would miss most of the wisdom here. They don't even understand each other very well."

"They need you to teach them," Gustav said, making his case. She considered this. She had never imagined anyone needing anything from her, aside from her own hoped-for babies. Nor had she imagined people lived in want; the forest was plentiful and she assumed the village must be even more so, explaining why they stayed there. What did they lack that she could teach them? She thought of the Rogues; they were not so admirable or teachable, and she certainly didn't want more of their kind visiting the forest.

"I'm not sure I want more people coming into the forest," Sparrow said, wondering to herself.

"The forest is such a beautiful place, can it really exist only for a few royals?" Gustav asked. But, hating to see her lips in a sad pout, he leaned over and kissed her before heading back to the lodge.

6

Castle Under a Cloud

As Gustav and Sparrow made their way back to the hunting lodge, they heard bursts of shouting and laughing; four men were playing gameball. Harz and Vatra consisted of one team, while Boris and Trevka were the other. Magnus sat by the front door, ostensibly officiating but in fact there was little to preside over. The ball was a sack of leather filled with gravel. Each man, although in a team, had his own goal; a tree designated in one corner of the playing field (which had no boundaries, part of why officiating was so impossible.) Whichever man held the ball could earn a point simply be reaching his tree while he still had the ball. Any opponent who did not possess the ball could use any means possible to take the ball away. One's empty-handed teammate was supposed to be supportive in efforts to score, (it was the combined score of the teammates which determined the winners), however double-crossing was known to happen. It was only when both teammates were empty-handed that cooperation existed. The player in possession of the ball was therefore in rather a lot of danger from at least two, and possibly three other men. His only choice was to either run for his tree or throw the ball to his teammate. Sometimes a player threw his ball to his opponent and suddenly became the chaser instead of the chased. Using the ball as a weapon was not unknown. The ball was in play until someone scored, and play ceased until the scorer had etched a point into his tree. This often took some time while everyone caught their breath.

Trevka had the ball and was being chased by Boris. They had both headed off around the lodge, actually away from Trevka's goal, but Boris wasn't helping. Trevka thought of tossing the ball back to him, but that wasn't going to stop his getting run over. He thought of tossing the ball away, but that wasn't going to stop his getting run over either. He apparently had failed to support his teammate in some inscrutable way and now he was caught. He came around a corner of the lodge and both Harz and Vatra were waiting for him. He tossed the ball to Harz and the two brothers then ran behind him until he had reached his tree, and gratefully they all stopped to catch their breath.

"Point!" Magnus said. Gustav and Sparrow approached the yard and Gustav asked,
"Who's winning?" Magnus called out the score:

"Boris, seven, Harz five, Vatra four, Trevka two. The game is tied."

"In that case, time out to introduce a lady," Gustav said. Magnus stood up and announced,

"Time out!" The pages had been waiting for the Count to return, anxious to see if this supposed lady really existed. The others had already been introduced so they stood aside. Gustav studied his pages while they made their way to him, panting, perspiring and dirty. Sparrow took in an amazed sweep of them from head to toe. It was both that they were so gritty and so identical. Gustav sighed; they didn't look impressive to him. He said with resignation,

"Fair Lady Sparrow, your servant the Page Vatra." Vatra bowed and would have kissed her hand, if she had known to extend it. Perhaps she didn't want to extend it to him. It didn't matter, he knew what to do either way.

"Your servant always," he said and swept his hand out to indicate he was at her service. Then with even more bother, Gustav sighed and said,

"Fair Lady Sparrow, your servant the Page Trevka." Trevka went down on one knee, took Sparrow's hand in his and kissed it. Vatra nudged his brother's boot heel and Trevka quickly stood up. He added quickly,

"Your servant always." There were sighs all around and Gustav told them that the game would have to end, as play must with a lady guest present at the lodge. Trevka muttered *Thank Heaven* under his breath and headed for the cistern inside the corral. Nearby was the smoke shed, now fixed. Gustav noticed it and rapped his knuckles on it as he passed.

"Nice work," he said. Trevka was splashing horse trough water on his face with his brother right next to him. "That's sturdy and spacious enough to stuff a pig in," Gustav remarked. Trevka guffawed but Vatra kicked his boot again and splashed his brother's face, who returned the splash and they continued tossing water at each other. Gustav took Sparrow's hand and led her away.

Inside the lodge, delectable aromas were coming from the kitchen. They passed by the dining table as Liesse was bringing out crockery for it. Sparrow regarded Liesse, and right behind her Genivee. She smiled and nodded. She wouldn't know what help to offer and didn't know whom to thank for the dress, but she wanted to acknowledge them. Gustav took Sparrow's hand and led her over to a large chair by the fire. She was so much smaller than the chair that it fairly enveloped her. Gustav stood behind it and rested his hands on its back. There were a few moments of quiet before the men had washed their faces and Sparrow took in the lodge's interior. It was oddly similar to being in a grove in the forest, with all the animal heads gathered around listening and watching. What an odd way to honor animals – by killing them first! But that was better than not honoring them at all.

Boris came in explaining gameball logic to Harz but Gustav shook his head vaguely and so Boris changed his topic and said, "The lands of Wilker raise some of the finest cows in all the kingdom, and the milk from those cows will sustain a man for a lifetime, if he is of the ascetic persuasion and chooses to leave solid food to his fellow man." Harz acknowledged this fact and sat down at the dining table to drink a tankard of ale. The pages finally came in, Trevka shuffling his pictorial cards in his hands. Boris snatched the deck away and pitched them aside and produced the suit cards and they commenced playing As Nas. At some point Magnus had come into the room with a book. He glanced away from it now and then to listen to the general conversation, for to read avidly in front of a guest would be ill-mannered.

During dinner, the men spoke quietly of the things they needed to do tomorrow, who and what in particular, so that Sparrow was not made to be the uncomfortable center of attention. The table was cleared and Gustav turned his attention, in the usual fashion, to conducting some business. He could of course dispense with it altogether on a hunting trip, but his sense of loyalty to his realm caused him to be thinking of them, even when at leisure. He touched his brow lightly and they were all quiet. He said,

"It would be wise for a survey party to be fully outfitted and return to the Marianna Valley. They should make a complete assessment and talk to as many knowledgeable parties as they can." And then the simple, usual addition, "When we return to the castle." Gustav paused so as not to give the proceeding any hint of hurry or triviality. He rarely gave more than two commands while on recreation. Thus he continued, "And a large animal should be taken back from the hunt so that the family who has exhausted its resources through the greatest generosity may have the use of it." Gustav then gestured with his hand to his brow, showing he had removed his imaginary crown and official business was over. At that point, Sparrow saw in her mind the actual crown Gustav wore while on official business in his castle. It was a hammered gold band studded with green gems. It was worth a fortune, and was also heavy. She realized for the first time how powerful and weighty his position was, and that the wearing of a crown was not just an honor, but an onerous one.

Genivee came out from the kitchen and whispered to Sparrow, touched her shoulder, and led her to a banquette near the fire. She had a comb, one like Sparrow had never seen, and began to comb Sparrow's hair, starting at the ends and going gently so that none of the tangles became tight and difficult. She commented on Sparrow's long hair, let her examine the comb, and they smiled and nodded to each other. Liesse joined them and after showing Sparrow how she braided hair, began to make a small braid in Sparrow's long hair, showing her the results. Together, they quietly entertained Sparrow until a suitable amount of time had been spent by Gustav at cards. He then retired from the game, took note of and complimented the ladies' hairdressing results without hurry, then took Sparrow's hand and they went upstairs to their room.

The women had kept Sparrow occupied so that she was not "left alone" by the card playing (although she hardly felt alone in a room so full.) And along with the rule that no man shall touch a woman in other than a helpful way, there was also a rule that no woman shall leave another one alone unless she requests it. Gustav had not bothered to explain all this to Sparrow, and so the women kept Sparrow company. If Sparrow had known, she would have gone into the kitchen to spare them the bother. Sometimes, of course, women just did what they wanted.

Once inside his room with Sparrow, Gustav closed the bedroom door behind him and leaned on it. He was entranced by the creature standing in front of him. Hooking his fingers onto the laces of her dress he pulled her towards him. He wrapped his hands around her body and buried his face in her silky hair. He pulled her up to him until her feet came off the floor, twirled her around several times until they were next to the bed and then fell onto it in one inseparable heap. Last night he had made love with energetic wonderment; tonight he committed each moment together to memory, because it might be their last.

Back in the kitchen, Genivee and Liesse were commenting on the Count's good fortune, finding someone sweet and calm, and upon his ability to find companionship even in the forest. Liesse remarked, "Rather uncanny, I'd say. And look at the pickings we have to choose from." Genivee shook her head at her friend, knowing she'd be lucky just to be noticed by any of them other than the pages, who didn't amount to much yet. Genivee replaced the lid on the wooden box she had packed for tomorrow's journey back home and said,

"I'm going to bed, I'm worn out-" Liesse put her finger to her lips abruptly and said,

"Shh!" They both turned their heads to the outside doorway and listened. Genivee heard only her weary feet complaining. "Did you hear that?" Genivee shook her head, but Liesse went over to the door and put her ear up to it. "I think someone is out by the smoke shed." Genivee frowned and listened again. There was nothing out there.

"I'm going to bed," Genivee said. Liesse theorized however, that

"It could be- you know." Genivee shook her head and took Liesse's hand.

"Probably just a fox after a hen. Come to bed and stop this nonsense. Your plan failed as lousy plans usually do so forget it." They headed up the stairs and went to bed. The men in the main room were soon asleep as well and the fire in the fireplace dwindled down to ember and ash, casting a faint glow up into the room. After a while, even the sounds of snoring subsided and all was quiet. Then there were faint rustling sounds, like animals moving through the forest and into a clearing. It was midnight and the stuffed snowy owl perched above the fireplace swiveled its head and blinked.

My eyes are glassy marbles, yes. But I am here, nonetheless.

You think only people haunt, feel distress? Oh, there are many who taunt, cause unrest.

I no longer fly through the night catching mice

and ridding the fields of their scourge and their lice,

yet I am alive, and here I abide.

My glorious body, preserved in its hide, its gracefulness shows, its beauty ne'er died!

Oh, how I am deified ... to think on it, one's stupefied.

Taking such skill to commemorate me, 'tis rare, holy - devoted; I am now honoree.

With wisdom my spirit speaks out in beneficence; gladly reunited with all my magnificence!

My spirit still hears, my spirit still finds, and some of them here are united but blind

to the bond that will hold them together, in time. But first their true selves must they successfully find.

For now they are tethered to duty and others, but one day will confess to their hearts and their heads.

And be reunited, though it will take time. This body is wise down to every white feather.

I see them and hear them, for I am not dead.

Now the great room faded and they were all back in the forest, free to walk or fly or swim. The snowy owl flapped its wings and took off. The elk stretched its neck, its great rack swaying in an arc as it sauntered through a wood. The deer browsed on grass and made nibbling noises. The bobcat frozen in readiness to spring from a tree limb finally relaxed and curled up for a nap, its eyes happily closing. Trevka drowsily opened his eyes and looked up at the animal heads on the wall. *You see, nothing is moving,* he thought. He had just imagined he heard something. The sound of his brother sleeping next to him lulled him back to his dreams.

Gustav opened his eyes when light was just emerging on the eastern horizon. Through the window of his room and its open shutters, he saw the sliver of the crescent moon rising through the trees. He had never woken up to such a sight, so framed and perfect. He watched it slowly move out of the frame of the window, fading away as light filled the sky. He looked down at Sparrow and knew she too was a heavenly body. Would he be able to keep her beside him, or would she too fade to invisible with the light of day?

Sparrow dressed in her own dress, Gustav put on his travel clothes. As they came down the stairs to the main room together, Harz was at the table telling Vatra everything he was to check, and reminded him to be sure no tools had been left behind in the smoke shed. Harz turned and looked at the couple coming down the stairs, but as usual Sparrow had her eyes elsewhere.

They ate a simple breakfast and then Gustav and Sparrow walked out of the lodge. Harz followed at a distance behind the couple making their way up the hill. They went up the trail to the cedar tree. Gustav asked her where her home was and she merely indicated up the hill. He didn't know if she actually had a place, like a cave or a shelter, or if she didn't want him to know. But he trusted her to take care of herself, as she had done well enough before knowing him. In spite of this, he had a hard time just watching her wander off. He took a ring off his smallest finger but it was too large to fit on any of hers so he simply folded it into her hands. "If you ever want me or need me or want or need anything, show this ring to any person in this land and they will take you to my castle or give you what you want. Even if I am dead, they will do this." She knew he could have tried to force her to go back with him, and that part of him wanted to. But he was used to fighting against what he desired and she would be as easily kept from her path as the moon from its own.

She held the ring tightly in her hand. She herself didn't want to leave him, she knew she would be lonely without all of them near. But to live confined in a stone castle? No, her child must be born in the forest where it could live and learn as she had. She sensed a fox nearby and called upon it for help. She didn't want this sadness to be pressed into their memories. The fox ran between them and then to all three, the forest was filled only with trees; to Sparrow she was alone in it, and to the royals there was no woman there. The men headed back to the lodge, unsure of why they were so far from it.

The wagons were loaded and everyone made ready for departure. They spoke only a hushed word or not at all, then began to lumbered down the mountain through the pine forest deep in morning shadow.

At midday they came upon a rocky ledge overlooking an aspen grove and stopped to have a meal. As they ate and rested, below them they could glimpse a tiny village in miniature. As the sun passed across its halfway point in the sky, the light changed and the yellow leaves on the aspens turned into gold. A light wind and the murmuring of the leaves rose in volume, sounding like cheering, then applause. The zephyr died out and everyone was in a trance watching the leaves flutter and settle, some of them falling free, letting go of life, others still hanging on. A fresh breeze swept down the mountainside and through the pine needles, shaking the aspens awake, sounding like the soft roar of a spell-bound crowd of tournament-watchers witnessing the grand finale. The wind freed a flock of golden brown leaves into the air where they hung suspended for a moment, twirled, then floated to the ground like gently raining coins tossed into the ring at the winner. The show was over, the curtain down. Gustav was on the verge of going back to retrieve Sparrow, suddenly wondering why he had ever left her behind, but the girls were climbing into the wagon and the men were on their horses and they continued down the mountain.

They were soon out of the trees and into fields of golden grasses speckled with a few remaining summer flowers. The grass was tall enough to swish the horses' bellies and brush the bottom of the passing wagon. But the color faded from the wildflowers and the afternoon became gloomy as wispy clouds crept over the sky. They came upon a cluster of cottages with a small church at the center. They passed through and made the usual inquiries; there were no reports of any troubles or sickness in these parts. A girl with fresh bread brought several loaves out to them, glad that she had guessed the day right and been ready with them. Harz paid her well for them and she ran back into her home happily contemplating how she would spend the windfall.

They ate their bread and were leaving the hamlet as a damp breeze came up and the girls wrapped each other in wool blankets and huddled together. They were finally able to hurry their pace a bit as the road became better and flatter the closer they got to the castle. They rounded a bend in the road and the top of the castle keep came into view over distant tree tops.

Wilker Castle has stood for hundreds of years, through attacks early on, surviving them not only because it was well built, but because it was well placed. Behind the castle, the land rises up gently in meadow until the forest covers the ground and then the mountaintops' jagged peaks look down on all of it. The castle is set on a tall cliff of land around which a river flows in a huge loop. A stone bridge crosses the river and leads into a village. Fanning out from the village are farmlands and orchards encircling it all like a queen's robes spread out around her throne.

The castle is a broad C-shape embracing its inhabitants, for within that semi-circle is a park-like courtyard with crisscrossing paths and flower beds and a huge beech tree under which people escape the hot summer sun. The terminations of the two long wings are in rounded turrets with high peaks, echoing the mountains above them. The turrets just begin to close the circle, and across them spans an arched gateway. The castle walls have many windows, and window boxes overflow with flowers in the summer; pine garlands drape the doors in winter. The keep is three-quarters distance around from the gateway and stands tallest of all; just a square of bricks with arched openings at the top to look out to the mountains on one side and to the countryside on the other. When the Count returns, the flag of his colors will be raised again above the castle, but for now nothing flutters in the breeze.

The castle was now only twenty minutes away from the returning party, but seemed different from the sun-lit place they had left a mere week ago. Now it slunk cold and gray under the snow clouds gathering on the western horizon. The creaking of the wagon wheels and the thudding of the horse's hooves became loud and close in the still air. There should have been a clarion trumpeting their return, but there was none. There should have been subjects coming out to greet them but there were none. As they entered the courtyard, Gustav was relieved to see people going about their business, but when they saw the party of travelers, they stopped what they were doing and watched them pass. Some of them ran inside as if remembering something. And instead of Uncle Ambrose and several of his minions greeting them, there was only a person of low rank standing by himself with the news: The Count's Uncle Ambrose, Harz's own father, was very ill. Silence had been ordered.

The traveling party went to the dining room to eat and solemnly await the details. The women huddled together by the fireplace and rubbed their icy feet and hands but Harz went immediately with damp boots and empty stomach to his father's room, his steps loud and ominous in the hallway, alarming to the nuns and apothecary watching over the patient. Seeing Harz at the doorway, the nurse mopping Ambrose's brow stood up and stepped back. Harz blinked on the threshold and paused before entering. Harz was his father's only surviving child and they had been close. He knew Gustav had been counting on having Ambrose's counsel for many years to come, and Harz certainly had.

Harz sat next to the ill man and gazed at him intently. *Open your eyes*, he thought. He had never studied his father's face before, but now he needed to know why his father was lying here, apparently dying, when a week ago he had said goodbye to him in the best of health. The fevered man's eyes opened, looked up and smiled. Harz smiled back. His father said faintly, "Ah, you're here. I've been waiting." The older man had to close his eyes and catch his breath after each phrase. With each pause, Harz wondered if his next breath would be his last. Harz had so many questions to ask. *What happened to you? Why are you sick? Did anyone do this to you?* But if he could see anything in his father's eyes it was that he did not have long to live and had something he wanted to say. So Harz waited. His father's eyes opened again and Harz breathed relief, for the moment. His father said,

"Protect the Count – with your life." His eyes closed again, his breathing more difficult with all the effort now given to speaking. Was that all he was going to say? He didn't need his father to tell him this. Minutes passed and finally there was more. "If you don't - the line will die out." Harz's mind raced with questions. Was there someone in the castle who had harmed his father? Was such a person a threat to the Count's life? Would his father even know the identity of such a person, if they existed? He had to ask, had to have at least a clue of whom to be suspicious. Harz leaned close, both to hear any whispers and to keep others from hearing them, and asked his father,

"Is someone threatening to end the royal line?" The old man's face shifted side to side, seeming to see something behind the closed eyes. He said quietly,

"There is – only you – to ensure the line goes on." The old man exhaled long and slow after the effort of speaking. His breathing became inaudible and Harz made way for the nurse to return to his side, checking his head for fever and his neck for blood pulsing through. But she shook her head and mumbled a prayer over her patient. Harz stepped backwards and fell into a chair in the corner and put his head in his hands. He didn't know which was worse, losing his father so suddenly or having the duty to inform Gustav. The rhyme repeated in his head:

If two deaths close to a sovereign lie, Expect misfortune by and by.

If a third one happens then again, Expect the sovereign's line to end.

Had his father merely been thinking of this rhyme as he was dying, just being superstitious? If he knew of some scheme, he certainly would have told Harz. Harz got up from his chair to go and deliver the news. If nothing else, he was going to take to heart his father's dying wish and protect the Count with his life. It didn't make sense to him, because he would have done that anyway, but a dying man might glimpse some of the future that is obscure to those who are bound to live through it.

7

A Noticed Woman and a Questionable Man

By the end of fall life in the castle was calm and steady. There had been another funeral ceremony for the late Sir Ambrose in September, followed by months of mourning. Everyone seemed to be waiting for something else inauspicious to happen, but it was a quiet and even warm and mild fall and thankfully nothing of consequence came to Gustav's attention. He dispatched a party to the Marianna Valley, led by Vatra and Trevka, to ascertain more detail from the people there about the spring floods and the shifting of the river. They had left with great fanfare, the most in two months, with Trevka in the lead and ordering the party on horseback to step lively and Vatra at the end of the line watching his brother and making sure everyone did as they were ordered.

As winter began, there was a holiday to plan for and enjoy, the Lighting of the Longest Night. Gustav decided it was time to begin celebrations again, and this one would be subdued with the late

December cold, even though snow had not yet formed a permanent blanket across the landscape. As the days grew shorter and colder and winter approached in earnest, everyone's work outside became more hurried and more unpleasant. So the Lighting of the Longest Night reminded everyone that even in the midst of the darkness that seemed to be enveloping them completely, from this day forward, the days would get longer and longer until at last they were deep in the heart of summer again.

As many candles and torches and sconces as there were to be had were placed all around the village square as well as inside every shop and inn and gathering place. When the sun began to set on that day, a team of young men crossed the village lighting every wick, showing that the darkness could be held at bay and that light would always prevail if people insisted.

Gustav enjoyed the illumination ceremony and took a small party from the castle with him to see it. He of course wanted to be considered a part of the enlightenment going on, as well as to show that there had been nothing to the superstition that misfortune was on its way. As the afternoon gloom cast darker shadows across the village square under an overcast sky, the team of lamplighters quickly sped from one candle and lamp to another, lighting each one and adding warmth, joy and gentle cheers to the frigid air. The village was dressed up with holiday garlands, flags and vignettes and there was a puppet show staging homilies for children. Everyone was busy buying and selling, as the village was filled with both locals and visitors. A few people recognized the Count and bowed as he passed, but no announcement was made of his presence and therefore people were free to go about their business as if he were another villager.

They passed by a woman with no stall for her goods. She simply sat on a footstool in front of a tray full of coals over which she roasted hazelnuts, selling them hot from the fire. The aroma when one passed by was all the advertisement she needed and she as quickly sold one batch as she started another, tossing a handful into the pan and shaking it constantly while they browned and crackled in the heat. When they were done she nestled the hazelnuts in a big maple leaf and exchanged them for a few coins. The royal party passed by her and she looked up at them, smiling and roasting. They came to the center of the square and stopped to admire the entire effect. Gustav looked back at the roaster; her crowd was temporarily gone and she had reached under her footstool to pull out a baby wrapped in lamb's wool. It was staying suitably warm in its place near the stove, so she kissed its head, retrieved another bag of raw nuts also tucked under the footstool and put the baby back in its place to continue its nap. Gustav mused, *Sparrow would be four months pregnant now, if she were pregnant. But she probably isn't. She's too young and we were only together two days.* They left the lively square and headed back to the stone castle before darkness completely enveloped them.

By February the snow was deep and the stillness deeper inside the castle. There were no more festivities until spring and celebrating seemed like too much work anyway. People spent most of their time plotting how to get warm. Servants with jobs involving baking, black-smithing and fire-place setting kept to their work with stern devotion. The inner courtyard filled with drifted snow and crossing it became laborious and even comical, as long as it was someone else crossing. The Countess Gertrudis was in particular prone to late winter restlessness, and took to watching for any activity outside her window. There were still cows to milk, stores to be moved about and people still had to do their jobs. She looked down on them and their work, well removed from the realities of work and cold.

One day the Countess Gertrudis's baby son had just been brought in to her as she had requested, (out of boredom), but when he started to cry she quickly flicked her hand in disgust and he was carried out. She went to the window again, a repetitive tick now, and noticed Liesse coming from the dairy. She already disliked anyone of the same sex who was either prettier or more popular, which meant just about every female in the castle. But she noticed something about this girl that seemed different, and possibly surprising. She waved one of her underlings over to the window with a spastic, twirling hand and instructed him to find out the girl's name and what he could about her. When the underling returned hours later, aggravating her impatience, she found it was just her good luck that it turned out to be something she could use for her own wicked pleasure.

That afternoon she requested to see the Count, but alas she was informed that his day was already filled with appointments and she would have to return in several days time before he could give her the attention she deserved. She had no choice but to retreat in consternation.

Several days hence, she was made to wait outside the royal meeting room for over an hour while more "business with important agents" was conducted inside. The guard at the door assured her repeatedly that her appointment was duly noted and would be granted the moment the Count was free. From time to time, the door would open and whispers would be exchanged, the door would close and she would still be waiting. At last the door to the meeting room was opened and following one more exchange of whispers, Gertrudis was shown in. She probably should have wondered that there was no exit of anyone from the inside, "agent of importance" or otherwise.

She was so excited to finally have the Count's ear that she had to wait for her own short breath, coming out in little puffs and spurts, to settle down. Finally she was ready to blurt out her pronouncement of kingdom-wide significance: "One of the dairy maids is pregnant," she said, with pride and a protruding chest that seemed to suggest she, personally, was taking the credit for it. Gustav responded to this by saying,

"Congratulations, madam; wishes of hail and good health to you both." Gustav waved his hand to show she could now leave, but she did not. Instead, her eyes bulged from their sockets. She bleated,

"But that's not what I want!" Gustav answered,

"No? Then I shall send good wishes only to her." He went to a side table where Harz was seated and picked up a piece of paper off the desk; there was no reason not to get something done. Gertrudis was pink with fury. She bustled over to Gustav and grabbed the paper out of his hand and wadded it and then ripped it in a flurry. Fortunately, Gustav had picked up a piece of paper of complete insignificance. Gertrudis said viciously,

"I want you to find out who the father is, that girl Liesse is unmarried and in your household." Gustav lifted his shoulders and let them fall, saying simply,

"It does not concern us who the father is, so you'll have to ask her yourself." The thought made Gertrudis somewhat step back. She said with a shocked squeak,

"I should not speak to a harlot!" Gustav could not think what to say, other than *'how very fortunate for harlots.'* Instead he concluded,

"Then the matter is unresolvable, for I am uninterested and you are unwilling."

Gertrudis's eyes flitted and scanned around as if they wanted to flee her face. She didn't even know who she disliked more, a pregnant single girl (who at least had male attention) or her husband who might in fact be the perpetrator of this act, because really, who knew? She blathered out, "It's a good thing more people don't recognize what an ineffectual Count you are!" Harz bristled as his eyes were darkened. Gustav thought about what kind of Countess she had been. She never ventured to inquire after the needy in the realm, never made the usual gestures towards helping them as his mother, the late Countess had done. She did not show any affection for her child, but left him to the care of nursemaids. She even treated the servants close to her poorly, throwing trays of food brought to her after refusing to eat in the main hall with the others, slapping maids who failed in some slight way, blurting harsh words at the husband she had never made an effort to know or understand, and certainly never loved. Now she was blurting those words publicly. Finally he just said,

"That is your opinion." Again Gustav waved his hand to dismiss her but she flailed out both arms when attendants on either side moved close in an effort to escorted her out.

"I want that girl to be *made* to tell who the father of her illegitimate child is," Gertrudis hissed. Gustav paused while a deep sadness settled over him. Then he said,

"Madam: *that* is something that may have taken place in your father's realm, but I assure you it does not take place in mine. You will not harass or question her in any way and whether or not she is married or ever becomes so is of no concern of yours. She is in my castle and under my protection and I do not find fault with her. Nor her baby." Babies were never punished for being born, nor women punished for having them. Children were adopted by others if their mothers rejected them or died. Poor widows with children were helped in various ways.

Gertrudis was being turned towards the door by the two attendants, but twisted out of their hands to shout back at Gustav, "Because it is yours, I dare say." The attendants recoiled and released her as if she had sprouted plaguey sores. But he was not going to play this game with her; instead Gustav sighed heavily and said,

"Madam, if you have anything further to say, you may convey it through a messenger. We have more important matters consuming our time." Gustav turned away from her and she eventually backed off alone, followed at a distance by her own attendants. Gertrudis retreated to her corner of the castle and did not leave it. She could not make Gustav angry, she could not make him jealous and now she could not even make him listen to anything she said. She was a ship slowly sinking under its own rot. Her attendants were subdued and silent around her, and a few more of them scuttled away under dark of night.

Liesse was in her room with Genivee, lying on her bed with several pillows behind her head and one over her belly, upon which her fingers were drumming thoughtfully. Genivee had been desperate to ask her who the father was; Liesse had been strangely silent on the topic. If she hadn't come forth with the information, how would asking her help? But her curiosity was getting the better of her. So she ventured:

"I think Trevka would make a good father." Genivee stated, as if it were a fact and didn't need confirmation. Liesse didn't respond. "I mean, Vatra would, too. He's more, well, dedicated to advancing. Trevka, he thinks in the moment. But he does have bravery, I suppose." Genivee was not getting the response she wanted, meaning any response at all. So she became more direct. "Look, did you tell him, does he know, I mean I guess he has to notice, doesn't he?" Liesse moved the pillow from her belly to her face and covered her eyes. She had certainly been looking for the father to notice her; that would have been helpful. But in fact, she had not seen either of the twins since she began showing her condition. First they had been off to the Marianna Valley, and probably on to Elster, then who knew where. She hadn't seen them. Finally Liesse's silence made sense in one sudden bolt of understanding. Genivee burst out, "You don't know which one is the father, do you?" Liesse groaned. It was the rare occasion when the father knew more about the parentage than the mother. "Well, look, maybe we can figure this out," Genivee offered. "We left a note on the bed, right? All it said was, 'I need your help.' Real obvious, right? We left it where we were sure Trevka would find it, I mean we worked it out which side of the bed must be his and he always fell into bed first."

"Yes," Liesse asserted, "We worked all that out. But then he had to have the nerve to come back to the kitchen and try to get a pinch out of me, and who knows what Vatra found or read instead. The truth is, we don't know who found the note, but it's obvious now one of them did and I've got the proof of it right here," she moved the pillow back to her belly. Covering the evidence couldn't hurt. It had seemed at the time, what with him courageously saving an eagle and winking at her that Trevka would make a good catch. He had a good position in the Count's court, he would have income and social standing, assuming he advanced. And she was silly and thought she was in love, and thought Trevka felt the same way. She had drawn on the note a doodle of the smoke shed with a heart above it, hoping he'd figure it out, being too coy to say so exactly. Having convinced herself that Trevka had found the note (she kept getting winks from him), she snuck out to the shed after Genivee had fallen asleep. Someone met her there and embraced her with such lust and fervor, she was swept off her feet; she assumed it was Trevka. To assume otherwise rather implied she wasn't very discerning. But now she wasn't so sure and after six months she wasn't even that much in love with him any more. It was Vatra who was looking like a better prospect. Or maybe that was how he appeared, with one of the other milk maids professing an interest in him. She thrust the pillow aside.

Genivee tried to be helpful, or so she thought. "He didn't say anything? I mean sometimes, you can hear in their voice..."

"He didn't say *anything*," Liesse said with some disgust. "It was pitch black, no moon, and that shed is small. And, well, my back was to him."

"Mmm," Genivee murmured, having nothing else come to mind.

Liesse remembered for a moment. "But he was really good, you know? I was really surprised. I could stay with him." Genivee wondered, *Trevka was good?* Then Genivee began to suspect something she wasn't sure Liesse had considered.

"Are you sure it was one of the two of them?" Liesse rose up from her pillows, her hands planted on the bed, looking at Genivee with horror. After a moments' consideration, she really wasn't sure. She dropped back onto the bed and groaned louder. Finally she stopped moaning long enough to say,

"I want to be married. I want to be a real wife and mother, not just someone whom everyone *helps*. I really thought I loved him at the time, and I thought he was serious." Genivee wondered at what basis there was for this thought. How would it sound to ask each man on the hunting trip in turn whether or not they made love to Liesse in the smoke shed one night? What if it was Vatra who figured he could point the finger at his brother and who would doubt him? Maybe his quiet composure was a front taking advantage of his brothers' conquests. What if it was really Trevka, who could be the same immature sport he was so often, and not wanting to take on a serious responsibility would deny it all, claiming it was his twin, and would know the difference anyway? Any child would look like both of them. Had the twins consulted Boris about a note, who perhaps told them to ignore it (which is what they all should have done), but in fact followed its request for himself? What if, in fact, Magnus had done some more investigating and found the note? Wasn't a widower supposed to be lonely and more experienced at love as well? Gustav was otherwise occupied that night and that left Harz, but Genivee dismissed that possibility. He was an absolutely honest man, whatever else he might be. He also knew when someone was telling the truth. Genivee watched her friend moan on the bed and considered whether he might be able to help her now, with a little discretion. She could ask him.

That evening, Gustav was in the game room where he often played cards or drank or just lolled about at the end of the day with the other men who weren't married, or men who were but preferred gaming and drinking. Gustav and Harz were playing Merels and drinking brew. They moved pieces on and off the board by turns, winning or losing their mills and appearing to take great interest. Gustav asked Harz as he often did at the end of the day, "What do you hear?" Harz studied the board, then said,

"A messenger came this evening saying that the party from Marianna is returning soon. Trevka and Vatra will be back tomorrow." Gustav finished the thought with,

"And will surely hear the gossip imparted by the charming Countess." They both wondered in silence who the father was, but how can another man speculate on such a thing without appearing to either take credit or be desperately wishing to be absolved of credit? So each said nothing. Gustav had no reason to care who, but he did care how.

"I would like to know that she – agreed." Harz nodded. That was the important point. Some women might accuse a man immediately of a disagreeable act, others might not want to tell anyone, others might be so confused and frightened they did nothing. Gustav added, "It should be easy to narrow the field to six men. Well, five because it wasn't me." Harz looked up suddenly. He apparently wasn't on the same line of thought. Gustav explained, "The hunting trip, it had to be." Harz leaned over the game board;

"Make that four," looking him straight on. Gustav made a dismissive gesture. "But it could have been right before, or right after." Gustav didn't think that was likely, saying,

"Too many people around, too much routine. Just doesn't seem right. And Magnus told me, they were acting strangely. Creeping around, giggling and other such pointless behavior. Can't be sure what was going on." Harz did some fast concluding and said,

"Must have been one of the twins." Gustav nodded in agreement. Then Harz added jokingly, "Assuming we can rule out the Countess's notion." Yes, the Countess had ideas but they were baseless and presumptuous. It hadn't been that her accusation might be true or not, but that she had tried to make it *her* business and of *public* interest. For the Countess to announce her mad ideas about the Count's personal comings and goings was unthinkable, especially when she was so unconcerned for him to begin with. It showed shameless lack of discretion and respect. Gustav responded to the Countess's idea with another dismissive gesture. He had been glad for the opportunity to be rid of her. Back to the matter of which twin, he suggested,

"Maybe you could bring it up, just see which one is lying." Harz didn't care for such a task and besides, the twins knew better than to let such a familiar device be used on them.

"Not likely," he said. Thus ended a topic they both disliked but felt obligated to resolve, one way or another. It would have been so much easier if Liesse would just name someone. The following day when the twins did return, Harz met them in the courtyard and steadily watched Trevka as he talked animatedly about their long trip. Trevka seemed utterly unconcerned with anything that had gone on during his absence and in fact was more interested in all the people they had interviewed and met on their trip to Marianna and Elster. He boasted that,

"When I told them I was the Count's deputy they really began talking, especially the Elster farmers. They sure have a lot on their minds and everyone else is tired of hearing it, so I-" Harz broke in,

"You told them you were the Count's deputy?" Trevka suddenly seemed to remember that he wasn't a deputy – the lie had come to seem real to him on the long trip away – and lowered his eyes and said in a solemn voice,

"I shouldn't have done that I suppose, but it did get them talking-"

"That's fine," Harz dismissed the issue. A bell sounded announcing the welcoming banquet and Trevka headed into the castle for some hot food. Harz marveled that while Trevka could make up a lie, he could not possibly hide one, or even keep from blurting one out. He wasn't hiding anything as far as Harz could see. He surely would have wanted to boast about good luck with Liesse. Harz watched as the two twins walked through the door to the castle, side by side and wondered about Vatra.

When Genivee saw Harz in the courtyard deep in thought, she trotted over to him from the milking parlor feeling fortunate to have a chance to speak with him alone. She called to him before he also headed inside,

"Pardon the intrusion, but might I have a word in regards to a lady in need of help?" She said. He stopped in his tracks and turned to her, looked her in the eye and said,

"Who needs help?" Genivee stopped to catch her breath, realizing this was probably going to be embarrassing. But she forged ahead.

"Liesse – isn't sure which twin it was." Harz blinked and tried not to lean away; she was serious and here was yet another reason to be sure females were inscrutable and untrustworthy. "She says, well, she would like to know herself because she would like to get married. But she doesn't know who to ask and neither of them has come forward." Harz nodded, but not really with much sympathy; he could only think that because *both* twins were keeping silent that perhaps they were in on the secret together, quite likely given how close they were. Harz could only think of one way of making them speak out about it, and that was to defend themselves. He rocked back on his heels and thought about it, then proposed,

"We shall have a reception, and I think it shall be a small and carefully chosen one, resembling very much the party of last summer. I shall invite you and Liesse to be guests. We shall see which twin acts the most guilty. Or perhaps they are both guilty." Genivee rolled her eyes around, wondering how very far mistaken her friend might have been, and in what capacity the twins might both be guilty. But then Harz began to smile and he winked at Genivee. She relaxed and felt assured that with Harz in the room, they were sure to find out who the father was. And she was rather amazed to have been winked at by Harz.

8
Cards at Play

In late February, there was a private midday meal in one of the smaller dining rooms. Only eight people were present, the same party as the hunting trip last summer. The twins, having returned successfully from the Marianna Valley, had a notion that this dinner might be in their honor, but no one would say. When Liesse and Genivee arrived, the six men, already seated and comfortable, began noticing something. Most of them had had little or no contact with these ladies since last summer. The women sat down but the men sat up straighter in their seats at the same time. Gustav decided not to prolong the suspense. He walked over to Liesse and took her hand, saying

"Liesse, a happy new year to you and your child and good health to you both." Liesse thanked him and lowered her eyes, realizing the voluminous dress she wore had not fooled him. Genivee sat next to her and held her hand in agreement with Gustav' sentiments. It was common for other people to then make similar remarks. But no one else spoke. Eyes grew narrow and jaws grew tight. The men looked at each other but with sidelong glances. Trevka and Vatra turned to each other and exchanged identical, accusatory glances looking not only like twins, but twins in a mirror, each one pulling away from the other with furrowing brows. Magnus had watched it all impassively, concluded it had solved nothing, so rose and approached Liesse, saying,

"You are a clever girl to find a husband in such a way." He had thought the word *sly* was more appropriate, but didn't say so. Genivee suddenly thought she had discovered the father, and in a flash was jealous.

"*You* got Liesse's note?" Genivee asked. Magnus just shook his head with vague disinterest. Genivee clarified: "Liesse left a note. For Trevka." Magnus shrugged.

"She left me a note?" Trevka interjected, jumping up.

Genivee ignored this and concluded, "Then Vatra got the note."

"You got my note!" Trevka accused, twirling around to face his twin.

"I didn't get any note," Vatra said with apathy.

The twins' eyes now turned to the others in the room. They had each known at once that neither one had gotten anything that night. Then there was a sound, like the squeak of a bat being woken up from a cave nap. Everyone turned to Boris who said simply, "I found a note," in an innocent tone that affirmed there was no crime in doing so.

"You got my note!" Trevka complained, whirling the other way.

"I got a note," Boris said, "I thought - it was from Genivee." Genivee glared at him momentarily but she was more dismayed at how poorly they had managed to put the note in the right place. She knew the plan would backfire, but would Liesse listen? She turned to Liesse, unsure whether to squeeze her hand or toss it aside in disgust.

Finally Gustav summarized: "So, Liesse left a note, which Boris received. And then conceived."

"I want my note!" Trevka protested, no direction left to twirl in. Gustav stood, flung his arm across Trevka's shoulders and turned him towards the door, the others following. Trevka said to Gustav in one last appeal at the doorway, "That's my note." Gustav smiled and nodded, and Liesse and Boris were left alone in the room together.

Boris approached Liesse but didn't know what to say. So he sat next to her, thinking perhaps he should say he was sorry, but actually he wasn't, really. Liesse felt as if she owed someone an apology, but it didn't seem to be Boris. There was a long silence. Then Boris took her hand and said, "I didn't really think it was Genivee. I just said that because you never said anything to me about our - time together." Now that she knew the truth, Liesse realized how much she had assigned guilt to Trevka simply because she had expected it of him. She was glad now she had not asked him about the episode, for his consternation would have been dreadful. After the long silence following Boris' confession and realizing that in a way she had ignored him unkindly after rather inadvertently inviting him, she said in all truthfulness,

"I'm glad it was you." They looked at each other and both smiled. Boris said in a timid voice,

"Would you marry me then, Liesse?" She nodded her head and said yes.

At the end of May Liesse, now married and living in better quarters with her husband and father-in-law, began to feel terribly uncomfortable. She called for her friend Genivee, who brought the midwife. Together they sat with her and tried to soothe her, but after twelve hours all three were worn out. Far away in the forest, her screams had reached Sparrow, who had tried to send reassurances to Liesse, but she was not getting through. So she sent a messenger hoping they might be able to communicate. A hawk arrived at the castle at dusk and perched on the keep ledge. Sparrow asked the hawk, "Are you there now?"

"I'm here."

"Can you hear her?"

"Everyone hears her."

"Tell her this: Your child will be here soon, so be happy, not afraid. I am a new mother, too. My child came yesterday and he is a fine little boy. Now your girl is on her way. I know, looking at the stars they are being born under, they are coming to this world together from another. They are star-crossed, it is very special." There was a pause as the hawk flew to Liesse's window and conveyed the thoughts. It then responded back to Sparrow, *"I told her. A lot of bother just for a baby. Mine fly away and I never see them again."*

"Yours come out as little eggs, quiet and small; but thank you for helping, it is important to us."

"That's fine, I see some good rabbits here. We're done?"

"Yes, we are done."

Liesse finished thrashing and fell back on her bed. A calm came over her and she decided to stop fighting; maybe she'd die quicker that way. Half an hour later she was calm and exhausted when Genivee put her baby girl in her arms, wrapped up in a blanket. The sun was just setting and a full moon rose over the eastern horizon and shone into the room. "This must be Luna," Liesse said, and fell asleep.

Announcement of the new arrival came to the Count's chamber where he and others were playing cards and backgammon. The news was greeted with desultory congratulations to the father, who had refrained from telling tall tales since becoming a married man. Gustav wondered to himself if somewhere in the forest he was himself becoming a father. Then he remembered he already was. No, Sparrow was too young and they had not been together long enough. But he should have brought her back with him anyway.

On market day, Genivee was in the village and noticed a small crowd gathered around the new stall of a young man whom she did not recognize. He had obtained a pack of pictorial cards like Trevka's and was now soliciting advice for people who consulted him on matters he claimed to have prescient knowledge of. A sign over his booth read: *Coffers empty? See mine.* Genivee watched his business proceed at a brisk pace and became suspicious, so she set down a coin for him so that she could test his ability with the cards. She asked him about a single friend who had become unexpectedly with child, and the young man, Derth, gave her the following prediction:

"Your friend will find no one to help her, save yourself. You should tell her that no man will find her attractive now; they will be repelled by the sight of her and will not even sit with her. The man who is responsible for this will never come forward or confess his deed. She should give the baby up to an old couple who will care for it. Otherwise she is sure to be ruined."

This was already after Liesse's wedding and the birth of her child. Not only was Derth a poor predictor, but he didn't keep tabs on the gossip or news very well. Genivee would have merely been amused by this folly and left it at that, but she noticed that a great many people were consulting this charlatan, (and whose coffers were being filled?), and she felt the dishonesty should be investigated. So it was that Harz and Genivee came to be walking through the village one day a week later.

"I just don't think he should be taking people's money when he obviously doesn't know his business. It's not right, and he could get someone in serious trouble. Imagine if Liesse had taken his advice to heart? Why she's so happy now I can hardly stand her company!" In actual fact, Genivee loved helping take care of Luna.

Harz took a deep breath and agreed. It would be interesting to see what this quack had to say to *him*. It was an unhappy fact that he would be enriching him slightly by doing so. But first they were going to see the old woman who made the cards. He asked Genivee where they would find her and Genivee pointed to a side street, and they walked together to a small abode at the edge of town. As members of the royal household, they should have been riding horses, but they had wished to conceal themselves and their mission. The shelter at the edge of town was a humble, tidy place. A low fence surrounded the yard around the house, nothing a dishonest person would have trouble with. Inside the fence, a round form hidden behind a voluminous blue skirt was bent to the flowers and herbs in the garden, planted not in neat rows or concentric circles, but as they grew and re-seeded, with various companions of blooms coming up together in new patterns. She hummed to herself, weeding a little, picking flowers. Harz and Genivee stood by her gate, not wanting to interrupt, not wanting to intrude on her trance-like concentration. They looked at each other, wondering who should say something, when they realized the old woman had stood up and noticed them.

"Come, come!" she exhorted. "I have visitors, how nice. Let's go inside and make some tea, I have a cake." She walked to them with hands outstretched, as if they were her favorite grandchildren. She took each one by the hand and led them through the little yard. "I've been thinking of you, I'm so glad you came." Genivee and Harz looked at each other over the short woman's head with an exchange that conveyed perhaps she was touched. She kept talking in a sweet, unhurried voice, "I was picking flowers to make things especially nice. Come in, come in." She opened the door to her small home and all three went inside. The central room had one large chair and loveseat. These were covered with fine lace doilies and on the back of the chair a topaz tabby cat snoozed without interruption, its furry tail, thick as a fox's, slowly swishing. Harz and Genivee sat on the small sofa as the lady indicated they should, but it was so old and sprung their hips sunk together.

The old lady moved a large and heavy kettle from the top of her wood stove, which emanated an aroma of roses from a pot full of petals in water. She hummed to herself, gathering little plates and forks and indeed, producing a cake from a pie safe along with teacups and saucers, all on a tray that seemed much too heavy for an old lady. Harz jumped up to help her with it. "Allow me," he said.

"You're a kind young man, I knew it when I saw you. You help your friends in many ways, I'm sure," she said. They all sat again with the tray on the table. She placed cake and tea in front of them and they looked at each other wondering if the cake was laced with something. "It's not tinctured, my dears," the old lady laughed. To prove it, she began eating and slowly the guests ate too as she gazed at them unblinking and cat-like. Genivee took one bite and noticed the cake was flavored with some kind of flower, something she had never tasted before but sat wondering what it might be. The old lady looked straight at them steadily, in such a way that made Harz himself uncomfortable, but averting his eyes did nothing to stop her from concluding, "You are a lovely couple." Genivee and Harz glanced at each other with surprise and busied themselves with tea and cake. Finally Genivee brushed cake crumbs off her fingers and said,

"My name is Genivee, this is Harz, and I'm sorry I don't know your name."

"You can call me Mona," the old lady said with a wink. She smiled a lot, like a little girl who thought she had a secret.

Harz began, "Mona, I understand you make pictorial cards, of animals and nature scenes. Is that right?" Mona did not ask if they were interested in buying a deck; it seemed she knew they were not.

"Yes, dears I do." She waited for Harz to speak again.

"You sold a deck to a young man named Derth?" Harz asked, supposing this was all true and preliminary. Mona waited a while before answering. The smile did not entirely leave her face, but it became less genuine. "No, I didn't, but he seems to have gotten one nevertheless."

Genivee was alarmed, "You mean he stole it from you?"

"No, he couldn't have done that. He must have traded it somewhere." She seemed only mildly concerned.

Harz continued: "Well, he is selling 'advice' based on these cards, and we think he is untrained in this. His advice is not worth much."

"What advice is?" Mona asked them. "People will always ask others what they think, then never listen. That he has cards does not change this."

Harz noted, "Well, true, but he is taking a lot of money for this and people seem to believe him, or at least want to hear what he says."

"Yes, they want to hear what he says. They think because he has some device – cards – he has greater wisdom. They think because they pay he must be real. They think many things but never do they think for themselves." Mona ate her cake and seemed to have dismissed the matter. Harz and Genivee glanced at each other. Mona noticed this and perked up.

"But here you are and I am glad of that." She leaned over the table and took their hands again, smiling. She brought their hands into hers, clasped them together but said nothing. It was a silent blessing, and when it was over she said, "Don't worry for me or for others, my children. Every one must find their way through the garden and pick what flowers reach up to them. I only feel sad for those who trample through life without noticing any flowers at all." She got up and went over to her table near the stove and took the bouquet of flowers she had brought in and gave it to Genivee. "Here are some you almost missed," she said. Genivee felt they were on the verge of being at the end of their visit, without having accomplished anything of what they had planned, so she asked Mona more about the cards.

"Could you show us these cards? We would like to understand them, and why you made them and how to use them rightly." Mona thought, then said seriously,

"To understand them takes much time. I used to explain to people how to use messages from nature to help them with their problems, but they often forgot the meaning. So I made cards to help them see and remember; show them how the squirrel works and prepares for the future, how the wisent embodies both the common and the divine. I am too old now to see so many people, so I make cards and hope they will use them well. It is unfortunate they do not always do so." Mona reached under the table and produced a deck of cards from a small hidden shelf. She shuffled them, fanned them and held them out to her guests. Reluctantly, they each chose a card and she put the rest of the deck aside.

Harz turned over his card with a dubious glance. Mona looked at it, the *grackle*. She closed her eyes and spoke softly, "It is time to free yourself from some chains." She opened her eyes and saw Harz unconvinced. "This is for those you love, even more than yourself. It is selfish not to do it." Genivee was gazing at her own card, a butterfly. Mona seemed very pleased, her smile huge and genuine, as if that was all the explanation necessary. Finally she said, "How beautiful is the butterfly when the sun dries its wings and its colors unfold, and its antennae reach out into the air. My dear for you, the sun is just coming up."

They cleared their throats, got up, thanked her and walked out with Mona standing in her doorway, watching them go, smiling and raising her hand in benediction, and they walked out of sight. They went back to the market place in silence, befuddled.

They arrived at Derth's booth in the village and stopped in front of it. A new sign said, *Futures predicted, lives improved, one coin.* Harz glanced at it and then at Derth.

"That's a wide claim," Harz said. Derth spread his palms and displayed a varnish smile. He gave away smugness for free.

"It is the cards that predict, not myself."

"And if the cards are wrong, do I get my coin back?"

"For what?" asked Derth.

"For having paid for worthless advice," Harz stated. He could already see in his eyes that Derth didn't give refunds. Derth had worked out that he should always give bad news, and if it turned out better, people weren't inclined to complain but rather to brag. If the outcome was bad, he looked good. If his predictions were quibbled over, he would say that things would go better 'if you travel far,' or 'work hard', both unlikely to happen, and this usually sent them away. He wondered what he could say to send *this* one away. Harz said,

"I'm going to make a bet with a friend, and I want to know if I will win or lose. I don't need to win or lose, I only need to know one way or the other. If you are wrong, I insist on getting my coin back."

Derth did not like this man's unwavering eyes. "I do not predict games of chance; it is unsavory behavior."

"You gamble every day, don't quibble now." Harz slammed his hands loudly on Derth's table, leaning forward and staring him down until Derth squirmed. "Never mind, I don't need your prediction, I have won the bet." Harz leaned further over the table as Derth shrank back in his chair. Harz picked up the deck; he was tempted to confiscate it but instead he simply flipped it over and splashed the cards onto the table. The card now facing up showed a magpie. Harz picked it up and flicked the card off his middle finger and into Derth's face. As he turned to go he purposely bumped Derth's table, upsetting the cards further and knocking a few onto the ground. Derth started to get up and go after him but noticed how tall Harz was and instead busied himself gathering up his cards.

As they walked away, Genivee said, "I can't believe he's still in business, or that people take him seriously." Harz shook his head with regret and noted,

"It helps that he only tells them what they want most or fear most. No, he doesn't appear qualified for it. He might as well be selling magic mushrooms."

"At least when someone buys magic mushrooms, their plan is to get muddle-headed. With this, they think for some reason they will get clear-headed." Harz considered what might be done to get rid of him, but it seemed he wasn't doing anything worse than being silly, and the condition was somewhat contagious. But Genivee thought he was more than just silly; she had a disturbed feeling about him.

"Can't someone just keep an eye on what he's doing?" As they walked away, Harz looked back at Derth's booth where already someone was seated for a fortune-telling. He said absently, "I think that much can be done." As he turned back around she smiled her thanks at him. He wasn't often shown appreciation for simply conducting his office. He had only made such a scene with Derth to impress Genivee. Alone, he would probably just have asked a few questions and dismissed him as worthless.

As they walked back to the castle, the warm summer air made it pleasant to be outside for the first time in many months. The stone bridge that crossed the river had been soaking up sunlight all day and now radiated back its warmth as they walked over it. Genivee stopped at the crest of the bridge and gazed out over the river. She leaned on the chest-high wall, craning her neck to look down at the river below, a lazy drift of water right now.

On the bank below she saw lily pads and exclaimed that they were frog traps, something she wanted to see up close. They crossed the rest of the bridge and made their way down the bank to the water's edge. Genivee sat on her heels at the shoreline and reached over the water to touch a lily pad, tapping lightly on it and watching little ripples radiate outward, making the other lily pads bob up and down. She waited and then tried it again, saying "This is supposed to make the boy frogs think there is a lady frog on the lily pad and that makes them come up to the surface." She watched and tapped a third time, waiting silently but the boy frogs were not responding. Harz watched from a few feet away, wondering about lily pads and Genivee.

They were on a narrow strip of land now between the river and the steep cliff below the castle heights. They were cast into shadow, even though it was just past midday. When Genivee finally looked up at Harz, he was in darkness with all the sunshine behind him, and she could not make out if he thought her completely childish or, as she hoped, inquisitive and beautiful. Something in Mona's cake had made her fall in love.

9

An Assignment

A few days later, Harz and Trevka were in the village square together leaning against a wall-mounted shelf outside the pub, drinking cider. Harz had said there was an assignment. They had walked to the square together, not taking horses, and now Trevka was drinking his cider and wondering why it wasn't ale, why they were there, and whether he had misunderstood what "assignment" meant. Harz held his tankard up to his lips and said over the rim of the vessel,

"See that young man in the booth over there?" He tipped his tankard in that direction. Trevka glanced over; he saw a stall with a sign and several people milling around. Trevka said,

"The one with the sign, *Your fortune is waiting?*" Harz nodded. Trevka studied the booth, then noticed the peddler was using the same pictorial cards he himself used, although mostly to pass the time and play a sort of solitaire. Trevka said, "Aren't those the same cards that I-?" Harz nodded. "I didn't know you could make money with those..."

"You can not," Harz corrected him sharply. "And neither should he. He wasn't trained by the maker of the cards, and it isn't likely he's doing any good at all for the people whose money he's taking." Trevka thought about this for a minute, then suggested,

"Should we make him change the sign to, *Your fortune is waiting to be taken by me?*" Harz shook his head. He tried to explain,

"He's not disturbing the peace or committing a crime, as far as we can tell. But we can't tell much. Your assignment-" Trevka perked up, "-Is to learn as much as you can about that guy. See what you can find out." Trevka had imagined at first that perhaps they were here to make some sort of arrest or seizure of prohibited items. But with no horses or guards, it now dawned on him that this was to be ~clandestine~. A smile came across his face as he pondered the possibilities.

"Mm hmm," Trevka mused, tapping his chin and nodding his head. Harz said sternly,

"Trevka, this person is to have no idea who you are; don't let him see you on one of the royal horses. There's likely very little to come of this, but nevertheless I want you to report to me what you find out about him."

"Right," Trevka said slowly, still nodding and contemplating. Harz wondered if he'd picked the right man for the job. He'd come to believe that it was best to keep Trevka busy, but he wasn't sure this is what he should be busy with. He sighed and reached into his jacket, pulling out a sack of coins.

"Take this and use it to buy fortunes and drinks. I want to know who this man is." Harz yanked Trevka's arm, pulling him near, "It's information for the Count." He handed the sack of coins over. Trevka took it and felt the weight of it, impressed because he'd never held so much money all at once before.

"Your servant always," Trevka said, acknowledging the end of the conversation. He would have also bowed, or at least nodded, or even saluted but they were still in view of the illicit peddler. So instead he tilted his head and rolled his eyes towards the booth as if to say, *I can't acknowledge your status when you-know-who might see.* Harz continued his steady gaze into Trevka's eyes. He might not prove competent, but he was determined to be diligent. Harz put his tankard down and headed back to the castle. Trevka ordered another drink and sat down at one of the outside tables with it. The pub was busy and he sat where there were others already drinking. He made friendly conversation with the strangers while glancing at the booth from time to time, drinking for over an hour.

When he had returned to the castle, Harz told Gustav that Trevka would be reporting on the card reader in due time. Gustav was satisfied with this course of action but was more curious about Mona. He wondered if maybe she was related to Sparrow, maybe she was actually her grandmother. It might interest Sparrow to know she had a relative who was still alive, that she was not alone in the world as she thought. Perhaps she would want to meet such a woman. He asked Harz,

"And how was this old lady, she wasn't living in a hovel, was she?" Harz merely shook his head. "Hmm, well keep in touch with her now and then, just casually, and make sure she is getting along." Harz nodded, but he didn't like the idea. He didn't like Mona. She was a straightforward old lady who served laced cake and tea and had the scent of flowers all around her, who smiled and giggled and was warm and harmless, and Harz had decided immediately never to visit her again. He had looked into her blackish brown eyes and seen two deep wells, and at the bottom a disquieting reflection.

Gustav turned his attention to Magnus, asking him, "Any news of the ambassadors from Elster? Weren't they supposed to be coming?" Magnus answered,

"Yes, they weren't very happy when our messengers arrived in January with the proclamation that the river has shifted under its own power and the land previously theirs is now ours. They replied that they would be sending ambassadors to discuss the matter, and I think we can expect them to make a bit of fuss over the loss of that field." Gustav nodded and said,

"Knowing them, they won't be traveling until all threat of bad weather is past. When they do get here, make sure they are well hosted and looked after. Even if mother nature isn't always generous in her favor, at least we will be." And since that was all the official business presenting itself, they all relaxed for the rest of the day. It was much quieter now that Gertrudis had been banished from the audience chamber.

The next day in the village square, Trevka arrived near lunchtime and bought a double portion of food from a street vendor frying pork and onions on skewers. He took his sticks of food over to the fortune teller and sat down. "I hope you're good at this, because I'm in need of a lot of advice," Trevka said. "The name is Velkro, pleased to meet you and none too soon it is." Trevka held out his right hand while both skewers wobbled in his left.

"Derth, the Diviner," the young man said as he returned the handshake, but only limply. Trevka took out his sack of coins and reached in. Derth eyed it curiously and said, "Three coins, sir." Trevka nodded and smiled and pulled out the coins, replacing the sack in his jacket. He continued chewing on the pork skewer and noticed Derth looked both thin and hungry, but he ignored this and said,

"Now how does this work, do you tell my fortune right out, or can I ask questions? For instance, can you tell me if I'll ever be wealthy and important, well known and revered?" Derth shuffled through his cards, then arranged them in a strange configuration on the small table between them. He proceeded to tell a fortune so fantastical that Trevka doubted anyone could be so gullible as to believe it. Derth had seen the sack of coins and was going to give the best predictions he could dream up so that Trevka would hand over more of his fortune just to keeping hearing such wonderful pronouncements. "That's amazing," Trevka muttered, then waved his second skewer around as if about to pitch it to a mongrel saying, "I can't finish this." Derth intercepted and grabbed the skewer. Trevka said to him, "You must come from a long line of fortune tellers, as you are obviously very good at it – was your mother a diviner too?" Derth frowned over his skewer and said,

"Not that I know of. She doesn't do much, that's why I'm out here earning the family keep."

"Oh, you have a whole family to support? That's awfully decent of you to make a living for the sake of your family; how many are there to support? Lots of children I imagine?" Derth shook his head and said,

"Just us, me and the folks." Trevka nodded sympathetically. He surmised,

"Yes, taking care of your parents is a noble thing to do, they must be very grateful." Derth grunted with some disgust but didn't elaborate. Finally he added,

"They are old is what they are. Old and worthless." Trevka wondered about this. He guessed Derth to be no more than in his early twenties, maybe even still a teenager. It was hard to tell if his face had an incipient beard or was just dirty, probably both. Trevka wondered how old and said,

"Oh, then they must be your grandparents. That is noble of you to care for them." Derth stopped chewing and looked over his skewer at Trevka. He seemed to be realizing something for the first time. He recommenced chewing and mumbled,

"Yes, my grandparents." Several girls came up to the booth then but Trevka quickly asked Derth if he could buy another fortune-telling, he had some relatives to ask about. He pulled out his sack of coins and Derth wiped his greasy mouth with his shirt sleeve, waved the girls off and said to Trevka, "Three coins."

The following week, after several fortune-telling encounters between Trevka and Derth the diviner, Trevka was sauntering through the village when Derth spotted him and called out, "Velkro, my friend come over here. How's that sister who got pregnant and still doesn't know who the father is?" Trevka smiled and shook his head. "I think I should read her cards again because she's going to need help finding a home for her unwanted child. Sit down and hand over five coins." Derth began flipping through his cards in what seemed an obvious attempt to find a particular one. It was late in the day, and Trevka had not made himself seen until Derth was just about to close up his booth, so Trevka said,

"It's getting chilly; why don't we go to the pub and discuss the possibilities. I'll buy." Derth slammed shut the window to his booth and they headed for the pub. Inside the tavern Trevka led them to a dark corner, having come to see Derth as an outstanding member of that coarse portion of humanity with whom he did not want himself associated. As they made their way to the back, Trevka refrained from returning the glance of the serving maid carrying a full tray of drinks and smiling at him. They came to a small table but before Trevka was even completely seated, Derth blurted out, "Tell me about this brood- sow sister of yours." Trevka paused, then dropped down onto his chair. He said to Derth,

"You're interested in girls with babies, aren't you? What is it with them, anyway, knowing you can't get them any more pregnant than they already are?" Derth's eyes shaded over. The topic of girls often made Derth mumble. Trevka had wondered if perhaps he just preferred boys to girls. That wouldn't be so odd, but he didn't believe this was the case. Trevka suspected that in reality, Derth harbored something evil, that in fact strange reptiles might inhabit Derth's brain.

"They're useful," Derth offered. Trevka couldn't imagine why, but looked at him steadily and asked,

"For what..." Derth took up the tankard of ale that had just been placed in front of him, swilled half a draft, swayed, leaned over toward Trevka (who wanted to lean away but braced himself), and said,

"The folks." Derth leaned back, Trevka blinked. Yes, reptiles.

"Which folks?" Trevka asked slowly.

"Mine, idiot."

"Ah, yes," Trevka asserted, but in fact had no idea. Those folks were old, by Derth's admission, and poor. They certainly couldn't raise children on a fortune-teller's income and old people tended to like a quiet and settled life, which was not one filled with children. Slave labor? Held for ransom? Trevka thought maybe his imagination was getting to him. Derth seemed rather harmless, but Trevka thought he should at least know where they lived, just in case. He said to Derth, "Why don't I take you home and you can drink with them for a change." Derth downed his drink and waved his hand for another. "I'll buy you a bottle to share with them," Trevka added. Derth looked sideways. "I'll buy two," Trevka said. They made the purchase and set off. Trevka held onto the bottles until they had reached the cottage, whereupon Trevka handed them over and edged Derth towards the door with a final shove. He watched to make sure Derth entered the house and stayed there. Trevka wondered what kind of bizarre family life went on in there. He began to walk away from the dark hovel, then crept back to listen under a window.

Once inside the door, Derth immediately hid one liquor bottle behind a spider infested stack of wood next to the wall, then brought the other one over to the kitchen table where an old couple were seated, picking bits of meat off a cold chicken carcass whose wiry ribs poked into the cold air like bony fingers begging heaven for mercy.

"Drink this," Derth said, preferring them drunk. But his mother, or rather his grandmother said in a singsong voice,

"Got news today. Her majesty is sending us a couple o' kids to put the noose around." The word *majesty* was drawled out in a syrupy tone with a chicken-greased tongue and a single-toothed rictus. Derth turned away in disgust. The old woman crooned at his back with condescension, "You can prove how manly you are." Again the word *manly* was spoken with such contempt it made Derth cringe. Still, it was something to look forward to, a trapped female under *his* power instead of the other way around. That would be a satisfying moment to savor, until the next one came along. It had been a while now. The old man at the table, all but ignored and insignificant, chewed absently on the wishbone until it broke in his mouth. No one said anything more. Outside, Trevka walked away and wondered. He had only heard their conversation, not seen it. *Kids*, meaning baby goats, *to put the noose around*: They must butcher goats for some extra money, with Derth doing the slaughtering. Rather an insignificant way to prove one's manliness, but then he wasn't much of a man.

The next day Trevka gave Harz his report on Derth. Trevka didn't quite know what to say; Derth hadn't done anything, wasn't robbing people, hadn't bragged about anything unsavory. He didn't even hawk for his business, never pestered passers-by. Finally he said, "Well, nobody knows him at all; he's pretty new to these parts and he's not quick to make friends. He came here the same time as the Countess Gertrudis; a lot of people from her realm followed her. Thought he might even find a place in the castle with her, the half-wit." Trevka snorted thinking of all the stupid ideas Derth had. Then he added, "Oh, and he's lousy at fortune-telling." Harz said,

"He doesn't know you're associated with the castle, does he?"

"No chance, I always came through the village from the tavern, gave myself a made-up name. He seems like a weakling actually, though a little odd. He lives with his grandparents."

"All right. If that's all he's been up to, I guess we can't keep people from listening to him and handing over their money willingly." Harz dismissed him and Trevka was tempted to ask for his next assignment, but perhaps he hadn't done very well on this one. Or maybe there just weren't any more right now.

Genivee was visiting Liesse and little Luna in their new rooms in a better part of the castle than what she and the other dairy maids had. Liesse's father-in-law, the once- physician to the last Count, also lived with them. The man was nearly sixty and no longer had the energy to go about sewing ax wounds, pulling teeth and cauterizing cuts. He sat quietly sipping his hard cider and dozing in a corner while Genivee bounced Luna on her lap and made happy faces at her. When she got hungry she handed her over to Liesse for a meal. Liesse gave Luna a nipple and leaned back in her chair. Amazing how pleasurable breast feeding felt now. She looked forward to the fact that soon Boris would be walking through the door, and he was such a devoted and passionate husband. How Trevka would have paled in comparison, she both giggled and shuddered to consider. She opened her eyes and looked at Genivee. "So who are you going to leave a note for?" she teased her friend. Genivee grimaced.

"No notes, Liesse, that was dumb."

"It turned out well in the end." Genivee wanted to roll her eyes; was she yet again going to be regaled with the merits of a husband and child? "Maybe a hint then, for Vatra perhaps?" Genivee looked dubious. "Sorry, too young, isn't he? And he looks too much like his brother." She considered some more. "You know, there were times I thought Magnus would look at you, and he must be an awfully lonely man."

Genivee watched as Luna's little hand reached out, landed on flesh and gripped.

"Stop match making, dearest," Genivee said, "All unmarried men are awfully lonely. And most men look at women." She really wanted to keep secret from her dear, but sometimes indiscreet friend, the man her heart and mind were on these days. She had not noticed Harz in the past, but since their visit to Mona, the idea had lodged in her mind that he might be in love with her. She closed her eyes and saw herself at the river's edge beneath the bridge. She tapped the lily pads and looked up at him. But instead of the sun shining into her eyes and being blinded, not knowing what he thought, he reached down his hand to her and pulled her up into his arms because he did love her.

Genivee opened her eyes and noticed Liesse dozing off in her chair, head tilted back. The old father-in-law's head tipped forward on his chest and he snored. Luna's head rested sideways on a breast. No one knew her secret daydream and it would just stay that way.

10

A Trap is Sprung

Genivee left her friend napping and nursing and went to her evening milking. It was peaceful work with the quiet munch of hay in the cow's mouth, the occasional soft shift of her hooves, the squirt of the milk in the pail. She rested her face against the warm, round belly, the soft fur against her cheek and each hand wrapped around a teat. The cow was happier with every tug, her heavy udder relieved, long exhalations of contentment from her belly. Thinking back to Liesse's nursing, it seemed nature rewarded mothers with a good feeling. Genivee sighed, at her age, would she ever have that? She had had two offers of marriage when she was younger, but had turned the proposals down, thinking she was too young and they were too average. Now she had no prospects. The cow's tail swished in gratitude and Genivee kissed the big round belly before her.

She heard shouts in the courtyard and saw people going for their horses and yelling questions. Harz came across the courtyard and yelled her name; she was barely up off her milking stool when he reached her and grabbed her arm.

"Where's Liesse?" he demanded.

"In her room, with Luna and the old man. They were sleeping." Harz took both her arms in his hands and shook her as if she hadn't heard a word, repeating,

"Where is she, how did you leave her?"

"She's with her baby. She's in her room!"

Harz corrected her: "She's missing. Boris says she's gone and the old man said you were there and that you both must have left together. Where did she go?" Genivee just shook her head in confusion.

They stared speechless at each other, Harz looking for any truth in her eyes than her mind had forgotten. But there was only what she had related and Harz suddenly seemed to come back to himself and realized that he was gripping her arms. There were more shouts and galloping horses pounding the ground around them; riders were gathering in the courtyard and Boris was yelling at each in turn saying, "You two, head to the village; you take the forest path, you-" Then Trevka came galloping up to Harz saying,

"I think I know where they are." Trevka pulled another horse after him and Harz let go of Genivee, even though he doubted Trevka could know anything at all relevant. Over the shouting and noise of horses stamping all around them, Harz took the reins he was handed and swung himself onto the horse's back demanding,

"What do you know?"

"A cottage at the edge of town, follow me," Trevka yelled, and dashed off ahead of any other instruction, and as Harz followed, so then did a string of other riders. They all raced off and suddenly it was quiet again. A moment later a trio of riders left which included Gustav and Magnus. Genivee watched them all go in disbelief while her cow glanced backwards, curious at the break in routine. She steadied her hands on the cow's flanks, lowered her forehead and sank down beside it. What had she done in leaving Liesse and Luna alone?

There had been a soft but urgent knocking at Liesse's door and while still blinking from her nap, Liesee opened the door and thought she vaguely recognized the woman there as someone she'd seen around the castle. "Are you Boris's wife?" the woman asked, seeming concerned and anxious.

"Yes," Liesse answered cautiously, clutching Luna against her body.

"There's been an accident. Boris is bleeding, calling your name."

"Where, how?" Liesse entreated, but the woman only grabbed her arm and said,

"Nearby, come, I'll take you there." Liesse left with the woman, Luna in her arms. She didn't consider leaving her baby with a groggy old man. When they had turned a corner at the edge of the castle grounds, two more women appeared, gesturing frantically. While these women each took hold of Liesse's arms, the other snatched Luna from her grasp and began running. If nothing else, Liesse endeavored to keep up with the woman who had taken her baby. It all seemed fantastical, but the women seemed determined to help Liesse, and she didn't have time to argue about their methods. She called out questions, but the women answered with, 'this way' and 'hurry, he may be dying.' They took a path through the woods Liesse never used, and finally came to a cottage hidden away in it. Liesse couldn't imagine what business her husband had here, but that was for later. The door opened and the woman with Luna ran through it. The other two followed, and then all three of these strange women disappeared entirely, suddenly gone. Liesse stopped suddenly, just inside the cottage. Across from her an old man was holding Luna stiffly, while an old woman cackled triumphantly from the kitchen and a young man near the door kept her from turning and leaving. A sickening dread overcame Liesse, and she wanted to leap at the man and grab Luna, but she was rooted to the spot, trapped and outnumbered three to one. The front door slammed shut and Derth stood behind her breathing down her neck.

At that moment, in the forest, Sparrow was sitting near her home, rocking her baby and smiling in the sunset when a pall came over her. She checked her baby all over, wondering if a poisonous spider had crawled onto him, but there was nothing. Then she realized the dread was coming through him, not for him. She put her hand against his face and tried to calm him and detect the source of his despair. He squealed and squirmed and she sensed, *Luna – danger!* Sparrow pictured Liesse in her mind, asked her where was her baby. She then saw the image now before Liesse, and was chilled by the emanations from the three people around her, cold and decayed. She hoped she could reach Liesse, who was so frozen with fear she might not hear a thing Sparrow said to her:

Don't frighten them - They are like rabid animals. Stand still. Liesse had this thought come into her mind, too frozen to think for herself. She was dumbstruck that *she* could frighten these people. She was gazing numbly into the man's face; it should have been a fearsome sight, but instead it was pathetic and hopeless. A life of denigration had left him feeble, a witness to depravity had made him paralytic. The old man gazed back at Liesse, seeing an understanding in her eyes he thought did not exist in others. Liesse heard another thought; *They will come soon, be quiet and wait.* If it weren't for the calm but insistent voice in her head, she felt certain she would fly from her spot. She kept staring at the man; the others didn't bear looking at. Did she hear hoof beats? The woman turned to something in her kitchen, Liesse didn't want to know what. The room was cold and dank and reeked of something sour. Behind her the boy made strange noises. The man was stiff and motionless, possibly about to drop the baby. Liesse softened her eyes, gently held out her arms. The woman saw this and whacked a long wooden spoon she was holding hard onto the stove. The crack in the air made the boy jump, and he took Liesse's wrists and yanked them behind her.

The voice in her head continued to comfort Liesse, who stayed rooted to the spot with her eyes fixed on Luna. *They know you are missing now.* The voice reassured her. How many minutes passed? How long did she stand with the old man seeming to sink into the floor, Luna gripped stiffly in his hands, the baby calm with all this madness around her? The boy acted tough, but in fact seemed uncomfortable holding Liesse this way, unsure what to do next. The woman cackled and shrieked. But still, none of them did anything. *They are on their way to you.* A stupor had befallen them, time was held still and to the predators it seemed only a second between when their prey had been shoved through the door and her rescuers followed. To Liesse it felt eternal.

They were all startled back into reality by the troop of men who suddenly burst into the house. Boris was through the door first, shoving the pathetic Derth aside with such force that he scattered to the floor like a broken toy. Liesse was free and pitched forward, taking her baby out of the old man's outstretched arms. She spun around and both of them were clutched into Boris's embrace. Trevka was on Boris's heels and stepped over Derth on the floor, strode to the old man and pinned him to the wall. Several men at arms followed and restrained the kidnappers.

The sun was disappearing and the evening gloom was settling in. The inhabitants of the hovel were made to stand outside against a wall and as several guards stood over them and held torches lit from the kitchen fire, Harz stood behind the light, watching. The three were quiet, amazed by the crowd of men around them. Harz overheard Liesse telling Boris that nothing had happened to her or Luna aside from their being brought to this hut under false pretenses. Not a large crime. But kidnapping rarely ended in favorable ways for those abducted. It was a common crime against the well-to-do, who would gladly pay for the return of their loved ones. But there were also kidnappers who demanded nothing, never contacted anyone at all. Stealing of people, assault, imprisonment and murder were not unknown. Neither was unexplained disappearance. That such people had been living so close to the castle was especially disturbing to Harz.

Also greatly disturbed at the same moment was Sparrow. Although she felt the relief when Liesse and Luna were rescued, Liesse's consciousness lost the sharp focus which had served her well during the crisis. Sparrow called out desperately for any animals nearby the hovel to communicate with her, but there was a shocking lack of them. Squirrels, rabbits, foxes and birds were all well clear of it and even mice and shrews did not respond, there being none around. There were insects galore, but they were rarely helpful, being uninterested in talking with Sparrow. Finally a screech owl, who had heard the commotion, told Sparrow he could observe from a tree, but refused to go closer. Now she had an idea of what was going on. It wasn't hard to yet again sense the dark odor of the old woman who had been taunting Liesse, the old man who had held her baby and the young man who had held her prisoner. Not difficult to sense, but difficult to abide. Their memories of other people they had tormented replayed in their minds, it was the strange sustenance on which they fed. Even the cries and screams of those victims still rung in their ears, a sort of howling melody.   Sparrow heard the echoing despair and choked with horror. She shuddered with the knowledge that these three were near to her Gustav and all his kind, and she had to do whatever she could to stop them in their unnatural, evil ways, which they had hidden well. Thus it was that her consciousness quickly came into tune with Harz, who stood watching the scene with the same protective thought and as much disdain.

Boris kept busy ordering a complete search of the house and grounds, making sure no one else had been kidnapped or was being held against their will and that there was not so much as an animal being kept unkindly. He kept giving orders and keeping men at arms moving busily about until his rage began to come under some kind of control. If they left too soon, not only might he do something unworthy of his position of power, but he might overlook something they should attend to while there. He glanced often toward Liesse and Luna, who were safely in the saddle on a horse next to Vatra, who held the reins tightly and guarded them closely. Amid all the commotion, Harz focused on the old woman's face from twelve feet away in the gloom. Vacant eyes caromed in oversized sockets staring like rotting onions looming out of the dirt. Her cheeks were gray hollows, the lines around her mouth were a sunken wheel of deep spokes. Harz both waited for her to look at him and anticipated with horror that she would. As he thought it, her gaze turned to him. He had never before looked upon someone whose soul had fled, but it was not that absence which made his blood run icy. It was the presence of what he did see behind her eyes; not a soul, but something evil. Memories filled the air around the three and their history became clear to Harz in a hazy mix of images and sounds, all of them dreadful.

Gustav himself had been on the heels of the skirmish to find Liesse. He had been talking to Trevka when they heard shouting and Trevka suddenly broke away and ran off to them. Gustav followed, but further back in case another ambush was afoot. It was a common enough ploy to catch a Count. He had several men with him, including Magnus, and they trotted along, quietly following the trail, and came upon the party of prisoners just as it was being led back. As Gustav watched the three walk by, Harz came alongside and told him the facts of the arrest. Then he tried to convey what he sensed, but had no facts to prove:

"Gustav, these people have committed many crimes, though most of them in Uluvost. It has been going on for many years." Harz hung his head, wishing it was not filled with the images now in it. "But I doubt we will find any proof of that. I have a feeling all their victims are silent." Gustav asked in dismay,

"Dead?" There would be bodies if that were the case.

"Silent, one way or another," Harz answered.

"How do you know?" Gustav asked. Harz wondered to himself; it was odd but somehow true that a little bird had told him. But he only said,

"I just know." Just then the old woman turned around to them, as if she had heard their conversation, although she was too far away and the clopping of horse's hooves made much noise. She said in an insect-like squeal which traveled far,

"Say hello to her *majesty*! Her old nanny is here." Harz felt cold air around him. He said to Gustav,

"She means Gertrudis." The old woman turned back around and kept walking, apparently unconcerned for her situation. Gustav said to Harz,

"Lock them in the the dungeon. Keep them separate from each other, and give only bread, water and one blanket."

The screech owl flew off. Sparrow breathed a sigh of relief; they would be locked away. The voices faded from Sparrow's head as the party drifted off back to the castle. She knew Liesse was safely back with her family and it felt bittersweet. A year ago Sparrow had imagined that having a child would replace the family she lost when her parents died, but there was still something missing. Her child not only had no father around but all the other people who were part of something larger, something Sparrow had never thought she was missing. Living was more than surviving, even more than surviving well. It was having around you people to care about.

The owl who had helped her sense what was happening at the squatter's hovel had flown off and now there was no one nearby to communicate with; no one who was listening and understood her. If even one of them had the same finely tuned sense, she could converse with them. But as it was, with no familiar animal nearby to hear and care enough to help, it was like asking a stranger in a foreign language to find a friends' home and talk to them for you. She kept her mind drifting over the landscape where the rescue party was even now making its way back to the castle, their vibrations fading as they left the place. She might try to follow them, but already they were absorbed back into their immediate surroundings, no longer crying out into the ether for help, certain their world was again as close and safe as their skin. Sparrow's thoughts floated like a feather in the breeze, faintly calling, *Does anyone hear? Is there a friend about?*

She had begun to drift off into a sad sleepiness, her baby in her arms, when suddenly she was startled by the sound of an old woman's voice. Fortunately, she knew at once this person was not on the mountain beside her, but was somewhere in that landscape she had been drifting through in her mind. Sparrow kept her eyes closed and repeated her mind's call: *You hear me?*

I hear you, came the answer.

My name is Sparrow.

My name is Mona.

I am far away from the castle, are you near it?

I am near the village in its shadow. You know the castle?

I have friends there.

I have friends there also.
Do you know the Count?

The Count's cousin was here.

You know Harz?

A little, he hides well, and is lost. I tried to help.

Tried? Is he still lost?

He lost his wife, and the one he could have married and had a son with is drifting away. Oh, he let her go too easily. A son is important.

Suddenly their connection ended, Sparrow could not know if it was because of some interruption in Mona's life or simply Mona's ending the conversation. Without a physical presence, Sparrow could not see Mona's face, know if she was just contemplating something, or if something more abrupt had happened. Sparrow called out again but could not bring her back. It was the first time she had conversed with someone like that in her life. Sparrow had tried to send reassuring messages to her mother a few times, but her mother might only get a word or two, or none if she had become very worried. She had tried sending Gustav thoughts, but he disbelieved them, attributed them to his own imaginings. So Sparrow had mostly given up trying to communicate with people that way. Mona must have good practice with it, or was perhaps just naturally a very good listener, hearing even the fluttering of a bird away up in the mountains.

When the rescue party rode into the castle courtyard, Genivee was still on her milking stool by her cow's side, slowly stroking the calf that was now finishing her job. While the others occupied themselves with the business at hand, Magnus left the group upon noticing her still at her cow. He had seen her in their hurried departure but thought no more about it. Now there she still was, pathetic and worrying in ignorance. Harz saw her too, imagined he saw red marks on her arms and looked away. He was too busy now anyway. He saw Magnus go to her and so returned to the business of the prisoners. Magnus got off his horse and spoke to her, "They are all right, it's over." Genivee stood up in his presence but her legs were uncertain, the words not quite taking effect. Magnus thought she was about to faint, she was pale and trembling. Her best friend and goddaughter had just been kidnapped and she had been made to feel responsible. Magnus put his hands on her shoulders and said again, "It's all right, they are fine now." He learned this from having been married; women needed to be told things firmly and repeatedly. She started gasping in sobs as if she had not breathed in the last half hour. Magnus took her arm and led her away from the cow shed and over to a bench against a wall.

He sat her down near the entrance to some servant's quarters and looked down at her, wondering when she would recover sufficiently to be left alone. She was still gasping and hiccuping, so he took her wringing hands and pressed them together. "It's all right now," he said. Magnus glanced around, hoping to ask someone where she lived so he could deposit her there and end his obligation. Then he heard Genivee's timid voice reaching up to him,

"They're all right?" He nodded, his gaze falling from her tear-filled eyes to her lips, the top one wet with crying and the bottom one half-bitten in her own teeth. He was gazing at her mouth when she suddenly jumped up and left him, back to herself all at once.

11
Condemning and Promoting

There was a courtroom of sorts in Wilker castle. It was on the ground floor, close to the dungeons where criminals were kept and far away from any living quarters. It had no windows and was not very large; there was room for only a dozen or so interested people to sit along the side and watch the proceedings. On the morning after Derth and his family had been captured, Trevka was in the courtroom giving his account of his dealings with Derth. Listening along with Gustav were Harz and Boris as well as several guards, scribes and a representative for Gertrudis. Gertrudis herself had declined to attend the proceeding, but Gustav insisted that someone close to her attend and listen. Trevka was recounting what he had learned about Derth, concluding with "He seemed too immature to be threatening, but I wanted to know where he lived." Gustav answered,

"That was very good of you, Trevka." He smiled and paused, thinking it would have been easy enough not to bother walking home with Derth one night, or not to put together a missing woman and child with a wayward fortune teller. "But how then did Derth know, if you were being so careful to hide it from him, the identity of Liesse and her baby, where they lived and even her husband's name?" Trevka's eyebrows crossed and he was suddenly worried. He'd been certain to reveal nothing of his real name or status. Had someone *else* been spying on *them*? He tried to answer,

"I don't know…I always walked to the village and came through the tavern." Had Trevka suddenly fallen from celebrated hero to unwitting informant? In a blink, a demotion to cleaning the dog stables flashed through his mind. Gustav tried to reassure him,

"I don't think anyone followed you, Trevka. You say you were careful and I believe you. What you found out saved Liesse and we thank you." Gustav then dismissed Trevka, but once outside the courtroom Trevka was informed that the prisoner would be brought in next and that he had been instructed to listen out of view in a hidden area. He was directed through a disguised doorway behind which was a long and narrow hallway; at its end there was a portion of wall near the ceiling with a carved wooden panel through which everything said in the courtroom could be heard. Trevka sat in the only chair and quietly waited. He marveled at being in this place he'd never known existed, wondering briefly if he'd ever been listened to by someone seated here. Gustav turned to Harz and said quietly,

"Time for the prisoner. I expect he will be lying." Harz nodded. He sat down at a table behind stacks of books and small objects, arranging papers, pen and inkwell. These things tended to distract persons being questioned so that they gazed in Harz's direction. Honest people looked earnestly at the Count when being questioned; dishonest ones were quick to look elsewhere. A silence filled the room and instead of whispers and chatter, there was only the shuffle of feet. Gustav was glad of it, for although he seemed to be just contemplating the questions he would ask, he was in fact listening for any noises from behind the wall where Trevka was hidden. He was glad to detect nothing of his presence.

After a time, Vatra led Derth into the audience chamber. Derth had been trying to talk to Vatra on the way out of his cold cell, saying, "Tell them I'm just a fortune teller. I had nothing to do with that girl being there. It was all my parents' idea." But Vatra, a stranger to him and uninterested in his pleas, just moved him along the halls and stairways to the courtroom. As Vatra instructed him to keep moving, Derth noticed in his voice a slight difference from what he had remembered, not to mention a lack of recognition he found perplexing. The entourage of guards and prisoner finally arrived at the door to the court and stopped. The sentry outside the court knocked on the door sounding three distinct raps. A minute passed and the door opened. Derth was led in. Inside everyone watched his progress down the center aisle until he stood in front of the Count, whose intense scrutiny soon made Derth avert his eyes to the table of objects and the bored-looking man behind them. Immediately Gustav asked,

"How did you know the woman and child that were brought to your cottage yesterday?"

"I didn't know them." Harz scribbled, looked up.

"Who were the three women who brought her there?"

"I never saw them before in my life," Derth answered. Harz merely scribbled.

"Why was she taken there?" To this, Derth shuffled uncomfortably.

"Don't know," he mumbled. Harz turned a paper over crisply, the sign of a slight lie. Gustav didn't suspect that Derth was an actual mastermind to crimes, but he must know more than he let on. He asked, "Why did you change your residence?" Derth replied,

"Came along when the Countess did, thought to maybe work in her service one day."

"But that didn't work out, did it?" Gustav asked him.

"No, sir," he smiled humbly.

"How does your family know the Countess?"

"Don't know her at all, we're just loyal followers." Harz cleared his throat and Gustav warned Dearth:

"The punishment for lying to the Count is the same as for kidnapping. Now, you know her very well indeed. Tell me how or you shall spend the rest of your days in the same dark hole where you spent last night." Derth shuffled and shrugged as he glanced at the warden who stood very close to him, ready to restrain him if he made a move. He smiled wanly and said more loudly,

"Oh, you mean, did we know her back in the old country, before she came here. Yes, we knew her there."

"And here, too." Gustav completed the statement. Derth weighed his loyalties, his options, his future. Each was slim. It was little surprise to him that Gertrudis was not there to say anything in his defense. He said gravely,

"I have not seen her in several years and I barely know her at all." But Gustav insisted,

"Nevertheless you worked for her here, didn't you?" Derth paused in answering. Gustav gestured and Vatra slapped his prisoner's shoulder to turn him around and leave. But Derth had only just begun to thaw in the warmth of a room above ground and the thought of another moment in that black dungeon made him fold. He did not want to be led away and the truth was he hadn't done anything. He protested,

"My mother was friends with Gertrudis, but she exiled all three of us when she became engaged to be married. My mother was a nursemaid who had charge of her as a child. The future Countess remembered how – I mean *her* and sent all three of us away, I don't know why. But we didn't go, we followed her instead. We felt loyal to her." Derth looked around, wondering if this might count in his favor. It did not. He continued, "When the Countess found out we were in the village, I guess one of her attendants saw us, she sent an envoy to tell us a girl and her baby were being sent to us, and that if we 'took care of them like mother used to take care of her', we might be pardoned and allowed to go back to our home country quietly. I didn't care about going back, really, but we couldn't refuse her. She said she'd denounce us all as exiled criminals if we didn't help her with this and that we would be arrested and locked up. She promised us some little money to help with the journey back, and lots of clothes and things for along the way." *I haven't done anything*, Derth thought. *Not here, anyway, not anything you know about.*

Gustav pondered things he had only suspected about Gertrudis. She wasn't a right woman and he'd always thought it was because she was hopelessly spoiled. Now he saw that she had been left in the care of a deranged woman who should never have been allowed in the presence of children, let alone given the raising of one. The old woman had probably stolen Derth, probably used him to help her abduct women and children. Gertrudis was a victim, but not powerless any more. She could have informed her Count that there were criminals in his realm; he would have seen to their punishment. She could have been an eyewitness at this very proceeding but wasn't, instead hoping for more trouble for Liesse and Luna (whom she obsessed was Gustav's). She wanted to give the pain to someone else.

Unfortunately, there was no hard proof against these three. Gertrudis could have given it, and it would have made their punishment clear and final. But she was being her usual isolated, unhelpful self. Gustav knew it would be foolish to let these people go and hope they behaved. Harz's impressions – and he was emphatic about them – was that they had committed crimes in the past and would plague any village, anyone they lived near in the future. Sending them back to Uluvost would be to knowingly inflict that on their world. Gustav contemplated cutting off their hands, but instead determined to put them to some good use for this world. They would learn duty and a proper place in society in his county, at the very least. He dismissed the prisoner and court was ended for the day. Behind his screen, Trevka wondered what would happen to them.

Several days followed during which many inquiries were made. Gustav informed Gertrudis in private that she could punish her tormentors and see justice done, but she remained aloof, as if taunting Gustav to take some action. Gustav consulted with members of the court from outlying areas and devised a plan to possibly awaken penitence in the prisoners, but if not that then to at least keep them from harming others. The three prisoners were brought into the courtroom, led down an aisle packed on either side with curious onlookers and made to stand stiffly and silently for their final pronouncement. The prolocutor read the edict:

"...these three people so named have been found guilty of occupation of a cottage not owned by them, paid for by them, nor given as a gift to them. They have not been stewards of it while staying there. They have failed to be usefully or helpfully occupied at any time during their stay in this county. They are not natives or citizens of Wilker and are not invited guests. They have conspired with others to do harm. They have waylaid and detained others against their will and no one declares them to be of decent moral character. Finally and most egregiously, they came here against the expressed wishes of the Countess Gertrudis. For these infractions the following sentence is hereby delivered: The above-named persons shall forthwith reside in the royal domestic farm in the low lands. Shelter and occupation shall be near and for the attending of the piggery. Food and clothing shall be provided as long as work is done." The prolocutor lowered the page he read from. Everyone looked at each other. There was no time limit on the decree, no final sentence such as, 'And this decree shall be in effect for a term of five years,' which always came after such decrees. That meant it was for life. There was a roar in the room to that effect and the three were led away in a daze.

The following fall, a report came of how the trio was managing in their new home. They were confined to a small hovel next to the styes and had adjusted to the smell and the duty. The hogs they tended were huge and aggressive animals, capable of harming any human they didn't like. The convicts had no tools to use for their job, not being trustworthy, but they were given a little wood for their stove and fresh food from the farm. The old woman, although able-bodied, soon refused to work however and so was not given her ration. Although her husband and Derth shared what they had with her, she refused this after a time, too. She stopped eating and slowly died. The two men continued on, coming to care for their swine charges with affection and kindness, perhaps the first real friends they had ever had. They were eventually given implements and allowed to mend stye and home with hammer and nails and make minor improvements if the materials were earned through good practices. They never tried to leave and in fact became thoughtful pig-keepers who tended their animals well and had the cleanest stables in the compound and a very humble but decent home. Derth was allowed to take his cards with him but never again told a fortune.

Gustav, meanwhile, had another problem to attend. Gertrudis had been a child when she was at the mercy of a debased nanny. She never grew out of that child, never became a woman, really. But still, as a Countess, she could have had her tormentors prosecuted, being well in a position of power to do so. Instead, she perpetuated the wrong by seeking revenge against a woman she never knew, but who had gained a happy home, a child, a loving husband, and all by merely being a milkmaid with a generous heart. That Liesse lived happily on the castle grounds and had the kindness of the Count galled Gertrudis, who felt entitled to these things yet lacked each one. The idea festered in the hole where her heart should have been until, by chance, an underling told her that she had seen her old nanny in the village. Gertrudis then coerced them into subjecting two strangers to the same tortures she knew as a child, and enjoyed the idea.

Gustav considered what to do with Gertrudis. She was a menace to his realm and his honor. In the end Gustav concluded that Gertrudis, still a child really, should go back to her home. It seemed the most merciful thing he could do for her. She was called to Gustav's audience with only a minimum number of witnesses present. She had been told to wear the vestments of her office; her crown, her robes of fur and velvet, her scepter, all the things given to her upon their ill-fated marriage; things that had later been confiscated.

When she arrived, she approached the throne next to Gustav's, the one she had not occupied in so long a time she felt eager delight upon seeing it. Gustav put up his hand to stop her advance. He felt only pity and disdain for her. He spoke plainly, without anger. "Madam, we are aware that you have been unhappy in this place. People here have not understood your situation, and you have mistaken the places and privileges of certain others." Gertrudis took another step, encouraged, but again Gustav raised a hand to stop her.

"As such, it is apparent your happiness cannot be attained here, and we therefore seek to provide you with the means and situation in which you might find it." Gustav and Gertrudis looked at each other; two people so far apart in temperament, so bereft of mutual affection, and so dissimilar in their life's purpose. This last encounter was possibly the most caring thing Gustav had ever, would ever do for her. She had no idea what was coming but she had, it seemed, resigned herself to having lost his favor, and she had at least enjoyed a brief moment of fantasy that it could all be made new again. Maybe it would be.

"Madam, this place does not serve you. You should never have been removed from your home of origin, as you never grew out of it true and whole. I send you back there to recollect that, to find what is still lost from you, and to find some consoling. The evil you encountered there is gone now. Your rank is not removed from you, but rather you leave it here, an honorary presence. Place your crown and robe and scepter on your throne, for it is not free for another to fill." Gertrudis took in the words, stepped uncertainly forward, extended the hand with the scepter; it started to fall and Gustav took it and placed it on the throne. She seemed suspended for a time, dazed. The robe more fell off her slumped shoulders, and Vatra took it, handed it to Gustav, who placed it across the arms of the chair. Finally she seemed to feel the weight of her crown, now a heavy burden, and she took it from her head. She gazed at it, admiring its beauty, for both the first and last time, and then placed it gently on the seat of the chair. She didn't know what to do next. Vatra barely touched his hand to her elbow until she just felt its presence. She looked at him, eyes wide and child-like, as they had been before her marriage. He turned her gently around, and led her slowly out of the room. They were all so calm and gentle with her, a treatment immensely new and soothing.

A week later, Gertrudis and all of the people she had brought with her were helped into several wagons along with their belongings. Gertrudis had on simple clothes, and had composed herself admirably. She declared, and everyone agreed, that leaving was her idea, as circumstances had become too unpleasant here for someone as high-born as she, and thus she was taking her people and returning home until such a time as she might fancy to come back. The maids who went with her were despondent; one wept and covered her face as she leaned on another. Some laid down in the wagon in despair, ill- accustomed to long trips and having no desire to see Wilker castle fade into the distance behind them. They had been maids and attendants to a Countess; now they were servants to an exile, returning to damp, primitive Uluvost. Gertrudis even pretended not to care about leaving her son behind, bizarrely claiming she had no son.

Gustav watched the entourage leave from an upper window and listened to the creaks and groans of the wagon wheels fade away into the sky like a flock of moths with no light. The sounds of voices and weeping drifting up from the attendants jumbled in the wagon dissipated and the ensuing peace and silence heartened Gustav like dawn dispelling the gloom. *Now there is room for Sparrow*, he thought happily. Counts in years past might have as many mistresses as a Countess would put up with; his own mother stood at least one he knew of. But Gustav always thought that left an unpleasant frisson in the air as if someone had guffawed at a wrong moment. He looked again at the empty path by which Gertrudis had left; so marvelously empty and serene he wanted to have an artist paint it to preserve its beauty forever. In a few months he would be going back to the hunting lodge where, the gods willing, Sparrow would be waiting for him. He wouldn't leave her there this time. When he came back she would be with him. As he thought longingly about her, far away in the forest she sensed his happiness about her, sensed that there was a place for her in the castle, heard the last creaks of a retreating wagon and knew that Gertrudis was in it. Sadness lingered behind it like dust settling to the ground.

One more matter was at hand for the royal audience. Trevka and Vatra were told to appear in their best apparel. Gustav had consulted with his senior officials and they endorsed his planned announcements. For once, he had a pleasant duty ahead of him. The twins entered and stood in front of the Count. Everyone else stood in rank as usual, but with a crispness and perfection of line special to the occasion. Gustav noted to himself how identical in features they were, exact same height, exact same weight, and yet how opposite in their apparel. Trevka's clothes were flamboyant, adorned, full of swash, almost sweeping the floor. Vatra's were simple and trim, utterly complimentary to his body, reserved and elegant, perfect in their simplicity. Gustav admired both styles and smiled to himself that at least there was one way to tell them apart. He spoke: "Vatra, the older, step forward." Vatra quietly took one step ahead of his brother and put one knee on the floor and put his hands on the other bent knee. "For your straight and moral handling of those bound and under the question of the law, I dub thee Squire Constable of Wilker. Harz is your superior; attend to matters of arrest, detention and disposition of questionable characters as he so orders or in his absence as you see fit." Vatra bowed his head while Gustav tapped his shoulders with his sword, placed a medal showing his title around his neck, and told him to rise. Vatra put his hand to his forehead and swept it out and down as he rose and stepped backward.

Gustav waited a moment. He dragged out matters of bestowing honor and left great silences in between, to show the proper seriousness and certitude for the honorees. "Trevka, the younger, step forward." Trevka's foot rose with a kick and sharply planted itself. He elaborately brandished his long cape out behind him so that it re-settled around him like a thousand lesser worshipers bowing down, his metallic adornments sprinkling the same flourish with a chorus of tinkling like the applause of miniscule fairies. After making a wide arc with his arm, his hand at last came to rest on his bent knee and finally his head slowly descended in a bow until his forehead nearly touched the top of his hand over his knee. Gustav waited, fascinated, until the entertainment was completed. Then he spoke: "In measure for your reconnaissance service lately rendered most expertly to the realm, I dub thee Squire Watchman of Wilker. Boris is your superior; you are the eyes and ears of the castle in all things not usually seen or heard." Some of the men in attendance shuffled and Trevka's eyes jerked towards them, but that went unnoticed thanks to the low aspect of his face. Gustav touched both shoulders with his sword, handed Trevka a stiletto with identifying marks of the castle on it, and told him to rise. Trevka did so with a bow and sweep even lower than his kneel had been, and backed away obediently, head down, stiletto clutched close to his heart. After another silence of recognition, Gustav raised his arms, the newly appointed young men turned, faced the audience, and great applause rose up for them. They were no longer pages, they were now squires.

12

Wayward Woman

A midnight summer thunderstorm was beating against the castle's walls, pouring down its sides and running in rivers across the courtyard. Genivee was outside in the darkness of the castle's courtyard soaked, shivering and alone. She couldn't go inside. She was still waiting for the men to come back. How long ago had the men rode off in search of Liesse? It seemed they would never come back and Liesse would be lost and Genivee would be standing in this rain forever. She couldn't hear anything over the constant explosions of thunder and splashing of water. She looked down and saw rivers of mud splosh over her cold bare feet. She shivered again, hugged her wet shoulders. Lightning flashed and she saw someone on a horse coming towards her in a hurry. But as he rode towards her he wasn't seeing her. It was the horse that made its way in her direction, then it turned abruptly when she appeared in its path. The man on the horse tried to pull the reins over, unaware of why the animal was shying. The foot in the stirrup nearly kicked Genivee in the face as the horse swung hard around. She flinched, amazed she had missed being hit, then reached up with her arms; the rider was going to be thrown off if he didn't take control. She called out to him; *take my hands.* But the rider didn't seem to notice her. With a bolt of lightning the horse reared up and with one toss threw the rider off backwards. The horse fled and Genivee fell to her knees and groped in the pitch black mud looking for the rider, but he had disappeared too.

She shivered again and finally being so cold, Genivee woke up. The rain was spattering into her room and onto her feet through the open window, the shutters of it banging periodically against the wall. Her feet were cold and wet and she had only her arms wrapped tightly around her naked body because she had gone to bed when it was a sweltering hot night. Even crickets had been silent under the burden of humidity. She had left the window open for what little waft might come through, and now a storm had invaded the room. She sat up; the only blanket was in a chest at the foot of the bed. She bolted out of bed and opened the trunk, grabbed the blanket and wrapped it around her. She turned to the window and was leaning out to latch the shutters when a flash of lightning illuminated the courtyard with the horse and rider in it. She looked again, trying to see through the splatters of rain, but the lightning was gone and so was any illumination of the courtyard. She stood by the window waiting for another flash, listening to the rain die out on the castle walls. The storm was fading and when the last silent flash of lightning illuminated the courtyard no one was in it.

She huddled back into bed, warm and drying under the blanket, her shivering subsided. She fell back to sleep and the rest of the night was still and dreamless. In the morning she woke up hearing a measured *tock, tock, tock* outside. Genivee got out of bed and opened the shutters, looked out. There was water dripping from a scupper to the ground below, rhythmic and flat. A few clouds drifted across the orange and lavender sky, the sun was not up just yet. Turning from the window swiftly as she dropped the blanket, she reached for her dress and put it on. Her cow was waiting to be milked.

It was the middle of summer and thunderstorms often threatened. The mornings began with a damp coolness from the night before, but quickly dried out as the sun blazed down and made anyone working outside nearly faint. People would retreat to the shady sides of the castle, and a heavy stillness crept over everything. Clouds began as fluffy, pink-edged wave crests low on the horizon, then insidiously crept across the heavens, piling up into vast, nebular mountains. While people lay dead to the heat, the burgeoning clouds crept together unnoticed. The sky darkened, thunder rolled like an avalanche and lightning flashed with foreboding incandescence. When these attempts of mother nature to waken the sleeping afternoon went ignored, she paused patiently with a leaden silence. Then her patience ended and a sudden downpour woke everything up and cooled everything off. Sometimes, though, she just lost interest or turned it elsewhere and the cloud masses brushed past each other and then dissolved. The day would drag forth hot and unrelenting, with barely a shadow to relieve the heat. It was on such days as these that storms might finally coalesce late at night into flashing thunderstorms followed by cool breezes and ever-vanishing rumbles of thunder, and people would lie awakened, contemplating their life and nature's grip on it.

Preparation for Gustav's hunting trip to the forest was the main activity occupying the castle in July. Although Gustav was only taking a small party with him, the other members of the castle became busy with their own plans. While the Count was away, a substitute court would be in place. They had little actual power, but enjoyed themselves immensely, pretending to carry on the business of the realm, staging mock trials and pretend executions, royal promotions and regal weddings, even spooky funeral processions and make-believe burials, complete with cryptic eulogies, fainting ladies and costumed children throwing straw. Boys dressed up as melodramatic fainting ladies to make fun of them. It was their summer recreation, and everyone looked forward to it. Older and less interested members of the court merely retired into quiet recreations and easy outings around the countryside to avoid all the silliness.

One such ambulation had been planned by Magnus, who had a desire to leave the heat and possible juvenile goings-on early. He walked his mare across the courtyard, tightened her straps once more, then shoved his foot into the stirrup, flung himself across the beast and plonked down into the saddle. Meanwhile, the horse turned in a circle under him, its typical reaction. Magnus had learned to mount fast because of this habit of hers. He started away but realized he had forgotten something and turned back to get it. As he did so, the flash of a bare body in an upper window caught his eye. He looked again more carefully; but the windows now were all dark. He yanked his horse away again, dismissing the forgotten item and deciding to leave immediately. Of course he had not seen a woman's bare back, completely naked, from her neck to her legs in an instant, her long blond hair swishing across it. It was just a curtain being pulled back.

As sunlight began to clear the mist of early morning, Harz was leaning against the wall under the archway of a dark passage that connected the inner courtyard to the outside of the castle, although few people knew this. The entrance where he stood on the courtyard side led to various working rooms, mostly for storing extra tack, wagons and garden equipment. These rooms were used quite often but did not appear to lead to the outside of the castle, being dark and dead-ended. However through one of those storage rooms was another door which opened to a hallway that connected to the outside of the castle, far above the village it overlooked, but unseen behind thick trees. From the outside, it was a secret entrance that could only be accessed if one knew exactly where it was and what it was.

Eleven frames resembling stable doors were permanently fixed to one facade of the castle along the outer wall; a twelfth one was actually a door. Pulling on door knobs would not open any of them, however shifting a lever sideways in one door would unlock the actual door right next to it. Unlocked but still shut, this door had to be known to the would-be entrant. It was rarely used now, and few people knew about it. In the past it had served as a way to gain entrance unseen by anyone watching the main gate. It was also a way to escape out of the castle without having to pass marauders lying in wait at the main gate. Now neither of these necessities came up. Before dawn, once a year, Harz checked the secret passage to make sure it still worked. He began by walking the narrow path that led from the mountain side of the castle, checking that it was still passable and yet untrampled by anyone recently. He reached the secret door, yanked its squeaky hinges open and entered the gloom beyond. Down the dark hallway and through another doorway, he then emerged to stand at the edge of the castle courtyard under an archway and casually watch the activities going on.

A sound came to him which, echoing off stone walls, was hard to identify. *Brush, brush, brush*, it continued quietly, unrelenting. He glanced toward the dairy and then walked over to where he could see into it better. Of course, it was the sound of milk squirting into a milk pail. The woman was bent to her work, her face turned away. But her blond hair was braided up around her head, the color of it perfect next to the caramel brown of the cow. The morning was still too quiet and calm to interrupt her. In the afternoon there would be lots of activity around. He watched her until she finished, raised her head and kissed the cow's side. She carried her milk pails to the buttery and Harz watched her go. In the rooms above him, Harz knew Gustav would be making his way to the main chamber and expecting Harz to be there already. Glancing one last time toward the dairy and knowing he could not keep his eyes on both of them, he headed upstairs.

In the main chamber already, Gustav had watched Magnus gallop away from the castle, wishing he could be doing the same. Soon Harz came in and Gustav began the business of the day. He asked about preparations for their trip to the hunting lodge, again. It wasn't that hard to get ready for a simple trip. Then he asked if he had gone to visit Mona lately. Harz hesitated, decided against pretending to have been busy and then simply said *no*. Gustav, vaguely surprised, asked him to be sure to do so before they were to leave for the forest. He somehow thought it would be important to be able to tell Sparrow that this lady was well and looked after. They might be related, after all. "In fact, go today," Gustav instructed. Harz's tried to think of something more important. But then he nodded.

At midday Harz was slowly making his way on horseback through the village. He was telling himself it was just a stroll, he was just out walking. It was too hot to be doing anything else. An old lady in a small abode would be napping at such a time and he would not think of disturbing her. But as his horse made its way to her home, she was not napping, but rather sitting in a chair under the shade of a tree, gazing across her garden at something far away.

She saw him approaching and stood up, limbs akimbo, looking peevish. Harz got down off his horse, tied the reins to her short fence with more care and time than it normally took to saddle the beast, and looked up as if noticing Mona for the first time. Her stern gaze had not wavered, though.

"Good afternoon, Madam. I'm glad to see you looking well," Harz said as he stepped through the gate and approached her. She was fixed in place, studying him, not speaking. She kept staring at him and he tried not to notice, but she wasn't trying to hide it so the effort came off poorly. Finally she said,

"Well here you are, anyway, so come inside for some tea." Harz followed her in, feeling like a youngster caught stealing candy. They seated themselves with cups of tepid tea. She had not bothered to reboil water, whether from the heat of the day or general pique, he didn't know and wouldn't dare ask. Finally she said, "And where is Genivee?" Harz was surprised by the question, and couldn't provide an answer.

"At her work, I suppose." Mona stared him down, clearly unsatisfied. She slowly started to shake her head, saying,

"No, she's not." Harz wasn't sure how to respond to this. Was he supposed to be keeping track of her? As well as Mona? And why wouldn't she be in the castle, probably resting from the heat of the day? Finally Mona sighed wearily and declared, "You're never going to make a woman fall in love with you by ignoring her." Again, another statement Harz had no response for. Wasn't he supposed to be interrogating her about her situation, her needs, her safety, all that business? Instead she had found fault with him where he was already feeling it and not saying anything helpful. Finally he muttered,

"We are just acquaintances, she's hardly my lady."

"Of course she's not!" Mona declared as if Harz were simple-minded. "Not the way you treat her!" Mona's eyes narrowed and she stared him down, poking her index finger at him accusingly. "You have already let her wander out of your sphere, and there are plenty of other men in this world, plenty even in this village for a princess like her." With disgust Mona retracted her finger and reached for the cards under her table. She didn't offer them to Harz, but instead slammed the deck onto the table, cut the deck and turned up the exposed card. She looked at it, grunted *gecko,* and mumbled something as if this card obviously confirmed everything she had said. She turned away from him in her chair and he felt he had taken enough abuse. He stood up, but suddenly wondered what he would tell Gustav, who expected a report on *her* condition, not his.

"Do you need any help, Mona?" It sounded hopelessly silly, but he was duty-bound to ask. Mona looked at him, now with deep sadness.

"You are asking the wrong woman, my dear." They studied each other. But Mona wasn't lying about anything, wasn't trying to trick him even though she was a tricky woman. It wasn't easy to see one's self so clearly reflected.

Harz left her and when he had vanished over the road Mona looked back down at the card. The gecko was a wonderful guardian, ridding a house of pesky and harmful insects. Mona whispered to herself, *Clairvoyance without sight; the gift of voice that goes unused.* She shook her head and mopped her brow and glanced at her cat napping in the shade, her only company. She sensed that in spite of the heat, it wouldn't rain.

After her milking and in the still coolness of the morning, Genivee had decided to take a walk away from the castle. She preferred walking to riding and didn't plan to go far. But she was determined to find some flowers to pick. That morning she had discovered in her room that bundle of flowers Mona had given her all those weeks ago, having been pressed under some things in her trunk. She had taken the flowers carefully out, but they had disintegrated onto the floor. Suddenly she realized she had been deluding herself about Harz. Merely because an old lady had batted coy eyes and made sweet insinuations, she had imagined Harz was madly in love with her. Now he had barely spoken to her in all that time, and she was silly to think she meant anything more to him than a shallow milk maid who couldn't even keep a keen eye on her best friend. She picked up the pieces of dried bouquet and threw them out her window. Walking outside to face the sunshine, she took the road that led straight-away into the countryside, thinking it was the road on which she was least likely to meet anyone.

She walked briskly for quite some time, spied a cluster of red poppies far off in the lee of a hill, and determined to walk that much farther to pick some. By the time she had reached the spot, however, the sun had risen high and was beating down upon her. Her clothes were soaked in sweat and she was beginning to feel faint. She thankfully fell into the meadow of poppies and wiped her forehead. A cloud passed overhead and she felt better, but still spent. She would rest here and then pick some flowers before turning back. In the meantime, she laid down on her side to rest.

In the countryside further away from the castle than Genivee's resting spot, Magnus was on his horse at a leisurely walk, headed home. It was too hot now to canter along, even though clouds were beginning to offer moments of relief. The heat and dampness in the air made his clothes twice as heavy and his vision occasionally wavered and shimmered. He had brooded all morning about his imagined vision of a woman's bare back, her hair sweeping aside to reveal creamy skin and curves. He hadn't thought about women that way in a long time. It would be pointless. After his wife died, he was too bereft to think of such things. Later still, there was no point in thinking of such things. Now however, the pleasures of female companionship occupied his mind and would not be displaced.

As he crested a hill, he spotted a woman in the distance who, having staggered along, collapsed onto the ground. She rallied a moment, then fell sideways into the tall grass. Was she trying to escape some pursuer? Was she running away from the castle or village due to some calamity? Fainting in fear of him? He spurred his horse towards her, curious. It seemed the image of a woman had him mesmerized this day, and he fantasized that here was his bare-backed beauty, fainting away at the sight of him.

Genivee's head was pounding from the heat when she suddenly heard horse's hooves beating towards her. It was as if the dream of last night was replaying itself here in clear daylight. She sat up, shading her eyes to the glare, trying to decipher who it was. She knew at once this mare was Magnus's. She was exhausted and thirsty, suddenly thankful she was not alone and stranded on this long road. She stood up in his presence, but her head spun and buzzed. She swayed in the hot sun.

Magnus leaned down towards her and asked her, disbelieving, "Did you walk all this way?" She looked back towards the castle, but oddly it wasn't there. She had walked much farther than she realized.

"I guess I did, I hadn't meant to come this far."

"Would you like a ride back?" She nodded and tugged at her dress; it was immensely uncomfortable and difficult to breathe in. He had taken off his jacket early on but now even one white shirt was too hot. She must be roasting in that heavy dress. He reached down to her. "Give me your hand and put your foot on top of mine." He twined his arm around hers until he had her by the shoulders. "Jump up with your other foot." Genivee followed instructions blankly, thinking she would never be lifted off the heavy ground. But amazingly with a tiny push from her foot Magnus pulled her up as if she were weightless and she settled down in front of him and they set off on an easy walk.

Genivee hadn't realized how exhausted she was and Magnus noticed how red and dry her cheeks were. "You need water," he said and turned the horse around, heading away from the castle. They rode back over the hill he had just crested, and soon came to a small pond. They stopped alongside of it and she slid off the horse, her body sliding down the length of his arm until only their hands were together. She looked up at him for a moment smiling her thanks, then turned and waded into the pool. When she got halfway into it, she let the rest of herself fall flat into the water, intentionally or accidentally, he wasn't sure. She splashed and dipped her head under the water, which was cool and deep in the middle. When she had found a depth she could stand up to her neck in, she lapped the water with her arms, dipping her head back and immersing herself, and breathing deeply for the first time since he'd come upon her.

He watched her cool herself off, glad he had noticed this pond and had seen her when he did. He doubted she would have made it back safely without someone coming to look for her. Feeling also hot and uncomfortable, he splashed his face and drank mouthfuls of water, then took off his shirt, swished it in the pool and wrung it out, put it back on and enjoyed the coolness. He avoided looking at her to see if she watched him do this. He turned from the edge of the pond and sat back down where the grass was tall while he watched her wave her arms around in the water, then undo her braids and let her hair float around in blond swirls.

Finally when she had drunk enough and felt cool and herself again, she waded out of the pond and plunked down onto the tall grass above it to dry off. She desperately wished she could remove her clothes and wring them out. They were dripping and clinging at her. She plucked at the dress uselessly. A breeze washed over them and she shivered slightly, taking the hem of her dress and wringing it out. Magnus stood up, took his horse from the water's edge where she had been drinking and said, "I'm going to take the mare over there and adjust her buckles. If you want to take that off and wring it out, I'll be facing away the whole time." He did as promised, and she watched his back. She trusted him, but felt strange removing all her clothes so near by him. But she only paused a moment before stripping the sticking garments from her body. She wrung out her dress and spread it over the tall grass, then looked down at her single undershirt; it was stuck to her skin in the same pestering, sodden way. Underneath she had nothing on but couldn't stand the idea of having it drip on her any longer. She dashed it off and wrung it out hurriedly, hearing Magnus's mare shake her head, rattle her bridle, stomp her feet and generally give him trouble. But the noises masked her own activity, to her relief. The sound of pulling wet and uncooperative fabric off her body, the drip of water onto the ground as she wrung them out, the shaking of her clothes and her bare feet crunching on dry grass, all sounded loud and ungraceful. She was glad the mare was a troublesome thing.

Thinking he should not listen to her undress, Magnus shoved at his horse and jostled its saddle gear unnecessarily, grateful for once that she was a generally uncooperative animal. She stomped and snorted, ringing the metal bit and snaffle as her head shook out, her mane flapping and flicking at his face. The horse protested being tugged suddenly, held firmly and soothed softly, and yet the sounds of Genivee's undressing and re-dressing still found their way into his head. Little muffles of breath and sniffles, quiet steps of her feet on the ground; they were sounds that he tried to decipher and ignore simultaneously.

She put her wrung out clothes back on, a much longer process with them damp as they were. But they felt wonderful in spite of it, as any movement of air cooled her whole body and she felt more revived every minute. She had not realized how heat-weary she had become. She gathered and wrung her long, dripping tresses and began to comb her fingers through them. She watched him now, still obediently looking the other way, and smiled at his courtesy and discomfort. "I'm done," she said but he didn't turn around, even though she was sure he'd heard her. She walked to him and reached out to him, tapping him on the shoulder and saying, "I'm done." He finally left off bothering his horse. She smiled at him and thanked him. He looked at her, noticing her hair, much longer than he'd realized it was. It was usually tied up into braids. She continued to straighten the tangles, moving away from horse and rider and then sitting down to braid her hair and wind it, tucking it in so it stayed off her neck. Magnus watched this activity with scientific fascination. How so much hair could be made so obedient with a few flicks of her hands, he marveled. She stood up and said, "I'm ready."

He considered whether to let her ride alone on the horse while he walked beside them, or put her back in the saddle as before. Although he didn't entirely trust his mare, neither did he entirely trust himself. She settled it, saying, "I don't think I can handle this animal myself, I'd much rather you stayed on her, too." So he hopped onto his mare and reached down to pull Genivee up in the same way he had half an hour ago. He cautioned her about the unpredictable nature of his mare and recommended he keep a steady hold of her. Together they rode slowly back to the castle, a trip that he made sure took most of an hour, not wishing to overburden his mare, already carrying two on a hot day near noon. On the way, they passed the cluster of red poppies that had been her pursuit on this venture, and he let her down to pick a bundle of them and then pulled her up again. She wished for endless patches of flowers to go by so that with each one, she could enjoy again the feel of him easily lifting her up. The countryside rolled by, the breezes cooled and dried them, the flowers bobbed and nodded to her. She smiled back at her bouquet in her happiness. Magnus looked over her shoulder and realized that for her, it was more than just gathering flowers; to do so would be a mere accomplishment to a man. To a woman, finding the beauty in the world was the accomplishment.

13

Invited or Not

In the week before the royal party would depart for the annual trip to the hunting lodge, Gustav was planning the composition of the party that would be honored to accompany him. Gustav liked to distribute the opportunity to different people as much as possible, while still keeping a few of his best friends in the party. Those whom he wanted to thank for their service who were not chosen to go were given the consolation of being a part of the Trappe Brigade, the name given to the group of people who remained at the castle and took the places of those leaving, pretending to govern, rule, protect and celebrate as they chose. In actual fact they did little more than keep the castle occupied instead of abandoned. Harz came into the room and Gustav looked up expectantly. Harz said,
"I visited Mona yesterday and she is in fine fettle with no complaints – regarding her situation." Gustav nodded and waited. Usually Harz had more detail, more insight to add to his accounts. Gustav

pondered, then asked him,

"Do you think there is a resemblance between Mona and Sparrow?" Harz looked at Gustav directly then, thought about the youthful beauty in the forest and said,

"No."

"Ah, well." Gustav imagined Harz hadn't taken much notice of Sparrow anyway. He turned his attention back to the Trappe Brigade and Harz took a seat at a writing table next to the window where there was good light in the morning.

As well as turning the castle over to the Trappe Brigade, there was also the planning of celebrations. A Feast was held the night before the hunting party's departure, which was also during the time of the August meteor shower. Tradition held that if one looked into the sky with a wish in their heart and happened to see a shooting star, the wish would come true. Thus, much celebrating was planned so that people would be up and about all night, ready to gaze into the sky and see their wish bestowed. Dedicated stargazers hoped all the celebrating would divert the attention of the less devout. This would mean more wishes granted to those glancing heavenward all evening, loyal and solemn. As well, it meant many people would be sleeping late the next morning and less inclined to follow the party headed into the forest, as there were always a few envious people who would have liked to go with them.

In the hot morning air in the courtyard, Magnus walked across the courtyard headed for the Count's chamber and spotted Genivee in the dairy. She set down some milk pails, obviously full ones, and used the hem of her dress to mop her face. Magnus watched her and wondered why she didn't get one of the stable boys to carry the milk pails for her. But it was like her; for along with her being pretty and sweet, she was somewhat silly. What was she thinking, walking out on a hot day to collect flowers? If he hadn't come along, she would have fainted for sure.

Harz was inside the castle at a desk. In front of him were various papers, including the list for the hunting party, and none of which held his interest. He glanced out the window towards the dairy and spotted Genivee setting down milk pails. Why wasn't one of the boys carrying those for her? She was dedicated to her work and was clever to put her hair up, keeping it off her face. The younger girls often let it sway and fly in the wind, probably to look more alluring, until it hung in limp, dirty strands.
Voices pulled him back to his work.

The castle steward, Talin, had come into the room and was quietly helping Gustav with possible names for his hunting party. He suggested two young men who worked in the stables, good horsemen who were always worthwhile on a trip away. When their names were spoken, Harz's attention shifted to the page in front of him and he wrote. Talin also named two women from the kitchen who had shown themselves to be more reliable and self-directed than the others. Talin knew every servant who worked inside the castle and kept record of all those who worked outside of it, though they had different overseers. He kept the castle running smoothly each day, such that meals were never late, floors were always swept and any dogs allowed in the castle were always well groomed. He had grown up in the castle as the son of the head housekeeper and rose up in position steadily until now at age 45 it seemed as if he had been running the place for centuries. Everyone knew him and showed him respect, and some few even liked him.

As Harz finished writing and Gustav was dismissing Talin, heavy footsteps approached outside the door. Friendly greetings were overheard, the door flew open and Boris marched in and stated solemnly; "Conveying the request of help from a woman, it is hoped I remain here at home to conduct my duty to wife and child." Gustav had figured Boris (via his wife) would be requesting as much, and had already made up his mind to not have him on this trip. However, he bestowed upon Boris the honor of his request being heard, considered and weighed. After a moment, Gustav nodded with a touch of affected regret and granted the request. He stated for the record,

"Of course, a man's duty to his family comes before the pleasure of a hunting trip. Commitment before adventure." Boris nodded, his mission accomplished, his appetite ready. He sat at a side table of food, always there for any sudden needs of refreshment. As Boris conscientiously sampled each item on the table, Gustav picked up the list Harz had written. Now Harz had nothing to study but the view out the window again. Genivee was sitting on a bench with another milkmaid against the cool stone of the castle.

Boris continued eating. Gustav made a few final scribbles on the list and put the page back down in front of Harz, who glanced at it, went to the door and spoke to the guards. The door re-closed and they all waited quietly for the summoned someone to arrive. As usual, he would discuss the appointment in detail with a person. Then it would become official at the Feast. If someone had a special reason for not wanting to go, (although it was rare), Gustav gave them a chance to say so.

Magnus arrived and took his usual place. Soon after, Trevka and Vatra arrived. Trevka scanned the room with a sedulous regard he had previously lacked with his buoyant curiosity. His new position as Watchman was either taking serious effect, or else he was still suspicious of his assignment and was looking out for someone to question it. Vatra seemed as if he had gotten taller since being addressed as Constable. Gustav waited for any theatrics from Trevka, but today there were none. He paused before speaking.

"Vatra, as Constable, duty calls you to remain with the Trappe Brigade and keep the peace and order." Gustav considered what disorders might be likely, although it was anticipated by everyone that there would be much lassitude from the moment he left. So he said, "Anyone attempting to conduct actual business shall be detained as you see fit." Gustav smiled to himself at the half-hearted rowdies who would always try to enforce new rules while he was away. Rules such as *no women shall drink less than 3 pints of ale a night nor go unaccompanied to bed*. Imagining that Vatra might be out-numbered on such an issue, Gustav added, "You may deputize as many men as necessary to enforce this edict." When Vatra was certain that the entirety of his office had been articulated, he bowed and said,

"It is my honor as your squire." Gustav turned to Trevka and looked at him carefully. He had talked with Boris about Trevka's new position as Watchman. They both hoped it would lead to Trevka's being more serious-minded; it seemed to have taken some effect so far.

"Trevka, as Watchman, you have an important assignment which, I am sorry to say, happens to be necessary in spite of the timing. It must not be interrupted nor delayed by a hunting trip; it is vital business." Despite the flourish to his speech, Gustav was actually very serious. Gustav continued, "In light of recent revelations regarding the future Viscount's lately departed mother and her unfortunate childhood, it is necessary that a discerning and discreet eye be kept on those who attend him." Gustav thought for a moment, then recalled the name of his son. "The heir Viscount Dane must be protected from anyone who may not be in complete possession of the highest morals. Any abuse or imperfect treatment must be detected and stopped in the most immediate manner. Boris can guide you in this, as an older man, he can be a better judge of situations which may be vexing or questionable." Boris was finishing his chicken leg and nodded when Trevka looked over to him; Boris saluted with the gnawed bone. Trevka realized it was time to bow and said,

"It is my honor as your squire."

The twins then turned simultaneously and left the royal chamber, so proud of their serious missions they didn't even consider fretting over not being a part of the hunting trip.

In the forest the sun was setting over a warm summer day. Sparrow and her baby had just returned to their shelter, a grotto hidden behind thick trees that her father had built a roof over. The grotto wasn't quite deep enough to be called a cave, but it offered protection and was well hidden. It blended in with its surroundings and Sparrow had never been molested there by man nor beast; men being few to find it and beasts declining to make a meal of a woman who spoke to them kindly. On this evening, Sparrow retreated to the grotto a little early, having felt a damp chill in the air. She sat down and began nursing her baby and a few quiet moments went by as she thought about Gustav's imminent return to the forest. This is the time her parents would have decided to take a trip across the ridge to another part of the forest where they had another, much less protected shelter. In the summer, shelter didn't matter as much. Now she waited for him to return and wondered what they would say to each other. She closed her eyes and contemplated him and her mind drifted miles away.

The Rogues had come over the ridge from the east and were wandering, as usual, with little intention to their steps. It had been a long year of foraging in the forest, simply wandering until they found some game to shoot with one of their arrows. Not really their arrows, they had stolen them. It had been just over a year ago that they made their escape out of the valley and into the mountains. It was a fortunate night for them when the guard at their prison cell made two mistakes in one night. Having just locked a cell, he failed to replace the keys to their hook because the convict in the cell, a rogue named Bit, immediately engaged him in conversation so prurient it shocked him into attention. The other convict, Maw, in the cell nearby, used a brick he had carved out of his cell wall where the mortar was crumbling to pitch the deadly object at the guard's head. When he slumped over, Bit was able to reach the keys and free himself. He almost didn't unlock the door to his companion's cell, but thought his chances of escape would be better with a partner.

They had roamed the countryside all night, then decided their best chance at permanent escape was in the mountains. They survived by poaching game, eating mushrooms and robbing whomever crossed their path. They murdered people with as much carelessness as they poached game, but since there were few people in the forest, that had only amounted to two so far. Where their education left off, their superstition began. It was a very uneven mix, having learned just enough by the age of ten to begin lives of crime. They crested the ridge above Sparrow's grotto and Bit sat down to rest. "My feet is plaguing me. We needs to rob someon' with good boots soon." Maw took out an arrow to sharpen it some more; they retrieved all the arrows they could from their game and tried to sharpen them but they were getting worn down, chipped and blunt. They weren't very efficient killing mechanisms any more. They also had leg traps and tried to retrieve these too, but some got lost. As Maw pulled the arrow from the quiver, he took the occasion to rap Bit's head.

"Shut yer hole," he said. He plunked down and examined the arrow point; it might soon get so blunt that if an animal had a tough enough hide, it would just bounce off. "Rot," he swore at the arrow, then picked up a stone and tried to give it a point. Bit took off his boot, peered into it, then put a finger through a hole near the toe and exclaimed,

"Shut this hole and rot!" he wiggled his finger through the hole, then looked about and gathered some leaves to make a patch; he folded them over and put them inside the boot, then put it back on. He swore again, kicked his feet in the dirt at the discomfort and ran the back of his hand across his mouth. Maw was running the stone across the arrow point and pondering.

"Ain't this place familiar?" he said to Bit. Bit looked around, but even after a year in the forest, he had not yet managed to remember its hills, vales and dells. It was one and the same to him and they wandered without understanding or reason. Bit didn't answer because he had no idea where they were. He only hoped they found something to eat soon. But Maw did remember. "This here's where that ma and pa were camped out with their little virgin." Bit looked up, surprised.

"Yeah," he said, "I reckin' yore right. She ought to be alone 'bout now, you think?" They exchanged dark leers and both got up and started trotting down the slope. "Me first," each one shouted at each other as they tried to get ahead.

In her grotto, Sparrow had begun to doze with thoughts of Gustav. He was busy preparing to come back, happy that the castle was emptier now and he was freer. She liked the idea and dreamed about it. Bursting through the silence a hawk swooped over the grotto screaming, tearing Sparrow from her reverie. It turned and flew back over her, screaming again in a raucous warning she heard only when its chicks were threatened. She perked her ears up and heard running footsteps, sensed two dank and filthy men moving towards her fast. She covered herself and her baby with her bearskin fur and huddled under it, but she sent her mind racing out to the two men as if she were the most ferocious mother bear in the forest about to spring upon them; a wild beast with blood-encrusted claws, drooling yellow fangs and nostrils flaring with the smell and remnants of her lunch. She called upon any animal nearby to add to her voice, and together the images and sounds made between them caused the men to stop cold in their steps.

"What infernal noise was that?" Bit asked, grabbing a tree to steady himself. "A bear?" he said, although he imagined a monster too hideous to name. Maw looked around, trying to figure out what he'd seen or heard. Some deer close by were frightened into charging across the ground around them, further disorienting the two men and making them feel as if they were surrounded by animals in headlong panic. If the deer were running off, the men were fools to linger on. "A bear that ate that girl for sure, I can smell it on his breath." The hawk overhead took a dive at the men, who turned on their heels and headed back over the ridge. Sparrow kept the bearskin fur over herself as she hugged her baby close to her. They had almost snuck up on her. She remained vigilant throughout the night; she couldn't expect the hawk to constantly be on her guard.

At Wilker castle, the Feast of the Shooting Stars was in readiness. Harz had climbed the rarely trodden steps to the castle keep to look out over the grounds and beyond the walls. It had occurred to him that with all the activity, villagers with bad intentions might find a way to sneak in and take advantage of the noise and distractions to steal food, rob revelers or even seize young women. He got to the keep and looked out over the landscape. People below were crossing the courtyard, some of them dressed in masquerades, some of them carrying heavy trays of festivity fare. The guards at the gate were there as usual, keeping watch. Perhaps there should be more of them on such an evening. He surveyed the grounds outside the castle, what he could see from where he was. No one was making their way up the path to the castle gate. The trees along that path had been cleared so that it was open and not a place miscreants could creep along unnoticed. Still, there should be more guards just in case. Harz spent a few more minutes surveying, then went back down to post more guards.

The revelers had gathered in the great hall and the Trappe Brigade had been announced and taken their places on a dais. Boris, Liesse and Luna were standing in for Gustav, the Countess and Viscount. Trevka and Vatra were there as officers in charge of keeping the peace and order. Boris and Liesse sat on chairs decorated to resemble thrones and had on sheepskin robes and flower garland crowns. In a private gallery above it all, Gustav watched the proceedings with the party who would accompany him to the hunting lodge this year. Quilin was the physician for the trip; he was a slight and inquisitive man who studied biology seriously. Two groomsmen, Ash and Morgan, would be driving the wagon and doing the heavy work. Ash was blonde and reed-thin; his friend Morgan was ruddy and muscular. They both hunted and handled horses very well. Genivee would be helped by Anna and Suzette, two girls from the kitchen who had received stern admonishments from Talin the Steward about the consequences of returning from such a trip pregnant. Magnus was also going, relieved to not be a part of the Trappe Brigade's escapades. Harz was going also, but had declined to take a place in the gallery; as Chief Constable, he was not quite yet on vacation.

There was food arranged in heaps on platters in the banquet hall; people would be wandering in and out all evening partaking of the fare. There were musicians in the ballroom nearby where there would be dancing all night. Harz was walking back from the main gate and climbed the back stairs to the musician's gallery overlooking the ballroom; from there he could observe the whole scene and make sure no one was up to any mischief.

He watched the dancers sway and step to the music. After watching for a while, he saw Genivee arrive with two other girls, presumably those going with her to the hunting lodge. He watched her whisper bits of information to the girls, who had certainly never been to such an event. It was likely that Genivee had only been to a ball once before herself, one year ago. Harz barely knew her then but she had a swan-like serenity and beauty he noticed right away, maintaining her equilibrium in the swaying wagon. He contemplated dancing with her, but she was a milkmaid. How would it be for a milkmaid to dance with the Count's cousin?

Genivee was standing alone now that Anna and Suzette had been engaged to dance when Magnus walked by her, no doubt headed towards some high-born lady he would ask to dance. Genivee curtsied almost imperceptibly as he passed, as she felt gratitude for his kind and saving presence on the hot day she wandered too far off, and for reassuring her after Liesse was abducted. He was a kind gentleman.

Just past her he stopped and smiled in return to her curtsy and then continued on his way, but further on stopped again and turned around. Her gaze had returned to the crowd assembling for the next dance. She was standing alone and as he glanced around, no one appeared headed in her direction. Once again on her own, he decided to rescue her.

She looked genuinely surprised when he came back and asked her to dance. She had been honored enough that he had noticed her at all, and probably he was just being kind. So it was unkind to refuse and thus she accepted his offer. She was surprised by how familiar dancing seemed to him. He caught her and turned her as if it were second nature. She hoped he did not see this as a tedious duty, although a duty it surely was to him. Halfway through the dance she remarked,

"It is very kind of you to dance with me. Your kindness, and the thoughtfulness you have shown in the past, I most sincerely appreciate." That was all she was going to say, she did not expect more from him than a polite nod. He nodded acknowledgment and studied her, gazed into her face and felt her warm skin beneath her dress. She became somewhat self conscious and wondered if she had said it right.

The dance ended and Magnus stopped moving but was still studying her. She was beginning to feel hot and self-conscious and the pinkness showed on her skin. Magnus said plainly, "Are you going to faint again?" She looked up, afraid he was finding her troublesome, but instead a sly smile began to spread across his face.

"I think I'll faint if I have to dance any more in this stifling room," she said. With that, he guided her away and they left through an open door and walked out into the moonlight. After a few steps, Genivee remembered that this was a good night to see shooting stars and began to glance upward hoping to catch one. Almost immediately she did and was so surprised she exclaimed suddenly and thrust out her arm to point in its direction. "I have a wish!" she said with such glee in her voice. They stopped walking and he followed the path her arm pointed in but it was too late and she lowered her arm and sighed. He glanced from the empty sky back to her and said,

"What do you wish for?" She blushed and of course couldn't say, as then it would not come true, so she just smiled up at him. She was so sweet and happy that he kissed her lips briefly.

They walked on in silence except for the sounds of their footsteps and Genivee's hem brushing the ground. She searched her mind for what to say or do, not knowing what he meant by that, and as she had been wondering if she was taking him away from some other business or person inside, she said,

"This is very comfortable out here, I shall be quite all right now." There was a long pause as Magnus thought. He asked her,

"Shall I take you back to your room?" To which she replied,

"Well it is still rather early..." she was hoping not to be dropped at her doorstep just yet. Again there was a long pause before he asked,

"Shall I take you to my room?" Her eyes opened wider and blinked.

"Yes," she finally answered, afraid he might not hear her timid voice. But he must have because he took her hand and turned them in a slightly different direction. They walked in silence across the grass, came to a path and entered a part of the castle she had never been in. They walked up two flights of stairs and down a hall and came to the door to his room. He turned the lever but didn't open the door and said as an afterthought,

"I never asked you if I should take you back to the dance. Maybe you should – think about this."

Leaning her back against the yielding door and looping her elbow though his, she pulled him across the threshold and planted him against the wall inside, closing the door next to them. She leaned into him, whispering as her cheek brushed his, "But I have thought about it already, a lot."

14

Observant Travelers

Magnus woke up to the soft swishing sound of hands braiding hair. Genivee sat on the edge of the bed, her dress already back on, her hair just about hidden back under itself. He touched her shoulder and she turned around and whispered quickly, "I have to milk my cow."

"But we leave early, won't someone else-"

"Yes, of course but I want to say goodbye-" Genivee stopped suddenly. She must seem silly or strange to him. She stood up and twirled in little steps, scanned the floor quickly, spotted her shoes and slipped them on, then was out the door with a smiling glance at him. He laid back and studied the ceiling, his hand drifting back to his forehead from its place on her shoulder. He had almost woken up to an empty room.

Genivee trotted to the milking parlor and arrived at her usual time. Settling down to her work, her heart calmed and as the cow munched hay she spoke to it softly. "Marta will be milking you for a little while, so behave for her like you do for me." The cow nodded its head, flicking hay around. Genivee began another instruction but broke it off when she heard her name blurted in surprise by a man and stood up quickly, thinking it must be someone with orders or questions. Had he just heard her talking to a cow? Surprised and a little disconcerted to find it was Harz, she watched him approach and say,

"What are you doing here, you disappeared last night, you should be getting ready..." and in those three sentences while she had looked him in the eye, he realized she was a little disconcerted and worried by his presence. He continued quickly, "No, you're fine, very good," and he was gone. She stood alone, staring at empty space. The cow turned to look at her with big brown questioning eyes, munching steadily. *Did he see me and Magnus leave the dance together?* she wondered, then sat back down to resume her work.

When she was done she went to her room to grab the few things she would need and stuffed them in a canvas bag. She flew down the steps and arrived just as the wagons were being loaded and Anna and Suzette were settling into them, each one waving her forward and saying,

"Hurry, we can't be late." But of course there was still time, even though Gustav was anxiously awaiting their departure, already on his mount and circling around, talking to Harz. When finally all the riders and all the supplies had gotten into their proper places, they set off for the lodge in the mountains just as the sun came over the tops of the trees that surrounded the castle.

Morgan drove the wagon full of supplies and girls, and Ash rode behind them keeping an eye on all the horses in front and turning from time to time to check the road behind him, which remained empty as it should. While they both would have benefited from the knowledge Trevka and Vatra could have given them, they were also glad to be on their own. The three girls took turns talking, watching the landscape and rearranging the bundles and boxes in the wagon, making the ride more comfortable or checking the contents. Several cages containing live chickens were moved about a few times, causing squawks to punctuate the trip. Genivee explained how they would set things up at the lodge and divide the duties. Ahead of them four men rode in loose formation with Harz riding a little ahead of the group and Magnus riding a bit behind. Gustav and Quilin ambled along in between.

Quilin was actually a young man still in his late twenties, but looked as if he were much older, perhaps because he tended to be bent over a lot, a habit he developed with years of poring over books and leaning over sick people. He was also of a very slight build, no more than 5 feet tall and wiry. His hair did nothing to add to his height, being straight and short and flat and parted down the middle. His face was proportionally small, with a pale complexion and little gray eyes. However his round little cheeks and mouth had a ready smile that was always sincere and caring. He tended to make people feel better just by sitting with them and listening as they talked. He was not a medical man in the same tradition as Boris, whom he knew and respected. Boris mended the obvious expeditiously; Quilin enjoyed studying the longer effects of certain herbs, the degrees of success of different treatments, divining the causes of mysterious ailments. He was always looking for better ways of treating sickness or mending bodies, and his scientific mind was bent on this endeavor. He had a child-like enthusiasm and a ready willingness to change his opinions, given fresh insights.

At first Gustav had listened with mere politeness as they rode along together. He was distracted by the prospect of meeting Sparrow again, wondering if she had even survived a year alone, and had quickly decided to leave much of he talking to Quilin. As their horses carried them further up the trail, Gustav began to realize that Quilin's chatter was actually very rational. He was bursting with ideas and noticed so much. He would always give Gustav a chance to respond, leaving silent spaces in his talking. But when these went unanswered, he would be off talking again about another topic that held his interest, and perhaps that of his listener, and Gustav began to see he was less bored by all Quilin's chatter than he thought he would be. Now Quilin was talking about cases of lunacy, a subject few dared speak of.

"Of course, the word lunatic may not be right for all cases, for there are many degrees of losing one's mind. Some people are merely forgetful or fanciful, or have imaginings that are quite extraordinary. Others, of course, are surely not seeing the world as the rest of us do. We call them lunatics, because they seem out of this world as if from the moon, but I would like to glimpse their world – while remaining in ours." Quilin paused, wondering if he would be too forward to ask the question in his mind. Then he asked,

"Have you ever seen a case of lunacy during your reign, Count?" Gustav wondered about Gertrudis. Maybe she was out of her mind, to a degree. Was her old nurse, Derth's mother, a lunatic? He wondered also about the prisoners still occupying the dungeons of his castle. All of them had been put there by either his father or someone else previous to his taking the throne. He only knew *of* them, and even that was more than he cared to know. Finally he was able to add his own voice to the conversation.

"I may have, but then I am not acquainted with the condition as you are." Quilin was about to add realms of thought to this, but they were interrupted by Harz who had turned back to join them and advise that they might stop here for lunch.

The meadow they had been riding through was lush with wildflowers this year, there having been good rain for the last two months. The dark forest they would soon enter was looming close by. They were upon the spot where last year Trevka had spotted the eagle's nest. With a signal of agreement from Gustav, Harz rode back around to Morgan and Ash and the whole party came to a halt. Genivee reached for the proper bundle and began unwrapping, handing Anna and Suzette a large blanket to spread on the ground for the three of them. Then they arranged the food onto the end of the wagon and everyone took what they wanted and began eating and drinking in various locations and states of relaxation. Morgan scanned the forest's edge while Ash checked all the horses.

Genivee was sitting on the blanket with the other girls, eating an apple. Suddenly, not having to hold herself steady against the rocking of the wagon, she realized she was dreadfully tired and sleepy, and laid down onto the blanket with her arm under her head, her apple nearly finished. The other girls watched the younger men. The older men let their horses rest and nibble grass, while they found boulders or wagon wheels to lounge against.

Morgan and Ash had walked to the forest edge, which was abrupt. Fallen trees made interesting planks to walk along and Morgan said it was a great place for a lookout, if there were anything to look out for. Ash agreed and they took to jumping up onto lower branches that had broken off and scanning the horizon for far-off invaders, then studying the forest for hidden bandits. Finally Harz whistled loudly and they jumped down. He noticed Genivee asleep on the blanket and wondered about her, napping soundly at midday, but suddenly she awoke to see the other girls gathering wildflowers and joined them.

They all began moving again, eager to enter the refreshing coolness of the forest. It was still several hours to the lodge. The party became quiet as women dozed and men concentrated on the path. Quilin refrained from any more speaking, and instead dedicated his attention to the forest, which he had only seen from afar before. There must be many medicinal plants here, and he tried to spy some out. The trail finally widened out at one point and Gustav rode forward to join Harz, talking about prospects for how boggy the mountain meadow might be, considering how lush the grass had been up to that point. Eventually Magnus caught up to the two as well and Gustav asked him for a weather prediction. Harz took that opportunity to make his way back to Ash and on the way noticed Genivee sleeping again amid the bundles in the wagon. And she had left early last night; maybe she was unwell; maybe she should have stayed at the castle.

They had left the castle at the break of dawn, so were at the hunting lodge well before sunset. Gustav had waited for all the riders and the wagon to reach the lodge, then took off galloping further up the mountainside. Harz followed at a distance but kept him in sight, "staying near" as his father had demanded, but not interested in eavesdropping or spying on the reunion ahead. When Gustav reached the crest of the path, Sparrow was waiting for him. After a long embrace, she and her baby and Gustav walked up the hill arm in arm, just moving out of sight as Harz reached the top of the hill. He dismounted and didn't bother to tie the horses up, but left them to graze figuring they were too worn out to run off. He himself plopped down against a fallen tree, ready for a nap.

Near her grotto home now, Sparrow stopped and glanced around, giggled to Gustav and asked, "Do you see it now?" Gustav looked around carefully. Finally he pointed and asked,

"That way?" Sparrow nodded and took his hand, leading him around the traps she had set. She had only just set them today, for it was last night that she had been frightened by the Rogues. If Gustav wanted her to come back with him this time, it worked to his advantage to have this happen. But she had already decided that she didn't want to spend all the rest of her years in the forest, even though a year ago she had been certain she did. They sat in her grotto and Gustav studied the home with amazement. It was warm and light-filled in spite of being so well hidden. Sparrow explained,

"My father constructed this and kept working on it all the time we lived here. There are other places of protection he built in the forest, but this is the best one. Even so, without him here, it needs repairs and I'm not as good at that as he was. The forest will take it back eventually if no one stops her." Gustav had spotted the bed at the back of the grotto and sat down; there wasn't anywhere else to sit, and he preferred it. Sparrow put their baby in his arms. Gustav looked down at the little creature, which he was certain resembled him. The baby was a calm and fascinated little person, unlike his half brother who usually focused his attention on wailing. Sparrow told him the story of being startled by the Rogues only yesterday at this very time.

Gustav listened, aghast at the tale and fighting the urge to run out into the forest and go after them. Sparrow did not want to hunt them down as Gustav did, she just found them unfathomable. She asked, "Are there many men like that, bent on killing for sport, wandering the countryside without family or purpose?" Gustav thought it through and said,

"No, they are likely from another province, another country even. They were probably cast out of their own village, maybe even escaped from prison. They will eventually die in the winter when they run out of arrows or other traps; as you say, they are crude and not terribly careful." Gustav wished he could be sure of this, but in fact had no idea how long they might live, or even how long they had been in the forest hiding. Sparrow sat down next to him on the bed and said,

"At least you seem to understand them." Gustav wished he did, wished he could give her - and himself - some kind of assurance. Finally he concluded,

"We may come across them, and if we do, they will be punished for poaching and harassing you, no small crimes in my domain." Sparrow pressed her hands together and said,

"I can't understand such people at all, I can only hide from them. That is all I could teach my son to do, and I do not want him to grow up so guileless. To frighten them off works for a woman alone. To truly conquer them requires facing them with wisdom." But Sparrow knew she wasn't the one to undertake such a task. She was only half-wise to people and knew that if she stayed in the forest her son would grow up only half-wise as well. It was not possible to learn about people second-hand, nor much of the world from just one place in it. She also had been thinking it would be good to give her child siblings such as she had never had. Since he had been born, she had sensed he wanted them. Gustav waited for her to finish thinking, then asked tentatively,

"So you'll come back with me and live in the castle?" Sparrow's hesitation made Gustav add, "There is much room, since the Countess became unhappy and went back home. You may live very quietly there if that is what you wish." Sparrow leaned her head onto his shoulder. Gustav glanced around for somewhere to put his little son. Sparrow took the bundle and settled it close by, but not on the bed. She went back to the bed and they worked on beginning a sibling.

Harz dozed against a tree as the horses wandered, munching grass. He dreamed of something that seemed long ago, or maybe it was last night. Newlyweds are spending their first night together, having married in secret. But in the morning she's gone, vanished. She'll never come back now. She even laughs about it, she is so unfeeling. Now *he* is the newlywed and she has left *him*. The angst of it wakes him up. Harz blinks his eyes. Coming down the hill towards him he hears Sparrow laughing as Gustav teases her. Harz sits up against the fallen tree and stands, brushing off the pine needles and kicking the mud from his boots. The horses are nibbling at a juniper shrub and he gets them. Harz wonders if Sparrow will ride on one of the horses or insist on walking, because if she does they will all have to walk. Fortunately for their empty stomachs, she and her baby (wrapped against her) get into the saddle with Gustav, but only after asking the horse first if it minds carrying three.

They arrived at the lodge and everyone was gathering for the evening meal. Genivee offered to hold Sparrow's baby while she dined, and it took Sparrow a moment to hand him over, realizing it was some sort of rule not to have a baby at the table. She wondered to herself if she would ever learn or get used to so many rules. She was settling into her chair when the last two to arrive came in from outside. Quilin was talking to Magnus, whom he had discovered had a wonderfully intelligent mind, although reluctant to share much of it. Quilin was saying,

"...and I have definitely noticed better health in married men. They have fewer diseases and most certainly fewer wounds. Why I'd say the vast bulk of men whom I attend to are unmarried, whatever age they may be." They both sat down, with Magnus right across from Quilin. Had Quilin's voice been louder or faster, it would have bothered the room like smoke, but being so soft was more like a butterfly flitting from flower to flower. He paused before speaking again, making sure no one else was waiting to speak. When no one did, he added, "And I would have guessed you to be a married man." Genivee kept her eyes planted on the baby in her arms, amazed at the frank outspokenness of this slight little man. He must be from another village at the very least. There was a short silence, then Magnus calmly answered,

"I used to be," and smiled politely. Quilin naturally assumed then that his wife must have died, and so said, "That is a loss. Was it an accident?" Gustav and Harz, the only ones in the room who knew the answer to this question, looked at each other and wondered how the reclusive Magnus would respond to such a bold question at a table full of people. But after a slight pause Magnus said,

"She died in childbirth." And just as quickly, Quilin followed with,

"And the child too?" It hardly seemed the diners could withhold another gasp, but they did. Calmly, Magnus nodded his head and looked down at his plate. Quilin spoke again with sincerity, "Then a loss doubly so." He paused for a moment of silent respect. Then addressing everyone in general said, "I hope you may forgive my curiosity, it is my life's hope to improve the physical condition of others and for that I am forever seeking to investigate it." After that he spoke no more, probably due to his ruminations on a woman dying in childbirth. Genivee focused her attention on the baby in her arms, glad it was a calm little thing but rocking it gently nevertheless.

The following day, after most of the men rode off on a trip to scout

out likely animals to hunt, the women stayed behind chatting in the kitchen. Sparrow said little, but had many questions to answer. Here was another court protocol she would have to get used to: not having the freedom to decide how she would spend her day or with whom. Anna and Suzette were inquisitive with Sparrow and competed for turns with her charming baby. Fortunately Anna was not holding the baby when she suddenly squealed as she spotted a small object run across the floor and scurry under the stove. "A mouse?" Suzette asked. Anna nodded and reached for the broom. Genivee shook her head and said casually,

"There is always a mouse or two when we first get here. We have set traps, it will be gone soon." Anna felt it could not be gone soon enough. Sparrow had seen plenty of mice but never a house cat although her mother had spoken highly of them. Sparrow asked why they didn't bring one along to take care of mice. Genivee answered, "They would probably run away into the forest. Besides, a trap works faster. The cats around our barn take their time about it and play with the mice. A trap asks no questions." Sparrow crossed her brows because something wasn't right. While Anna peered cautiously under the stove, broom at the ready, Suzette noticed Sparrow's confusion and said to her,

"Do you think cats are bad luck? Some people do, and some even think they act as agents for people casting spells." The three village women eyed Sparrow askance, wondering if she herself could cast a spell. Sparrow answered plainly,

"I don't think animals bring luck good or bad, only messages and wisdom. As for spells, I suppose they might work if one's mind is silly and stupid enough to let them." The women looked at each other, somewhat chastised. They hadn't expected this diminutive girl to speak so plainly and so dismissively. So Suzette asked Sparrow,

"What messages do cat and mouse have?" Sparrow thought a minute about general wisdom, not the specific messages she was getting from this particular mouse. She answered,

"Mouse pays close attention to detail, but can not do so for every detail, which can be dangerous. If a mouse ran under my stove, I would ask myself what little detail I have missed, for it could lead to missing out on something much larger which is important." She thought about this further, then she added, "But I would not set a trap for it."

"Why not?" Genivee quickly asked. Surely she didn't think mice should have free reign over a kitchen. Sparrow paused again before answering; she was listening to this mouse and it was distracting. Then she looked up and answered,

"Because I would be destroying the messenger before I could understand its message! Your cats are waiting, too. They know the mouse is as important as any animal and should not be ignored or killed straight off, even though it is so small." Genivee had no great love for mice so asked,

"And once the cat has killed the mouse and is crunching its bones?"

"Then it's too late; either you've caught the wisdom or never will." They looked at each other. The mouse was not an easy animal for Sparrow to understand, for they were often very busy little creatures with little time for idle chatter. This one seemed to be trying to bring someone else into the kitchen, but she couldn't figure out who. Or why.

Anna gave up and put the broom back in the corner. After a minute of silence, Genivee began relating the major events of the last year for Liesse and her baby Luna. Sparrow knew there had been an attempt to kidnap her, but she had not known that the father's identity had been a great mystery. It was quite unbelievable to Sparrow, who had chosen very carefully who her baby's father would be. Sparrow listened and watched as the two girls cooed at her baby, remembering how a year ago she had been just as keen to have one of her own. She asked in general about other goings-on in the castle, knowing she would have to get used to living among a vast array of people. She was aghast when she discovered by one of Genivee's off-hand remarks that the Count's one-year-old son was cared for by relative strangers.

"The Countess did not take her son with her when she returned home?" Sparrow marveled.

Genivee, Anna and Suzette all exchanged nervous glances. Genivee said, "No, he is the heir."

"But who are these nursemaids?" Sparrow asked.

"Members of the court, they are very competent." Sparrow crossed her brows, somehow this did not seem right and she wasn't sure why. Suzette wanted to bridge another odd silence and so asked Sparrow,

"What is your baby's name?" Sparrow paused and explained,

"It hasn't come yet. My mother told me that a baby has to reveal his name to you, through whatever makes him special. In my own case, just before I was born, a sparrow was making its appearance near our home every night. On the third night of this, I was born, so they named me Sparrow." She paused in her memories. "I haven't received a sign for his name, so I am still waiting." The other women pondered this and began to essay certain names, but Genivee frowned gently at them and they stopped. Anna then burst out asking,

"So what does Sparrow mean? You haven't told us!" Sparrow looked at them but didn't want to answer. What her parents had said was that the lowly sparrow was a symbol of triumph of the lowly - peasants and commoners - over nobility. And hadn't their lives been proof enough of that? But these women would make such tales of that and gossip about it. They heard the men returning and so she simply summarized, *It means awakening.*

Late that evening, long after dinner, Genivee was sipping a mug of cider as the sound of mens' voices from the other room drifted through. Anna and Suzette had gone off to bed ahead of her. She rolled the mug back and forth in her hands. She was enjoying the comforting warmth of the oven, still radiating heat. When she returned to the grandeur of the castle she would be as before, alone and a little older, a little colder. She took the last sip of cider and examined the empty bottom of the mug. She heard a man's voice approaching and wondered if she should have gone to bed with the others.

The kitchen door opened and Magnus came in, startled to see her still there. His immediate thought was that she had been waiting for him, so that in the moment she stood up, he was next to her with his hands on her face but they soon heard more voices approaching. Genivee grabbed his arm and quickly pulled him into a small game-keeping room just off the kitchen. They listened as the voices came through the kitchen door and continued talking. Morgan said,

"The ladies appear to have fled from us. And I was genuinely going to offer my services in the dressing of that animal hanging up there." Ash expressed his own squiffy dismay at finding the room empty. But quickly Harz came into the kitchen after them, saying loudly,

"A little late to be offering help, lads." There were grumbles, explications and the shuffling sounds of the young men reluctantly leaving. The voices trailed off as Genivee and Magnus listened and waited in silence. On the other side of the game-keeping door there was equal silence inside the kitchen, but Genivee wasn't sure that Harz had followed Ash and Morgan out. But then she heard the door open and close again, its tell-tale squeak on a rusty hinge. Behind her Magnus grabbed her up and kissed her neck with passionate suggestion. She wrapped her fingers around his wrists and squeezed, but then pushed the hands away from her gently. She said,

"It's not a good time. Nothing has happened, as it did for Liesse." They both were silent at the memory of Liesse's unexpected pregnancy and her even more unexpected marriage. "I don't want to become an obligation." Magnus lowered his hands from their hold on her ribs. Genivee smiled at him and then headed to her own sleeping quarters above the kitchen, hoping he would have the good fortune not to run into Harz outside the kitchen door.

15

Trevka's little ghost

Trevka stood in front of the little house on the edge of town. He squinted at the yard, blowsy with wildflowers and herbs, crazily fragrant. The little fence and gate kept him out. Soon however, Mona sensed she had a visitor and came outside to look at him. He took off his hat, still embellished with its eagle feather, and bowed low to the woman. He announced himself to her with,

"Madam, I am your servant, Squire Trevka." He stood up and waited for her to say something. She appeared to be trying to place him, but there was no reason why she would know him. Finally Trevka added, "I am one of the Count's squires and I believe you have met his cousin, Harz." Mona's head tilted back a little and then began to nod. Trevka hadn't taken seriously the rumor that this woman was just a little touched, but now he began to give it more consideration. Then she seemed to act normally, waving him inside the fence and into her house. He wove his way through the flowers along the overgrown, narrow path. He entered the house and glanced around. The topaz tabby on the chair back opened her eyes and regarded Trevka, then returned to dozing.

"Sit, young squire," Mona ordered, pointing at a chair. Trevka flung back the cape he was wearing before sitting down and it settled around him as he did so. Mona glanced back at this display, pausing in her tea-making. "Are you also Harz's cousin?" she asked. Trevka smiled inwardly; he always knew his ostentation would be noticed one day. But he had to correct her and began shaking his head with an appreciative smile. But Mona wasn't yet done with her appraisal: "Those heavy gloves – you work with falcons?" Trevka nodded, surprised. These were not his falconing gloves. Mona brought the tea over and sat down. She had a steady gaze, one like Harz used when he suspected Trevka was lying. Trevka let the woman study him, perhaps because few enough women did. He then remembered he needed to correct her assumption and said,

"You remind me of Harz, actually. But he's not my cousin." Mona's eyes drifted away from studying Trevka and became sad. She asked him,

"Did he send you to ask after me?" Trevka worried about the old lady, her moods shifted suddenly. So he launched into the reason for his visit.

"No, Madam. I am here to return your property to you." Trevka pulled his deck of pictorial cards out of his jacket and placed them solemnly on the table next to the tea. Mona glanced down at the deck as if it were a long forgotten item. She put her hand over the deck as one might touch a delicate pet bird. She said,

"These have been in your possession for a long time?" Trevka nodded and added,

"I am sorry they were not purchased rightfully; at least I did not pay you for them. I would like to do so now, as well as return them, for I am not instructed in how to use them and do not think it right for me to keep them." Mona picked them up and held them in her hands. She closed her eyes and weighed the deck, gently rocking it up and down. Trevka placed coins onto the table worth twice the price for the deck, and the coins tinkled into a silver pile. But Mona kept her eyes shut and held the cards as if listening to them. Trevka was getting up to leave, but suddenly Mona snapped open her eyes and blurted,

"Sit!" Trevka plunked back down on his cape as Mona slammed the deck on the table. "Cut!" she ordered. Trevka cut the deck and Mona grabbed his hand before he could take it back. "Again," she instructed, moving his hand to the half deck just created. Now there were three piles of cards on the table. She put her forefinger to her chin and leaned back deeply and slowly into her chair. It was a look that reminded Trevka of himself. He glanced down at the card stacks. Mona flew back to sitting up straight and flared out her fingers over the table, forbidding him to interfere with the prognostication to come.

She turned over the first card; it had a weasel drawn on it. Trevka did not think this looked good. But Mona sounded intrigued; she made a curious and interested sound in her throat and looked up at Trevka. "It is up to you to uncover something which has gone unnoticed." This sounded good to Trevka; it confirmed his new position as Watchman. Mona turned over the second card. It was a woman wearing long robes and a crown. Mona thrust her long-nailed forefinger into the air over Trevka's head and said, "Your future wife is nearby!" Trevka glanced around. Mona shook her head, correcting herself; "Nearby in time, young man." She glanced at him with squinting eyes. "You're not engaged already are you?" Trevka shook his head sadly. But Mona countered with, "Good." She then put her hand over the last stack, waiting to turn over the last card. She paused, whether from delight in the center stage or trepidation, Trevka couldn't tell. She flipped the card over and sprang backwards as if the card was suddenly hot. "Ha!" she exclaimed. The tabby cat looked up alarmed and swished its tail. To Trevka, the image of a cuckoo on the card seemed unpromising. He looked across the table at her dubiously.

Mona was studying him with wondering amazement. She noticed the eagle feather in his hat. Her smile was crooked and curious. She was watching something happening in front of her, but was seeing the scenes in her mind. Worried about his image and hoping it did not resemble a cuckoo, Trevka said,

"Do you think I'll ever be truly respected in Court?" Suddenly Mona burst out laughing. She was not cackling like a madwoman, but she was laughing with such amusement that when she fell back into the chair again the cat batted her hair. Finally, seeing his discomfort, Mona reached out her hands and covered his and finally her laughing subsided. She said to him,

"My boy, promise me that when you are a few years older, you will visit me again before I die. I want to see your face when you realize what I have seen." She leaned back and closed her eyes, still chuckling to herself. Trevka didn't like having to wait. The cuckoo not only looked silly but sounded silly. Mona looked up at the guest still in her house, picked up the cuckoo card and said, "He may look silly but those wild feathers on his head denote a clever mind and having two toes forward and two backward means he always has his balance. His showing up means things are going to turn out differently than you ever expected."

Trevka rode back to the castle thinking to himself. He wanted to take his task as Watchman seriously. He didn't know if his assignment to spy on the Viscount's nursemaids was real or just a tactic to keep him occupied and out of sight. Well, he was going to make it real, and find out things they would never suspect. He would impress them and they would never give him a merely diversionary assignment again. His first action would be to consult with Boris. That way, if anything went wrong; well, that way nothing would go wrong.

He found Boris and Liesse in the castle main room, acting royal by chatting, eating and lounging around. He made a formal show of asking for Boris's attention on an important matter and they went into another room for privacy. Actually, Trevka had been hoping for him to ask the others to leave instead, but he followed Boris reluctantly past the food table. When they were alone, Trevka asked Boris how he should go about spying on the nurses. Boris grimaced,

"Spying is a lurid word, man, don't use it. You are ensuring the safety of the heir apparent, without other people knowing what it is you are doing. It is vitally important work." That was all he deemed necessary to say, so Trevka asked,

"How do I do this vitally important work?"

"What are the options, man, come to me with options. It is not my job to do your job, it is my job to tell you when you are doing it wrong." Trevka considered the options, and not for the first time. It was just that all of them seemed - lurid.

"I can drill a hole in the wall and peep through it." Trevka stated. Boris narrowed his eyes, pretending he hadn't heard that and might possibly nod off. "I can drill a hole in the ceiling above, or the floor below." Boris crossed his arms, head tilting backward. "I can listen at the door, or in a room beside." This is where Trevka had run out of ideas. There was one main room in which the nursemaids, usually two or more, fed and entertained and watched the sleeping baby viscount, and at night some would sleep in the same room and some in adjacent ones. At all times, there were at least two people with the viscount, and it wasn't unusual to have four or more, depending on whom the nurses were gossiping about. Trevka envisioned hearing hours of fascinating, private information on the workings of female nursing. Boris finally said to him,

"Whatever you do, Trevka, you have to be sure they do not know you are doing it. I suggest you wait until they are outside with the viscount on one of their afternoon strolls through the inner courtyard, giving him fresh air. That way you can inspect the Viscount's quarters." Trevka looked aghast momentarily, then realized that by quarters Boris meant rooms. Trevka wondered what he would discover by examining empty rooms, but decided he would follow Boris's advice, because he had no other. Then Boris added, "It's called reconnaissance, man." Boris leaned in near to him and said in a low voice, "And be certain, no one knows you *go* there, *are* there, or *have been* there." Boris ended by poking a warning finger close to Trevka's face, then put the finger to his lips, smelled bacon, and returned to the outer chamber.

Trevka was not familiar with the part of the castle that the little viscount occupied. He found Vatra and asked for a briefing on the layout of those rooms, as he had had occasion to be there to escort the Countess to and fro. The twins stood at the window of Trevka's room and looked across the courtyard, with Vatra pointing out the various windows of the third floor and what was behind them.

"That was the Countess's bedroom, when she was here, and various closets and side rooms attach to it, but those don't have windows," Vatra said.

"Who is in there now?" Trevka asked.

"No one, they are empty. The nurses take care of the viscount in those rooms, further west. The nurses' bedrooms are next to that. The first floor is where the Countess would receive guests. The second floor is where she would have conducted business, if she ever had any. The fourth floor is storage rooms and extra space for more servants, all empty now." Trevka nodded, trying to remember it all. He had decided that making notes would invite sabotage from the enemy side (whoever they were), so he had sworn himself to committing it all to memory. He repeated in his head what Vatra had said, and when he was sure he had it down, asked,

"And there are stairways on both ends of the wing?"

"Yes," Vatra said. "Use the one on the far end; no one goes there now." Vatra turned and looked at his brother and asked, "You really think there's anything important over there? It's just a nursery." Trevka thought for a minute. He was remembering Gertrudis, wondering what she might have gone through as a child, with Derth's mother for a nanny. He said to Vatra,

"There might be. What did Boris say once, 'A group of women scheming together could overthrow a king'?" Vatra smiled. Trevka seemed to be seriously enjoying this job. Trevka turned back to looking across the courtyard and asked, "Everything is probably locked up though, shouldn't it be?" Trevka was familiar with the annoyance of locked doors keeping him out of otherwise interesting places, especially as a young boy. He and Vatra played hide and seek often in the maze of castle rooms that to a child seemed endless. Vatra remembered this too, but since being granted the position of Constable, he enjoyed an advantage that as a child he had not. He pulled a ring of keys from his pocket and fanned them out silently in front Trevka. The brothers' eyes met and they smiled at each other slyly.

It was their usual habit in the summertime for the nurses to escape the afternoon heat in their rooms and seek the shade outside with viscount in tow. The nurses gobbled and waddled like geese as they made their way to the beech tree in the courtyard and Trevka, toting a creel and rod, took this as his cue to saunter across the courtyard. He was hoping to overhear anything they said. He passed by them and tipped his hat and smiled, continued walking and eavesdropping, never once hearing anything amounting to the details of nefarious plans. Once out of their sight, he made his way in tip-toe fashion to their wing, furtively looking left and right outside its door, then jamming his key into the keyhole and pushing the rusty-hinged door open.

Inside, Trevka crept up the stairs and reached the second floor. He walked slowly down the hallway, pausing often, trying to make sure no one was moving up on the floor above, in the nursery. When he had walked the length of the hallway and back, hearing no sounds from above, he returned to the stairs and went up to the nursery. All was silent. He tried the doors to the nurses' bedrooms, listening closely for snoring first before entering. But each one contained only nursemaid flotsam; beds, clothes, mirrors. He entered the main nursery and prowled more closely. No instruments of torture were hidden under tables, no splatters of blood stained the walls, no screams of agony echoed in the room. He looked further at some of the items that were there; bottles, tiny spoons, little stuffed animals and cast-off blankets, along with needlework and artwork that kept the nurses occupied. It all seemed amazingly much for one so little. He had picked up and was examining closely an object that, he was sure, looked just like a woman's breast. It was a fist-sized ball of yarn wrapped in cloth; a small knob of cloth had been cinched with a string to enclose a nipple-sized protuberance. He held it in one hand, and was spronging the projection with an index finger when he heard something.

He crept out of the nursery and looked up and down the hallway, then walked to the Countess's rooms. He pulled another key from under his sleeve and slipped into the room, satisfying a curiosity he had long held, which was, *What does the room of a crazy woman look like?* But it was a bit of a disappointment, because it didn't look like much at all. There was only a minimum amount of furniture; a large but empty and unmade bed, a few chairs, one dresser. All of the personal belongings were gone, and Trevka felt deprived of what he considered to be one of the main perquisites of the job. He began following a trail of doorways that led to closets, dressing rooms with tall mirrors, a bathing room with a giant tub. Unimpressed, he made his way back to the bedroom.

He sat on the edge of the bed and looked about; spying was not going to be interesting with no one around. The silence and emptiness enveloped him and sighed in his ears. Then the sighing became a sort of whimpering. He turned around quickly to look behind him, but the sound was so far-off as to be possibly only in his mind or in the past. But it sounded like a girl crying, very faintly. Between whimpers were long silences. Perhaps he was imagining it. Then there it was again, young and very frightened, not the sounds he had remembered coming from the Countess; her voice boomed and crashed. This voice was faint and frightened. It must have been the ghost of the Countess's girlhood, crying for the terrors it had endured and it chilled Trevka to the bone. *The room was haunted, he knew it.* He stood up abruptly and stomped his boot on the floor as he did so. And it worked; the ghost's crying stopped. But instead of feeling relief, Trevka felt deep sadness as he left the room. He had only frightened the ghost further and imagined it running away to hide in a corner, no better off than before.

Trevka walked out into the hall and made his way to the staircase. He heard a noise far-off and began anew to worry about being discovered. Just as he reached the stairway doors he heard a noise and panicked that the nursemaids had returned and were at the other end of the hallway, spotting him. He leaped into the stairwell in one spinning move. He waited to hear the nurses shriek things like, *there's someone lurking in the stairwell!*, but no such alarm was raised and he breathed relief and padded down the three flights of stairs and back outside. When he had regained his own room, he collapsed on the bed, thinking this business was harder and less fun than he had imagined.

Trevka had dozed off in his room, then awoken with his unfailing punctuality for dinner. He joined everyone else in the dining room and afterward he and the rest of the Trappe Brigade were assembled in the main room, relaxing after the exertions of the day. Suddenly there was a pattering of feet not unlike the fluttering of startled birds' wings. One of the viscount's nurses came running into the room, her hands twirling, her long dress and wimple flying in her wake. "My lord," the small, round lady spoke out between pants. She looked around, wondering whom she was addressing. Boris stood up and approached her. "My lord," she panted, "We heard noises in the hallway, when no one was out there. We were all in the nursery, and there was a noise we didn't know what from." Boris had to control himself not to look in Trevka's direction, but of course he had been at dinner and then leisurely sitting in the same room with him for the past hour, and so was rather beyond suspicion. For his part, Trevka couldn't imagine how the noises he made earlier had only just now been heard. Boris patted the nursemaid's shoulder.

"Be calm and tell us what you heard." The nurse was beginning to get her breath back, and the others in the room had gathered to hear her answer. She darted her beady eyes across the watching crowd, the first time she had ever been an object of so much attention and suddenly asserted,

"A ghost, my lord!" The crowd murmured their dismissal. Boris shot them a glance and turned back to the nurse.

"Yes, well, describe this ghost; how did it sound?" The nurse thought for a minute, then with surprise said,

"I didn't hear it!" The crowd groaned, and Boris stifled his own.

"Who heard the noise, nurse?" She said,

"The other nurses, they said they heard something, and sent me to get help." Boris waved at Vatra to accompany him and the three set off for the nurse's territory, certain they were chasing loose shutters in the breeze or the groaning walls of a slowly crumbling structure. They gently interrogated the nurses, who were unable to take turns talking, each one disagreeing with the others as to how the noise sounded, where it originated, or what it might be. The two men glanced at the viscount, asleep and oblivious to all the fuss, and smiled to the ladies, thanking them for their attentiveness and charging them to carefully note any and all suspicious noises they heard in the night. By then, the nurses had forgotten the noise to the extent that it no longer seemed threatening, and since sleep was beginning to overtake them, they resigned themselves to that task. Boris and Vatra left, waiting until they were in the hallway to exchange dismissive glances.

When they returned to the main hall, Trevka asked what they had heard and Boris interjected with, "I defy any one of them to describe the sound of their own voice, although they are in use enough." Trevka himself tried to put into words the noises he had heard earlier that day. That didn't help much in trying to decide if their noises and his noises were one in the same. He glanced toward the nursery and wondered.

The following day everyone hoped things would be quieter. Already there was too much activity for the Trappe Brigade to be dealing with, but solitude was not to be. At mid-afternoon a group of five men arrived at the door of the castle requesting to see the Count. They were shown into a waiting room where Boris, Vatra and several other men received them. Boris stood with his arms crossed, asking what business they had here at this time of year. It sorely taxed tradition, protocol and courtesy to show up requesting an audience in late August; everyone in the realm knew better than that. The lead man stepped forward and asked, "Are you the Count?"

"I am the Count's deputy," Boris said. "State your business." The lead man thought for a bit, glanced at his companions and turned back to Boris saying,

"We are the contingency from Elster, come to discuss the Marianna River. But if the Count is not here, then we seek only a night's rest."

Boris and Vatra blinked in disbelief. They didn't look like ambassadors, but then they had been traveling for many weeks, possibly months, and how many ambassadors had either of them known, anyway? Having no desire to offend the contingency that had been so long awaited, Boris said to them with a flourish,

"Gentlemen, we are so pleased you are here! Please forgive us not having your accommodations ready. This page will escort you to our dining room where a meal will be brought. You must be weary after your long journey. When you have eaten all you care to, we'll show you to your rooms." The visitors were led out and toward the dining hall. When they were gone, Boris rolled his eyes to the ceiling and said to Vatra, "I can't believe they have showed up now, after the Count has waited months for them. If he comes back to hear they were here and left without speaking to him, he'll be appalled and the matter of the boundary dispute will be delayed another year. Who sends ambassadors to arrive in late summer?" He shook his head not knowing what to think of them. Vatra however knew exactly what he wanted to do with them, and told Boris in a determined voice,
"They are here to conduct serious business, which I have been

charged with disallowing. The Count specifically said I was to detain anyone with such intentions and I shall do it, on his direct orders." Vatra had every right to take the Count at his word and do the duty given to him, and since Boris had no better idea what to do with them, he agreed. They decided to lodge the contingency in comfortable rooms in a remote part of the castle. Then he and Vatra went to the dining hall to join them. Boris addressed them as the food was just being brought in.

"Gentlemen, you have come on a most pressing and important issue, which must not be delayed any longer than possible. You will remain here as our guests until the Count returns in a week or two." The group chuckled and smiled at each other, apparently happy already with the fine food.

Later in the day, Boris asked Trevka for a report on his reconnaissance mission of the day before. Trevka summarized; "A lot of rooms full of junk." This didn't sound like very successful spying, so he added, "Come to think of it, I heard something too." But then Trevka thought, "Maybe it was just some kids playing around, like me and Vatra used to do." Boris didn't like the idea of kids playing around or unexplained noises. If there was any object worth protecting in the castle, the future Count was it. He decided the flighty nurses who looked after the viscount might not be competent enough to ensure his safety. He wasn't sure Trevka's was either but he told him,

"Stay in the Countess's old room tonight, and do it without being noticed by anyone. You might be able to hear through the nearest wall into the nursery, and be nearby in case anything happens." Trevka bowed in acknowledgment, intrigued with a new assignment and wondering if his stiletto worked against whimpering ghosts.

That afternoon Trevka watched the nurses again escape the late-day heat of the sun against their side of the castle and head for the shade in the courtyard. With a sack of food he made his way into Gertrudis's old bedroom and closed the door. The bed did not have sheets or blankets, but it still had the remnants of curtains hanging from the canopy. He looked for the room he thought would be closest to the nursery and dragged a chair from the bedroom into it, hoping it was a common wall to the nursery. He sat and examined his stiletto, always hidden in his jacket, until he heard the nurses returning.

The evening dragged on with him listening to the nurses' murmurs through the wall; he had to press his ear to the wall to understand them, but heard them mention strange visitors and speculate on what that could mean. They discussed baby to-dos at length, many of which he failed to understand. One of the nurses was exclaiming loudly that the baby needed changing (was his personality so bad already?) As she spoke, the baby began crying and the nurses mentioned how hungry he must be. Trevka remembered the food in his satchel and pulled it out to eat. They complained loudly about missing the other wet nurse, and how fussy this baby was. Trevka puzzled over how useful a nurse who sweated a lot would be and shifted in his chair. There was lots of baby crying and criticism and advice going back and forth, until finally, with one of the nurses singing softly, the crying died down to a series of whimpers. Trevka, asleep in his chair, meat pie crumbs scattered over his lap, dozed thus for a while until his stiff neck woke him. All was dark and quiet. He made his way back to the Countess's bed and fell into it face first, fast asleep.

In the middle of the night, there was a creaking sound. Trevka awoke and had no idea where he was; a dark curtain was all around him and after a few moments he remembered he was sleeping in a crazy woman's bed in a haunted room. He heard light footsteps approaching. His eyes popped open to probe the darkness; there was only a sliver of moon to see by, and the curtains of the canopy bed obscured his view with strands of moth-eaten fabric. His heart began thumping when across the room, from the closet he had done his eavesdropping in, a figure dressed like one of the nurses drifted quietly out. He was frozen in place, too terrified to move, certain the specter was the former crazed Countess-child herself, and she was going to spot him in her bed and kill him in some unimaginably hideous manner. But instead, she merely walked quietly across and out of the room, pausing at the doorway and looking carefully up and down the hallway before leaving and closing the door silently behind her.

He shook off the last of his sleepiness and realized he was not seeing a ghost, but a live woman who was much smaller than the former

Countess. This woman must also be a spy, for didn't she just come from the same room, and didn't they both creep about on tip toe when they thought no one was watching? Well, he would beat her at their own game. He crept to the doorway and looked out, and she was indeed headed east towards the rest of the castle. Following her proved difficult, as she did not seem to know where she was going. She took a zigzag path through the hallways, pausing very often and sometimes even re-tracing her steps. Finally he began to hear talking, laughing and whistling, and knew they were approaching the quarters where the Elster ambassadors were being lodged and apparently carrying on a late-night celebration. She headed quickly in that direction, and he followed with increasing bewilderment.

She went into their room and there was subdued talking, the words of which were unintelligible to Trevka. He figured she must have wandered into the wrong room, and waited for her to re-emerge, but a quarter hour went by and she not only had not re-emerged, but the sounds from the room became increasingly muffled, and he finally decided they had all gone to bed. He didn't hear screaming or sounds of struggle or ungentlemanly behavior, so he went back to the Countess's room to wait until morning.

With the first light of morning, Trevka awoke and immediately investigated the closet from which his ghost had sallied forth. He got to the closet where he had sat in his chair listening, and could go no further. Yes, this must have been where he was last night; there were the meat pie crumbs on the floor. But where could she have been hiding? He looked around; the only possible hiding place was behind some old drapes that hung from a pole and pushed to one end. But he knew there was not enough room for a broom, much less a person to stand there unnoticed by him all evening, even as small as she was. Still, he pushed the drapes aside and stared at the wall one foot away. He was beginning to re-suspect haunting when he noticed a gap between the back and side walls. A peg for hanging was on this wall, and he gazed at it, realized it was more worn than the others equally spaced along the wall. He reached up to wiggle it and the wall drifted away from him like a cipher. Amazed, he followed the silently retreating hidden door into a tiny room with a heap of bedclothes on the floor and satchels for cheese and bread, now empty. The room was stuffy with the smell of long-confined occupation.

He quickly retreated back out of the space and went back into the bedroom to contemplate. Had this girl been left behind by the retreating Countess, locked up for punishment? Was she hiding from someone in this lonely part of the castle? Did these rooms of the castle have lunacy seeping from their walls? He went back down to the main room; it was still early, well before breakfast and there was no one to consult. He didn't want to wait long to interrogate the woman who must be hiding in the Elsters' quarters. When Boris finally came in, Trevka related all the strange doings of the night before, and Boris immediately ordered *all* the Elsterians to become his personal guests for breakfast. When they were ushered in, the five same men as had shown their faces yesterday stood at the table and then took seats. Boris looked at Trevka with a questioning gaze, wondering where his mysterious sleep-walking nursemaid was. Trevka ran to their room, expecting to find her hiding under a bed, expecting the Elsterians to follow him and try to stop his investigation, expecting to get some wild explanation from her. But none of these things happened. He went to their rooms, looked everywhere without interruption or discovery, and returned to the breakfast room only to find them all eating breakfast calmly.

Nothing further out of the ordinary happened all morning. By the time the nurses, with the viscount, retreated outside after lunchtime, Trevka had lost hope of discovering anything. He went back to the main room where people were gathered, relaxing. At least they were not talking about him, at the moment, although he did not doubt he had been the topic of much unworthy speculation for most of the morning. Vatra was near the door and the twins exchanged glances. Vatra had not seen the mystery woman either and raised his shoulders at his brother, then let them fall, sympathy and consternation on his face. Trevka crossed his arms and was silently brooding when a footman marched into the room and barked out abruptly,

"The Ambassador from Elster has arrived and requests to have an audience with the Count." The room went silent; Vatra and Trevka exchanged looks and for the first time knew what it was to have the identical twins game played on *them*. Trevka bolted out of the room and towards the courtyard. All of it was suddenly clear.

16

Revelations

Vatra ran out the door after his brother with several others following. When Trevka got to the courtyard, the viscount's nursemaids were in a cluster, hastily roped all together back to back. They struggled to move, but having eight legs and not a single mind was a hindrance. It was an enormous spider caught in its own web. They argued loudly about whether they should move towards the vanishing party that carried the viscount away, or whether they should head for the castle and summon help. Trevka might have laughed at such an image, but the situation was too dire for that. "Horses!" he yelled back to his brother, who was already headed for them. He took the most upright nurse by both arms and asked, "Which way did they go?" She jerked her head up the road and began her sorry tale, but Trevka didn't wait to hear it. The brothers were quickly mounted and headed down the road, with others following, all in pursuit of the criminals who had just kidnapped the Count's son.

The kidnappers had chosen an escape route around the outskirts of the village, but they could not completely avoid being seen by people who lived or walked along the road. It didn't take long for their short advantage of a sneak attack to wear off, and soon their pursuers were in sight behind them. Trevka spotted the small girl, now dressed as a boy, carrying the viscount. Her companions around her had scattered and were being apprehended. Trevka brought his horse quickly alongside hers and reached out to take control of her reins. He had imagined apprehending fearsome criminals, hardened to violence. He had not imagined halting a slight girl clutching a baby. Trevka said *whoa* gently to the horse and to her and with that simple admonishment she meekly gave up.

The five men who had impersonated the Elster contingency in order to gain access to the castle (and who were actually from Uluvost) were taken back to their quarters and two guards were now posted outside their door. The young girl, Beth, was taken to a small room in Liesse's apartment and was clutching Dane while Liesse sat next to her. Trevka waited outside the door and soon Boris arrived to question the baby snatcher. He entered the room and stood over her with his arms crossed and asked, "What is your name?" but the girl was so frightened she began to cry softly and hid her face in her bundled baby. Liesse looked up at her husband and shook her head. Boris threw his hands up and left the room, telling Trevka on the way out to find out what he could. Trevka entered the room and sat in a far corner beside an armoire, hoping to go unnoticed. Liesse put her hand on Beth's shoulder and said to her,

"It's all right now, you can just stay here and hold the baby as long as you want. He's good in your arms and I won't let them take him away." Beth tried to stop crying and slowly lifted her head. But she didn't want to examine her new world and her hair hung down in a semblance of protection around the baby. Finally she began to talk, in a voice soft like a mouse, saying to Liesse, "I'm sorry I ran off, but I was so heartbroken. My own baby died when he was only a day old. The Countess had just had her baby too but she wouldn't touch it, so they brought Dane to me and I took him to me just like he was my own, given back to me like a gift right from Heaven to ease my broken heart." Beth remembered how happy she was then, in spite of everything else that had gone wrong. "When the Countess was leaving Wilker for good, I was so afraid for my little boy. They said I had to go with the Countess. But who would feed my baby? Them other nurses, they never did take to him, or him to them. He always cried for me, and I was always there for him." Beth looked up from the baby and into Liesse's eyes, saying, "I was terrified that if I left him, he wouldn't eat and he'd die." She hugged him close then continued, "I couldn't leave him, he's all I have, the only thing I live for. I don't think his own mother cares about him. When everyone left to go back to Uluvost, I sent a letter with one of them to give to my cousin. I lied to get them to help me, told them Gertrudis would give them a right high place in her household, even though I know she wouldn't. I've been waiting for them all this time."

Finally Beth had found her voice, but she hadn't mentioned where her husband was in all of this, and Liesse doubted whether he existed at all. A girl so young might have been taken advantage of, especially under the lax security of the Countess's home court. Liesse had heard such and worse of the people from Uluvost. Beth continued explaining how she had come to be in this position:

"The other nurses lied for me when they found out I was pregnant, told Gertrudis my husband was a soldier in Uluvost out in the field, no place for a bride. I think some of them felt a little guilty about my getting – into the condition I had. It doesn't matter now. All I care about is my baby." Liesse hated to remind Beth, but she seemed to forget the fact easily and so said,

"He is the viscount, you must remember that." Beth began crying again and hugged her bundle closer. She felt certain it was only a matter of time before she was punished and sent away, or sent to the dungeon for kidnapping a viscount. Liesse tried to comfort her and Trevka had managed to hear the whole tale, even through her thin hair and thinner voice, for all else was quiet in the room, the baby calm for a change.

The nursemaids in the courtyard were untied and taken back to the nursery. They were reassured that all was well, but they too were worried about their fate as failures at protecting the heir. Boris questioned the oldest nurse, asking her carefully about how the viscount had fared since the Countess and her entourage had left. She protested that she did her job well and the heir lacked for nothing, but Boris wondered if she was trying to hide something.

Boris then went to question the impersonators being held in rather nice quarters for such a crime. They protested that they thought a crime had been committed when the Countess was taken away from her son and that their cousin and friend was going to help them set it right. No reward was expected for this heroic deed. They had encountered the real Ambassadors from Elster on their way to the castle, and having learned of their mission, raced ahead of them to use their tale to gain access to the castle. Their slow pace was exceedingly easy to surpass, but the lead had not been far enough ahead and when the real Ambassadors arrived at the castle, it was just in time to interrupt a crime. As far as Boris could tell, it was the cleverest thing the real ambassadors had done to date. Boris told the Uluvostians they would be held with a guard on their door until the Count returned. He would decide how to punish them for trying to take away his son.

When Boris was alone with his wife that evening, Beth and her baby being kept in a small room next to their apartment with Trevka watching the door, he listened to his wife make a confession. "I neglected Dane, whom I should have cared about and who has been right under our noses. We have left him in the care of those silly women, while we danced and were gay. This timid young girl is the only one who has loved him and truly cared for him. She spent weeks in that closet, running out of food, ready to nurse him again, and now she is terrified that she will be punished. The Count didn't even know of her existence, and we may well have only her to thank for what little there is of the viscount's good health." Boris snorted with doubt, certain his wife was exaggerating. But Liesse corrected him. "Haven't you noticed Dane is barely bigger than Luna? And he's nearly a year older. But he takes to Beth very well. I think she should keep looking after him, although she is very attached, even for a wet nurse, and I'm a little worried about her. She acts as if that baby is hers."

Late summer at the lodge high up in the forest was still warm during the day, but in the evenings the dying leaves shivered in the chill air. Harz spent most days around the stable with Ash and the horses. Much time could be spent feeding, brushing, examining and walking the animals not being used for the day's hunting. In the afternoons Ash worked with the wolfhounds. They were learning the command to lunge, and next would be taught the one to back down. Although they were rarely used for such defenses, they were always trained in them nevertheless. While his litter mates rested separately, the dog sitting in front of Ash turned his head sideways, listening to a new word being spoken to him and wondering about the treat thrown a slight distance away. Ash waited a bit, then repeated the word. Now the dog laid down on the ground and put his head on his paws, glanced up at Ash briefly, then lowered his eyes.

"He's confused right now, but he'll catch on," Ash said to Harz, who was watching the progress. "This one gives up a bit quickly. He wants to obey, but he doesn't know what to do. I'll let him think about it and watch the others. He'll figure it out." Harz said to Ash,

"You should go out tomorrow for the hunt, see these animals working. You haven't been out for a day since you got here."

"All right," Ash replied. They left the animals to their own interests, and Harz patted the slow dog on the head before walking away.

While the men stayed outside most of the day, the women enjoyed the privilege of having the lodge all to themselves. Sparrow didn't see it as a privilege and wanted to spend all day outside as she always had, but Gustav said she might as well get used to being indoors with other people and learn some of the things they did to occupy themselves. To Sparrow it seemed the women did nothing but talk and Gustav explained with a chuckle that talking was the main pastime of all the women he had ever known, that he suspected it was a way they had of doing less work, and that they all seemed to enjoy it. She followed along as they cooked and "cleaned." It was amusing and confusing, but she was also reminded of how her mother used to do this kind of work, and she felt a nostalgia for her old family life.

The women continued to look for signs that would tell them what Sparrow's baby's name would be. They seemed to take greater interest in this than Sparrow herself, who knew the name would come along and that looking for it was unnecessary. Then she came to understand that *hunting* for the name was as much fun, or more, than *having* it. In fact, she was beginning to simply accept what people said. At first she had found herself wanting to correct them, to tell everyone what they were really thinking, which often differed from what they were saying. But being reticent and still confused by them she held back. Then she came to realize that even though their thoughts and words differed, they had reasons for speaking this way. It might or might not be deception, but it was how they handled each other, and they did laugh a lot. Some of what they said was purely to make each other laugh. Wouldn't blurting out all their inner truths change that? What she didn't quite realize was that very slowly, she was becoming more like them, and not seeing past the deceptions some times, preferring instead to laugh as well. The more she talked, the less she perceived.

Equally keeping her in this new life was being in bed with Gustav. Every night her body looked forward to having him beside her, melting into the pleasure of being embraced by this man with a sensuous mind and talent, who delighted in delighting her. Bit by bit she was lured back into civilization just as her parents had been lured away from it.

It was the last day and the men were to go off hunting, although they had plenty of game and it would be more of a leisurely stroll. Harz was staying behind as the one to watch over the lodge and the women. He planned to spend the whole day outside. Sparrow watched the men ride off and would keep a part of her attention with them until they safely returned.
She heard sounds of tapping and clanging coming from the stable and looked over to see what it was. Keeping animals corralled and

"trained" was odd to her, and she indulged her curiosity and walked towards the horses to listen to them. Most were gone for the day but one, standing off to the side, watched her approach. She closed her eyes and reached out to the animal's mind. *How are you feeling?* she asked. The horse shook its mane and snorted, then swished its tail. *Good*, came the reply. She waited for more. *My hooves tingle.* She looked past the horse and saw that the tapping sound was from Harz removing the old horseshoe from another horse's hoof in preparation for the new shoe it would have for tomorrow's trip. Harz, as usual, was keeping whatever thoughts he had to himself.

She watched him work for a while but he didn't look up or take any notice of her. She wished she understood him better, he was certainly very important to Gustav. If she could sense anything about him now, it was perhaps loneliness. He stopped what he was doing but didn't look up. Then he gave the old horseshoe one more tap and it came off the hoof and into his hand. He examined it, flipped it over and seemed to notice something. *You are well accomplished, Harz,* Sparrow thought. Harz turned suddenly and threw the horseshoe across the stable where it hit the far wall and dropped to the ground. He paused before turning back to his work, noticing Sparrow at the edge of the corral. He nodded acknowledgment of her and then immediately went back to examining the horse's foot and its new shoe.

When they were alone together that evening, Sparrow asked Gustav about his cousin. "Can Harz read thoughts?" she said.

"He can always tell if someone is lying. He's very useful for that."

"Am I useful?" Sparrow asked, half teasing.

"Hmmm," Gustav commented. Then he teased back, "Did you tell him a lie today?" Sparrow thought that would be an interesting thing to try, if she could think of a lie. She said,

"No, I only complimented his horseshoeing skill. I think he's very disappointed with someone." Gustav scoffed and said,

"Harz? No, you must be imagining that." But Sparrow knew her intuition. She said plainly to Gustav,

"I don't know why I would imagine it; it seems plain." She didn't want to admit that it *was* hard to read him. Instead she added, "It would be better if you were more aware of what is going on with those close to you." Gustav was going to object to her giving him advice, but couldn't deny that she had a unique intelligence. So he concluded diplomatically,

"Then I shall have to rely on you to increase my attention where it is needed, unless of course you take it all," and he kissed her before she could say anything else and so began their last night in the lodge together.

In the great room of the lodge, the rest of the men were still awake.

Morgan was aiming cards into a bowl, Ash poked the fire and Quilin was meticulously examining each dog that dozed on the floor, happy to find and remove a splinter or palpate a lump. There was much less chatter with Boris away, and after Ash had stoked the fire he brought two tankards of ale from the kitchen and joined Harz working at the dining table. Ash drank from his tankard and Harz looked at the ale brought for him, then went back to his task of punching new buckle holes into a saddle belt. He took careful aim with hammer and awl and punched another hole into the leather.

Ash leaned towards Harz and said, "Do you think it would be gainful to tell a fair lady I admire how wonderful and fine she is?" Harz studied the hole he had made and said,

"No."

"I never did see such blonde hair around so lovely a face." Ash sipped more ale, obvious to Harz it was more than his usual. Harz kept to his work, so to further impress him, Ash slyly pulled a miniature loaf of bread from his pocket, "I found this in my jacket." Harz glanced at the bread, watched as Ash put the loaf to his nose and inhale deeply. "It's too good to eat." His eyes fluttered with the ecstasy of the aroma. Harz looked back at his leather, moving the awl to its next location. He said,

"Where did that come from?"

"I don't know, it just showed up here in my pocket. But I believe it is from the goddess in the kitchen." Harz took aim and whacked the awl into the leather.

"Which of the several?"

"Ah yes, there are many. But I hope, I believe, it is from Anna." Harz paused before speaking.

"And why do you think that?"

"Oh, I have reason. And I believe the others are otherwise, well, rather otherwise interested." Harz examined the back of the leather belt, frowned with disappointment.

"You seem to know a lot. Why ask for my opinion?"

"You'd never do the wrong thing by a lady."

17

Settling Down

After breakfast on the final morning before returning to the castle, Gustav conducted the short order of regal business that was standard. He touched his forehead and it began. He took his time with each statement, the first one being,

"Two favored members of the realm shall henceforth reside in Wilker castle." He smiled at Sparrow and their son. "They shall be given every extra attention and accommodation necessary to make them comfortable and safe. They are very honored residents." Everyone nodded in Sparrow's direction. Gustav thought about Sparrow's caution to be more aware of others' concerns and thus continued, "If the eyes and ears of my well-regarded subjects gain intelligence of value to my otherwise occupied eyes and ears, it would be of great service to the realm to bring it to my attention. The strength and goodness of a country is much more than one monarch, but lies in the sum of all its good people." He paused, touched his forehead, and then the last preparations began for the return trip.

As wagons were loaded and horses were assembled and bridled, Sparrow watched it all and held her baby tight against her. Gustav came up behind her and put his arms around her; he wouldn't be letting her sneak back into the forest again and leaving him worrying about her. As he held her tight she knew she could still call upon a fox nearby; she could cause a distraction and slip away, go back to her grotto, which was behind the traps she had set. Gustav pulled his arms back and put his hands on her shoulders, in case anyone glanced at them he should look dignified. But he was still close behind her and whispered to her, "I love you." Sparrow looked down at her baby. No, at their baby. "And I love you for coming back with us." She saw in her mind all of them living in a castle together. She asked Gustav,

"Could our son ever become the Count?" Gustav was silent behind her, either considering the possibility, or the impossibility, but finally just said rather casually,

"That is not likely." Sparrow turned and faced him with a smile and said,

"Good, for I do not sense it happening. Now I need not worry why." Gustav walked Sparrow over to the wagon where Genivee had prepared a comfortable spot for her. She knew Sparrow was not accustomed to riding in a wagon and might find it tiresome. Sparrow got into the wagon and Gustav got on his horse and soon after they set off for the castle.

When they reached the edge of the forest, the traveling party stopped for a midday meal. They had all settled down into restful spots and were in the stillness between food and sleep when a blackbird fluttered over the party for a moment and lit on the wagon's rim. From her arms, Sparrow's baby reached out a hand in its direction. Anna noticed this and said,

"It's a sign, just like with Sparrow! Oh, but we can hardly call him Blackbird." Roused from his contemplation of fauna, Magnus said,

"The name Kasch means blackbird." Sparrow liked the name. Gustav opened his eyes from near sleep and saw the bird just before it flew off again. He said,

"An excellent name, we shall call him Kasch." And with that business settled, they continued on their journey. As the wagon rocked and Sparrow began to doze off, Suzette leaned over to Anna and whispered in her ear,

"For a second when it landed and I saw that black bird I thought of a crow, but thank the gods it wasn't a crow, that wouldn't have been good luck at all." Anna nodded solemnly, for she too had been thinking the same thought. She added her own folk wisdom back into Suzette's ear.

"And if it had croaked while standing nearby, then it was bringing a message of death, everyone knows that." The two girls kept their eyes on Sparrow, who still appeared to be sleeping, not hearing the girls' whispers above the grinding of the wagon wheels and the breeze across the field. The party continued on its way, making good progress across the level pediment. In the forest above them, two humans still lingered behind.

The Rogues were hunkered down on either side of a small fire. Bit was roasting a very small squirrel skewered to a spit. Maw was watching and wondering why it was taking so long. He had brushed the squirrel's hide dry with a rock and wanted to make a hat from it, but it was too small and he became disgusted with the attempt and let it drop. He asked Bit, "Ain't that critter done yet?" Bit answered back,

"You want to gnaw on raw squirrel?"

"Ah don't want to gnaw on squirrel a-tall." There was silence for a while. There was a lot of silence between them. When Maw thought the meat was suitably singed he grabbed it, tore it in half and gave the smaller half to Bit. They ate in silence until they were licking the last fat off their fingers. Bit said,

"Ah don't want to spend 'nother winter starving. This here squirrel was obliging, but they's all going to winter down soon and they won't be nothing left to snare." Maw wondered if Bit had a plan or was just complaining. He added his own wisdom:

"We cain't go back south." That was all the wisdom he had.

"No we cain't, not with you a-wanted for murderin' a prison guard when you didn't even have to." Bit had pointed this out to Maw before, but to Maw it had seemed that throwing the brick at the guard's head was important; whether or not he died from it wasn't. Some things weren't planned.

"Where kin we go?" Maw asked. Bit was silent for a while. Then he said,

"I'm goin' north. I'm gettin' out-a these woods, which is haunted anyways with possessed critters." Maw observed,
"Ah don't know no one up north." Then after further thought, concluded, "Ah needs more in my head then what Ah got." Bit knew what he was thinking and said with disgust,

"You ain't goin' to try and snag another regal bird. Thet didn't work last time and it don't work even if you catch one. You cain't git wise just by catchin' a wise bird." *Hmph*, thought Maw. It ought to work, and Bit hadn't ever proved it couldn't work. But is was hard to catch one. Bit said flatly, "I'm goin' north. You kin stay here an' rot ifn' you want to." Maw had exhausted his own ideas, so even as unpromising as it seemed to go to a place they'd never been where the people might speak differently and the work might be harder, he decided to go with him. He said,

"OK then I'll go too." As if he had ever considered trying to make do on his own. But Bit had more to add.

"Then you have ta keep low. No killin' people just 'cuz. You git a girl in an alley, ya better be sure she don't scream or see you. There's more folks a-watchin' in towns. And there's prisons, too, you got that?"

Maw just grunted. What Bit didn't know didn't matter. Maw was tired of working so hard just to stay alive. In a town there would be lots of opportunities, unsuspecting rich people walking around and certainly girls on the loose. They'd find their way in somewhere, and then life would be better. They finished their scanty meal and stood up, gathering their few things and Bit looked up at the sky, made a show of determining north, then started walking. Maw followed behind him, for now at least.

The forest breathed a sigh of relief. Finally they were leaving. The hawks and ravens made noise on the south side of them to keep them moving north and out of the forest. The rabbits and squirrels cleared away from the path before the two men. And on a ridge far above them, a wolf sat on a rocky ledge watching them pass below. He had never been hungry enough or close enough or interested enough to kill them, and besides there were the two of them, always staying close together. It had always been more convenient to just stay away from them, but nevertheless the wolf watched them go and sensed the relief of many in the forest, mainly of those who had been close to Sparrow. But the wolf didn't wallow in the luxury of thinking they, or those like them, were gone for good. As guardian of the forest, he would always be vigilant to their presence.

Boris knew that today was the day the real royal party was returning to the castle. He had garlands and banners placed all around and great amounts of food were ready and waiting on the great long table in the dining room. There was a good deal of unpleasant business awaiting the real Count's attention and Boris was entirely ready to give back the title. Beth and Viscount Dane were practically inseparable and every day that passed Boris wondered if he should be separating them, sending her away, or rewarding her. The nursemaids had been giving him dire warnings about leaving Dane with this young girl, but one of them came forward privately to Liesse and confessed having been worried about the tyke. So Boris had trusted in her and Trevka's report that the two were now best kept together. Trevka continued to be a careful Watchman; this girl had come very close to escaping his or anyone's notice and nothing like that was going to happen again. He took to guarding her door most days, not as a guard but as a person still conducting surveillance.

Boris had turned the matter of guarding the prisoners from Gertrudis's realm over to Vatra, who took careful charge of his job as constable, arranging a schedule of men to take turns at the watch, assigning two at a time to the night watch, giving them cards and food and each others' company to make sure they didn't fall asleep while on guard duty. Once over dinner the twins discussed the odd family now held in opposite ends of the castle. Trevka asked his brother, *Do those schemers ever demand to know how Beth is being treated or what is to become of her?* Vatra shook his head and confirmed that they did not. Then he asked Trevka, *Did Beth ever ask to see her cousin, ever ask about them or what was to happen to them?* Trevka shook his head. One would hardly think they were actually related.

Finally, the party actually from Elster was becoming more vexatious every day. If Boris invited them to eat with the rest of them, they complained it was too inconvenient. If he left them alone, they protested they were not being shown the proper respect. They insisted on showing him their maps, and he assured them he had not the authority, understanding or interest to see them. In every way, they gave him more pains and worries than the other two problems combined. Boris looked forward to Gustav's return. When a scout on watch rode back to the castle to inform them the Count's party was on its way and would arrive within the hour, Boris called up musicians to play music in the courtyard for the entourage's return.

When the party of horseback riders and wagons finally ambled into the courtyard, a troop of servants were on hand to help with the unloading and unharnessing and other necessary tasks. Gustav made formal hellos to Boris but told him he was still Count until the end of the day, meaning tomorrow at sunrise, and with that he disappeared into his private rooms with Sparrow, Kasch and one wolfhound alongside him. Boris kept his mouth shut and watched him disappear into the castle, sympathetic but somewhat fettered as well. Anna and Suzette returned dazed and exhausted to their rooms above the kitchen, with Talin looking after them sternly, as if by staring at them he might detect hidden sin. Ash and Morgan appeared still full of energy and helped with the horses. Quilin made his way over to Boris and ask him how it went here at the castle. Boris rubbed his beard, put his other hand on Quilin's shoulder and said to him, "Quilin, my fellow medic, no one is unwell in body, but some of us are unsettled in mind." Together they retreated inside to eat and talk.

Harz was lingering in the courtyard, pretending it was necessary to direct Ash and Morgan and the others. He made busywork for himself while he casually kept one eye on Genivee, because it would soon be his last chance to do so. After this evening, she would almost always be out of his sight and sphere.

Genivee drowsily disembarked from the wagon. She looked around for Liesse but her friend was inside with Beth, who was suffering a trembling attack over the arrival of Dane's father, the man who would decide her future, and possibly break her heart by his verdict. Liesse had watched the party's arrival from a window above the courtyard, but Beth could not be convinced to come to the window and see for herself that Gustav was nothing to be horrified about.

Harz watched Genivee look around searchingly, but most everyone had gone inside by then. She limped and tapped her foot, asleep from its cramped position in the wagon. When Morgan walked by, Harz told him quietly to help her inside, where she was lopsidedly headed. Morgan didn't immediately do as he was told, it was too strange an honor. Harz looked over to him and added (because young men often forgot) "Ask first." He watched as Morgan walked off and then timidly offered his arm to Genivee and the two of them hobbled towards the servants' part of the castle with plenty of light visible between them. Boris came back out to the courtyard to find Harz, whom he had expected to be following immediately behind. Although Gustav had brushed off official duty for the day, he could always rely on Harz to be interested in important business. He started out with the simplest news:

"The ambassadors from Elster arrived while the Count was away." Harz watched as Morgan bowed to Genivee at her doorway and headed back towards the stable. Then he turned to Boris and said,

"Quite a feat. I thought they would never get here." Boris answered with,

"They almost didn't. They were waylaid." Harz became more interested. "By some men who thought to kidnap the Viscount."

"Thought to?" Harz asked sharply. Boris answered,

"He's fine, have no worry there. Well at least he is certainly getting great attention. A young girl is looking after him in my smaller apartments." Harz glanced up to the window he knew to be Boris' and for a moment saw a female gazing out, then disappear. She was too far away to see clearly. Harz asked sharply,

"What girl?"

"One as loyal to her duty as you." Boris assured him, and they headed inside for Harz's first course of food and Boris's second. "Trevka saved the day," Boris said, smiling broadly and knowing that this part of the story was the one Harz would be the most curious to hear. They went into the castle and now the courtyard was empty.

By then, Gustav had finally reached his own room and led Sparrow through the door. The room would not be empty any longer. Sparrow looked around, spotted the brightest window and went over to it. She tried to lean out to see more of the outside, but the window was narrow, the wall was thick and she couldn't see much. She rocked back onto her heels by the windowsill and gazed at what she could; a slice of the empty courtyard. Gustav came over to her and said, "You're safe in here." But she shook her head slightly and murmured,

"It's very dark." Gustav then took her hand and led her out the door. They walked through hallways and corridors and up stairways and finally came out onto the keep of the castle. It was seven stories up from the ground, higher than any other part of the castle. Four corner columns supported a square hip roof, but all was open between the eaves and the waist-high walls. Sparrow went to each wall and took in the view. After a time Gustav put his arms around her and said,

"It will be Vatra's job to make sure this keep is for you alone. Come here whenever you want. You will keep the crows from making a habit of it." Sparrow did breathe easier after being there a few minutes. In fact, it was rather nice to be so high above everything, removed and yet a part of it at the same time. And the crows would *not* be kept at bay; they would be interesting to chat with.

After talking with Boris at dinner, Quilin's main concern was with the fifteen-year-old looking after the one-year-old who was the heir to the throne. Although Boris had said they both appeared well and healthy, Quilin figured it would be best if he too could report to the Count that he had found them in the best of health. In the morning, Liesse introduced Quilin to Beth, who sat down next to her and explained who he was. He told her he had come from a village near to where she had, and this helped to ease her mind about being questioned by a relative stranger. (Well, he had visited that village several times.) Quilin asked her questions in a roundabout way, hoping she wouldn't become defensive or frightened into lying.

"Are you getting enough food to keep both of you feeling good?" Beth nodded. In fact, it was lucky she had escaped when she had, for the food had been running out and Liesse fed her very well. "Does Dane like to eat often or does he wait until he is cranky and cries?" Again she affirmed that he was always with her and nursed often. Finally Quilin asked her if she was happy here, was she being well looked after? She nodded fearfully, not out of any lack because they were very generous (much more so than Gertrudis had ever been), but out of a dread that now the Count was returned, it all might come to an end. Quilin could not reassure her one way or another what the outcome would be.

Quilin held Dane and looked him over, put his ear to the baby's chest, and concluded that the baby was healthy, if a bit small for his age. He gave Dane back to her, and then tried to comfort Beth with a smile and a firm hand on her shoulder. He left them and talked with Liesse in the hallway. She told him,

"Dane looks better since she has been taking care of him. He was thin when they tried to – when she came out of hiding." Quilin may have doubted that Beth was mature enough to be sensible. After all, an attempted kidnapping of a viscount was quite ridiculous. However, no one could doubt her devotion to the baby or his attachment to her. He simply said to Liesse,

"Yes, it is apparent that the baby is doing well now." He wondered what Gustav would think and started back to his infirmary. As he and Liesse walked away down the hall together, Trevka stepped inside the room. Beth looked up and noticed Trevka, whom she recognized as the one keeping post outside her door. She was a prisoner with a guard. Well, she had been a prisoner before, and then with no one to guard her. She smiled at him briefly and since she didn't seem to be bothered by his presence, he took a chair and placed it a little near her, sitting backwards on it and resting his arms across the backrest. He said,

"They give a good report." He nodded towards the open door, although Quilin and Liesse were gone. Beth smiled weakly. "And I shall too," he added. Beth relaxed a bit. At first she had been uneasy having someone guard her door, constantly there. At night the door was locked, and by day she hadn't had the courage to ask to go out. Now it occurred to her she could have. But what if she had gone to the door and found someone other than Trevka keeping watch? She managed to say,

"Thank you. You're very kind." Trevka looked past her out a window, drummed his fingers thinking, then said,

"The Countess was not so kind, I understand." Beth's eyes widened with the memories of Gertrudis, and she had to smile at how much was different now. She shook her head in answer to Trevka's question. He continued,

"Then I have to wonder, were you really going to take Dane back to her? Would you have handed him over?" They looked at each other. Trevka wished he had Harz's ability to see if people were lying. Beth herself had to contemplate the answer. Would she have gone all the way back to Uluvost, her home once? Could she possibly have given Dane over to that woman, and likely suffered punishment for taking such an unsanctioned risk? Finally Beth shook her head and looked down. She was terrified but she couldn't lie. Trevka leaned towards her and touched her arm. When she looked up at him he said, "That may count in your favor." They both smiled. At least she had until tomorrow before anything was decided.

The following morning Harz used the secret passageway that led from the cliff side of the castle, past many dark storage rooms in a ground floor hallway, out into the courtyard. He had only just checked it a few months ago. But having left by an outside escape route and walked all around the perimeter of the castle, Harz wanted to reenter the courtyard unobserved by the guards at the gate, whom he was certain were doing their duty well and truly. He was acting on the niggling sense that someone was prowling the castle grounds in the early morning hour. Or perhaps his imagination had begun to run wild, but the recent attempt to kidnap the Viscount left Harz feeling as if he could not guard both Count and Viscount with equal vigilance, and the deficiency worried him. He had made his circuit and found nothing amiss, so leaned against the arched passageway and watched the courtyard become illuminated with the sunrise. As he did, to his astonishment, he realized a girl was sitting under the beech tree. Her long golden tresses were drifting in the breeze and hiding her face, but he felt certain it must be Genivee. What Providence to be here now, alone in the courtyard together, and probably she was the one he had sensed ambling around in the pre-dawn shadows. Then the sun broke over the castle wall, the light changed and the tresses turned to brown and he realized it was Sparrow. She looked up and saw him and rose to walk over to him.

He studied her coming towards him and when she was near enough he said, "I did not think to see you outside your room; the grounds are very vast." Her sense of direction *had* been tested by these walls and doorways, so unlike the forest. But she answered him frankly,

"Being outside at sunrise is very natural to me, and also the quietest time of day for this busy place." She was able then, just for a moment, to catch his thinking, because for once it was accompanied by an overwhelming emotion. His empty-hearted sadness was impossible to miss. She wondered how he stood there composed and calm. She gazed across the courtyard now filling with people and said, "But yes, perhaps it would be best if you were to show me the way back to the dining room before I am lost and causing trouble." Harz thought a moment, scanned the grounds and realized that any danger he had sensed had vanished, and offered her his arm. They walked across the courtyard, passed by the solitary beech tree, and went back into the castle together.

When Gustav was finally satisfied with having learned everything there was to know about what had been happening in his absence, everyone, including Sparrow (who thought that in a roundabout way, nature had taken care of this child), was in favor of keeping things as they were. Gustav was only concerned with being certain that Gertrudis had no knowledge of these events and was not in fact expecting her child to be returned to her. For all they knew, she was behind the plot and Beth had simply changed her own mind about how it ought to be handled. So it was that Harz was present when Beth had an audience with the father of the child she loved so much, and whom she had never met, even when Gertrudis was still living in the castle. She knew virtually nothing about him other than that her future was in his hands and that her fate might be about to change swiftly and dreadfully.

Trevka escorted Beth and Liesse into the room where Gustav and Harz were waiting. Beth leaned on Liesse with her eyes cast down in a fearful shyness. Trevka stationed himself near the door. Liesse led Beth to the right place to stand and took the required step away from her, hoping the girl wouldn't faint. Beth kept her eyes intently down, her hands clutched together. Harz was waiting for her to look up.

Gustav and Harz finally glanced at each other with slight amusement. She was frightened quite out of proportion to how intimidating they were trying not to be. They looked back at her, and now Beth had managed to look up at them, but saw only Harz. She gazed at him as if daring him to change her fate. He stared back at her in disbelief. Gustav knew Harz was studying her to see if she were lying; had she planned this with Gertrudis? Harz began to slowly shake his head and Gustav was satisfied there was nothing to worry about. Gustav made a dismissive gesture with his hand and Liesse took Beth's elbow and led her away, uncertain she would be able to walk out under her own power. Outside the room Liesse told her that all would be well and she could go back to caring for Dane as before. Beth swayed, bewildered and weak. Trevka put out a hand to steady her and led her back to her room to gather a few things up as instructed, then showed her the way to the nursery and her new rooms nearby. Trevka left her, assuring her that Liesse would join her soon. He no longer had both obligation and enjoyment of standing guard outside whatever room she was in. He turned after a moment of contemplating this and walked away. When she settled down and her heart had finally stopped hammering, it occurred to her that she didn't even know which of those men was the Count.

She was alone for only a few moments before Liesse came in with an attendant and both babies Luna and Dane. Once Liesse had sat down and become comfortable, Beth asked her about her unusual meeting, anxious to feel assured that there would be no further trials to pass. Liesse smiled and explained,

"Yes, not much was said. But then Harz can tell if someone is lying even if they don't speak. They probably just wanted to know for sure that the Countess Gertrudis wasn't in on any scheme. Even though she is gone, they still have to take her into account on some things.

She is still the Countess after all." Liesse had picked up Dane and was bouncing him on her knee, glad that he felt a little heavier now. Beth said to her,

"So that was why he was looking at me so - intently." Liesse rested the baby on her shoulder and said,
"Don't let it bother you, he's like that. Really a good man, always looking out for the Count." Beth began studying Luna; she definitely resembled her father, Liesse's somewhat intimidating husband. Beth blurted out to Liesse,

"I want you to know that I never believed what Gertrudis said about you being pregnant because of the Count. I knew she was making it up just to be troublesome. She was like that." Liesse realized that Beth had had a very different experience of living in Wilker than she or anyone else in the Count's favor had. Beth was lucky not to be among the others who had all left with Gertrudis, and Liesse believed that Beth knew this very well. Just then Sparrow arrived at the door holding Kasch, who was unusually agitated. But when they came into the room and Sparrow sat next to Beth, still holding Luna, he began to giggle. Sparrow had been looking forward to meeting someone who was, like her, just getting used to castle life. She hadn't known what she was going to say, but sitting next to her it came to her exactly what to say, which fortunately also put Beth at further ease about her recent larceny, which she regretted attempting, but had been swept along with thanks to her troublesome cousins. Sparrow said,

"You should know that the Count is very indebted to you for staying here as you did and are now looking after his son. You are the best person for the task." Beth breathed a sigh of relief, for she half imagined that Sparrow would be somewhat of a scold against her, perhaps even a jealous one. But instead it was clear to her that Sparrow, like her in age and frame, was happy with her own child to tend, and the three of them together had much in common to share. The three children, beginning their lives close together, and would remain close for as long as they lived.

After having dismissed Beth, the band of kidnappers was brought before Gustav next. He had agreed with Boris that they were more incompetent than dangerous, but still, such a brazen act of royal larceny had to be punished. He told them he was sending them back to the absent Countess on the heels of a messenger who was delivering the news to her that they had abandoned their posts in her service in a futile attempt to seek higher offices and positions of favor with the Count. She herself could decide how to reward such traitors.

The former nursemaids to Viscount Dane were next brought before the Count, who told them firmly he was not punishing them for the viscount being kidnapped under their collective noses. This worked as intended in that they finally stopped talking. But their services were no longer needed here. However some children in the realm were in need of care and attention, and they would each be found a home where extra help with the children would surely be appreciated. They would still receive room and board. They were dismissed, and all departed in the firm belief that the lack of ample opportunities to gossip among each other daily, nay hourly, could well lead to the breaking of their spirits.

At last, the party from Elster had to be dealt with. Gustav welcomed them royally and praised their patience (Boris rolled his eyes), and told them their report was most anxiously awaited. (They began right then to unroll their maps). However, by royal decree, it was still officially summertime and such beautiful days were too distracting to be spent in serious decision-making. The court would be pleased to have them as their guests of honor for one more week before September began, at which time the matter of the Marianna Valley would be the sole concern of his undivided attention. In the meantime, their accommodations would be immediately elevated and expanded to occupy the entire, uppermost floor of the guest wing, they would dine every evening as revered guests, and would be taken on tours of the realm in extreme style. By the end of such a week, Gustav hoped, they would be more likely to see Wilker in a favorable, honorable and generous light. They thus retreated with grudging thanks and resignation, escorted by Vatra.

Gustav had one more thing to do. It weighed more heavily than all the others, even though it was the smallest. He headed for the nursery. He made sure they would be ready for his arrival by sending an attendant before him in a casual way to say that the Count was on his way up to visit with them. When he arrived and saw that the door had been left ajar, he knew he would not startle them. The women looked up and smiled as he came into the room. He sat down next to Sparrow and waited for her to find subtle ways to clarify to him which baby was which. He gazed at them wondering how women deciphered such things. He silently contemplated the fact that he couldn't have identified his own firstborn child, but then they were just infants. He would have many years to make up to Dane for the neglect of which he was to this point guilty. Kasch as well had been without his father for a time, but being raised together, each one with a mother of their own, they were sure to become close half-brothers. And with two older brothers, Luna would never again be threatened or stolen. The favoritism Gustav felt on the one side for his future heir and on the other for the child of his beloved Sparrow would dissolve. An old adage's prediction about the royal line being in any danger vanished with the sight of his two sons before him.

ACKNOWLEDGMENTS

I thank my mother, sisters and niece who
read my manuscript and offered excellent
advice on grammar, syntax and content.
I thank my husband for inspiring
improvements to a book that was
not even his cup of tea.

I especially thank Ted Andrews and his book
Animal-Speak for guidance about animal lore.

ABOUT THE AUTHOR

Jean Hudson is currently finishing the sequel to
Sparrow in the Keep, Crow Like Thunder,
which is due to be published in 2014.
She lives in New Mexico with
her husband and menagerie of animals.

Made in the USA
Charleston, SC
12 June 2014